MERCILESS
SAVIORS

ALSO BY H.E. EDGMON

Godly Heathens

The Witch King Series

The Witch King

The Fae Keeper

MERCILESS SAVIORS

A Novel

H.E. EDGMON

WEDNESDAY BOOKS
NEW YORK

First published in the United States by Wednesday Books,
an imprint of St. Martin's Publishing Group

MERCILESS SAVIORS. Copyright © 2024 by H.E. Edgmon. All rights reserved.
Printed in the United States of America. For information, address
St. Martin's Publishing Group, 120 Broadway, New York, NY 10271.

www.wednesdaybooks.com

Map design by Westley Vega

The Library of Congress Cataloging-in-Publication Data is available upon request.

ISBN 978-1-250-85363-9 (hardcover)
ISBN 978-1-250-85364-6 (ebook)

Our books may be purchased in bulk for promotional, educational,
or business use. Please contact your local bookseller or the
Macmillan Corporate and Premium Sales Department at
1-800-221-7945, extension 5442, or by email at
MacmillanSpecialMarkets@macmillan.com.

First Edition: 2024

10 9 8 7 6 5 4 3 2 1

For children who were handed scissors and punished for running.

I know you didn't think there'd be this much blood.
I know you were just trying to get away.

CONTENT WARNING

While this book is about magical powers and fantasy worlds, it's also an honest story about pain. It features a candid portrayal of mental illness stemming from childhood trauma, and a main character whose own mind sometimes seems to be working against them. Recovering repressed memories, and the questioning of reality that follows, is a significant part of this story. There are also graphic depictions of suicidality, depersonalization, and other symptoms that are difficult to stomach, which may make some readers uncomfortable.

Other potentially upsetting content includes:

- Incest, childhood sex abuse, and other sexual violence involving minors.
- General violence, including murder and torture.
- Horror, including anthropomorphic and body horror.
- Brief mentions of nonconsensual pregnancy and pregnancy loss.
- Animal death.

1

THE BLOODBATH THAT AWAITS WAS YOUR CHOICE ALONE

I t rains in the church attic, fat drops of warm water and thick shards of stained glass, while I take the Cyclone's life and the Reaper takes a bullet meant to end mine.

There is screaming. It could be lifetimes away, as muddled as it is, reaching for me through the bands of time and space and magic as thick and black as tar. The quiet sound of Zephyr Beauregard's last breath seems louder. Beneath my pressed knee, beneath the callous weight of my knife cracking through the eggshell of his rib cage to pierce the yolk of him, the rich boy gurgles and spits. In this moment, I know with certainty why they call it a death rattle.

Someone grabs my knife arm. They try to drag my shoulder back, try to wrench free the weapon buried in Zephyr's chest. Do they think to save him? Do they not realize they're too late? Too late for the Cyclone. Too late for any of us.

His blue eyes widen until they can't anymore, until they aren't blue at all anymore, color leaching away like oceans drying up, until I'm staring into ash that used to be a home.

Around me, I know the world is moving, loudly and quickly, and I know it wants me to move with it. But I'm trapped here, suspended in a cocoon; my body, my knife, the skin and bones and blood that used to be a boy.

The electricity starts like a tingling in my fingertips. Like the pins and needles of sitting wrong for too long, like part of me falling asleep while the rest is awake. Am I awake? Have I not been sleeping for weeks, for years, for lifetimes? Am I not only just now beginning to open my eyes?

It starts like a tingling and it grows like a fire, a cold burning ripping its way up my arm. There is screaming, and maybe it's mine.

Lightning touches my heart and my head tips toward my spine, eyes rolling back. The last thing I see is Christ on the Cross above me.

My last thought is that this god did not die for my sins. But others have. And more will yet.

In the Ether, I stand on the cliff's edge overlooking the shoreside cityscape below, as it falls victim to the ravages of the Cyclone's latest tantrum. The ocean swirls into hurricane gusts, and tornadoes of brine tear down whole houses, leveling generations of memories in seconds. Before this, the city was filled with screams of panic and disbelief as its people tried to escape what they knew was coming. Now those screams have fallen silent. There is nothing but the wailing of the wind and the cracking of wood as lumber falls.

The Cyclone is a fickle and merciless god, moving at random from one village to the next, demanding offerings from its people only to indulge in their destruction whether they sacrifice or not. There is no reasoning with him, no bargaining that may actually hold sway. He sets his course and cannot be moved from his path—unless, just as randomly, *he* decides to turn.

I've been following him for some time now. Something must be done, before he floods the whole of our world for his own entertainment.

"What about *him*?" I ask, waving my hand at the beach below. "You cannot look upon the Cyclone's actions and tell me you truly see no purpose for my weapon."

Who am I talking to? I'm alone on the cliff.

At least, I thought I was.

"The monstrousness of another does not excuse indulging in your own."

The voice comes from behind me, though I don't turn to face it. I must have known she was there, if I spoke to her, but . . . how? I don't remember her being there, I don't remember . . .

Who is she?

Some tangled consciousness, some part of me that is Gem Echols, desperately wants to turn around and face the voice. It's beautiful. Sultry, raspy, deep, and melodic, the way I imagine a jazz singer might sound. But I have no idea who she is.

But I do. The Magician does, I do, I know her, I came here with her, I must have. Why can't I remember who she is? If only I would turn around and look at her.

"It is not *indulgence* to create a safeguard," I snap. My hands curl into fists so tight my nails dig into my palms. I get the impression we've had this argument many times, I just . . . don't remember any of them. "I am the keeper of the scales. My place in this world is to keep the axis righted. How am I meant to do that if I cannot eradicate those who are bent on its collapse?"

"You are the keeper of the scales," she agrees. I can feel her disappointment, and it makes my chest ache. I don't know why, but I need her to understand me. I *need* her to forgive me. But more and more, I realize she isn't going to. "That does not make you our warden. Nor our executioner. The bloodbath that awaits was your choice alone."

"I don't know why you seem to think so little of me." I sniff, tilting my head back as a spray of salt water ghosts up from below, coating one side of my face in a wet shimmer. "After all we have meant to each other, I cannot accept that you would abandon me now. Not over this."

A wash of seafoam begins to swirl, tumbling round and round itself like soapy suds overflowing in a bucket, until finally the swirls give way, the sea parting. From its dark depths, the Siren emerges, body rising from the abyss until she can plant her feet on the water's surface. She tilts back her head and roars the Cyclone's name.

Her roar is met with distant laughter, carried down on a boom of thunder.

"It is only because of what you mean to me that I see this act for what it truly is. I know your heart, Magician, even the parts of it you would like to hide. Even the parts that you keep secret from yourself." Behind me, her voice cracks and I want to cry. "And I know the truth. It is *you* who has abandoned *me*."

Lightning strikes me in the chest.

I don't *wake up* so much as I realize my eyes are already open and I'm standing outside the First Church of Gracie. It's not like I'm unconscious one minute and conscious the next; it's like I'm stuck in some vivid daydream only to suddenly remember what I'm doing. Except I don't remember, not really. I have no idea how I got here.

Here. I'm on the sidewalk. It's no longer raining. There are cops, and parishioners, and crying parents, and old gods. Rory has an arm around my shoulders. Enzo is talking to an EMT, his parents in the back of their ambulance.

In another, my mom helps a first responder ease my dad onto a stretcher. The doors close behind them. I think I talked to her, but I can't remember where they're going.

Buck and Rhett are gone. Or maybe they're still inside the church. How long have I been standing here without being in my own body?

The sidewalk quiets when someone rolls a gurney through the crowd. There's a black sheet pulled over the corpse. I don't know if it's Poppy or Zephyr.

Rory's arm tightens around me. The ambulance takes Enzo's parents away. He walks back to us, his fingers threading with mine. None of us speak.

A cop snaps his fingers in Marian's face. He's trying to get her attention, but he catches mine instead. She stares beyond him, following the flashing lights as the ambulances careen away from us and toward Gracie's tiny hospital. Is her girlfriend in one of them?

How many people survive gunshots to the head every year? More than can call themselves gods of death, probably. If the odds were in anyone's favor, it would be Poppy's.

The cop raises his voice. Rory tenses. Enzo releases my hand.

Marian doesn't need us. She turns her cloudy eyes on the officer. She doesn't speak. I don't know that she can. But a Black woman in a pinstripe suit touches a hand to her shoulder and speaks for her. I don't know who she is, and I don't know what she says. But the cop rolls his eyes and leaves.

The woman steers Marian away from the crowd. Toward

a car parked on the street. Murphy's in the back seat, staring straight ahead, unblinking. Is this woman Murphy's mom? She helps Marian into the back seat. It strikes me like rotten food in the pit of my stomach that the god of battle has never looked more like a scared little girl.

Indy meets my eye from across the road, where he's standing next to his own truck. His expression is stone, eyes cold and harsh like black ice about to send us off the road. There is a world where the god of art paints murals with the blood of those he's massacred. I've never seen my friend look as much like that god as he does now.

Everything has turned upside down. Everything has gone tipped out of whack, out of order, out of balance . . .

Balance. My head hurts. I ~~am~~ was the keeper of the scales.

Buck's warning is as clear now as the day he spoke it. "*And the scales will tip . . . tip . . . tip . . . until they fall from existence.*"

What does a world out of balance look like?

I don't realize I asked the question out loud until Enzo says, "We'll see. Soon enough."

Rory kisses the side of my face. "Let's go home."

Home. I don't know what that means anymore, either.

2

THE BEGINNING AND END

Home, at least for tonight, means the log house where Rory's grandparents live. They don't come outside to greet us, the way I've gotten used to. I can't say I'm not relieved. On the list of things my fractured—still-fracturing?—brain can handle right now, they aren't present.

Rory turns off the ignition, their grandfather's ancient sports car going still and quiet. I miss the Jeep. I wonder if it'll ever be drivable again. How many bullet holes can a car survive? More or less than a god in the body of a teenage girl?

I don't know if I feel guilty, and I don't know if I should. It wasn't my finger on the trigger. I wasn't the one who ordered it pulled. *I'm not the one who shot Poppy.*

All I did was survive.

It's only when the silence stretches on for a beat too long that I realize Rory's staring at me. Enzo, too, bent over the center console, head tilted to face me. I can't read either of their expressions. Or maybe I don't want to. Something electric and heavy pulses in my temple, the beginnings of a terrible headache. Or maybe the end of one.

"What?" I don't mean it to sound angry. I'm not angry with them. I'm just tired.

Or am I even tired at all? Maybe I'm too awake, hanging in that space where exhaustion has gotten so bad that sleep is impossible. I don't know anymore. Upside down. Out of balance. Tip, tip, tip.

"How do you feel?" Rory finally asks. I get the impression they don't really want the answer.

"Fine."

"Fine?" Enzo repeats the word back to me, like he must have misheard.

I clear my throat and rub one fist over my eye. There's a vein twitching in the lid, like the flicker of lightning over and over. "Yeah. Fine."

It isn't *not* true. Fine is not healthy or happy or stable or sane. Fine is also not dead or dying or broken or gone. Fine is somewhere between. And I am, I guess, somewhere between, if that somewhere is that I don't know where I am, and I don't know how I am, but I think I'm fine. I'm pretty sure I'm fine.

"Gem—" Rory begins, and I don't realize they've raised their hand until their fingertips touch my cheek.

The unexpected contact makes me jump. I don't let them say whatever was meant to come next. "What happens now?"

Rory and Enzo exchange a look. That can't mean anything good.

Enzo looks back to me and touches his hand against the back of my wrist. "We go inside. We get some food in you. And then maybe we call the Evergod."

The Evergod. Buck Wheeler. The god of time.

"Why him?"

"Gem," Rory repeats, taking a deep breath. "Taking the life

of another god with the Ouroboros has been your greatest fear for as long as the weapon has existed. You said it yourself, over and over again. You were never supposed to be the one to wield that knife the way you did today. The balance . . . you warned us the balance would be thrown out of order if you ever did."

"Right. Yeah." I look at my hands. I can still feel the pressure of Zephyr's rib cage cracking underneath them.

"But do you have any idea what that means in practice?" They hesitate, tapping one fingertip against my knee. "Do you know what's going to happen to you?"

"I . . ." Heartburn crawls up the back of my throat, but the acid tastes more like burnt plastic. "I don't know. I can't remember."

Ever since Buck pulled down the wall between lives, giving the pantheon back all of our memories, things have been clearer than ever before. I've seen more of myself, in my every iteration, finally beginning to understand who I am and how I got here. But there's still a shroud of fog between me and . . . something. There are still memories I can't grasp, no matter how desperately I reach for them.

And right now, I can barely grasp at the *present*, much less the past, and certainly not the future. Ever since I woke up on that church sidewalk, my head is only on my body in the way of bone and muscle. My thoughts have gone wind-whipped. Reality, whatever that means, is happening at the other end of a very long telescope. I hardly know if I'm actually in this car at all.

"Right." Enzo trails his knuckles over my arm, brushing them against the inside of my elbow. I think he means it to be comforting. In reality, it tickles a little. I don't tell him to stop—it's himself he's really comforting. "But if anyone does know what's coming, it will be him."

"Sure." That makes sense. Buck Wheeler knows everything

and nothing, the most formidable and feeble among us in equal measure. Of course, it's *his* power that the present hinges on. Nothing can ever just be easy.

"Gem," Rory says again, and I find her eyes with my own. She has beautiful eyes. Dark brown, one painted with a bloom of green. She's beautiful. I miss her. Or I missed her. Or. "Why did you do it?"

"What?"

"Why did you kill him?" She shakes her head. Those beautiful eyes are wet and sad, and I don't understand anything, but I would do the worst thing I've done all over again if it meant she didn't have to look like *this* anymore. "We had a plan. What happened?"

"I—"

—don't have a good answer for them. The decision to kill Zephyr had been spur-of-the-moment, impulsive, reckless. I'd been angry at Marian, having just realized that she'd set me up, that there was no way the Lionheart was letting me leave that church alive, not if she was allowed to see her plan through. I was tired, tired of the self-flagellation, the apologizing, the grief of reckoning with myself. I hadn't had a new plan beyond wanting to hurt Marian and Poppy as much as I could, beyond wanting to do the most ruthless, brutal thing imaginable just to scare them both.

But it wasn't just the Reaper and her lover I'd scared. Rory stares at me with those wet eyes and Enzo watches me with his mouth set like barbed wire and I realize I'm shaking and I don't know when it started or how to make it stop.

"I thought I could trust her." I don't even know I'm talking about Marian until I realize it in the aftermath of my own words. Thunder rumbles outside the car, loud and close enough to shake the frame. "But her bullet was meant for me. The Lionheart will always have a bullet meant for me."

"And you wanted her to feel as betrayed as you did." Enzo doesn't pose it as a question, but as a mirror. The words are meant to show me something, but I don't meet the reflection to examine what.

"How did you even know about the gun? How did you—"

I cut Rory off again. "Buck."

It's the only answer anyone needs. The car goes quiet again.

Without distraction, my attention is drawn back to the unfamiliar hum of power in my hands. This uncanny spark just beneath my skin *begs* to be played with. I imagine the world like one of those plasma lamps, imagine pressing my palms against it and watching threads of magic leap toward me like obedient servants.

As I do, a bolt of lightning strikes so close to the passenger window that it blows the side mirror from the door. Rory and Enzo jump, all of us wheeling toward the charred-black hole, the smoke rising off the metal.

My partners are afraid. I can taste their fear, even without looking at them. I am not unafraid. But it's not just *fear* that wets my tongue and makes my heartbeat quicken. This lightning is mine. I summoned it here even without meaning to, and I can learn to control it. *This* was an act of *my* magic.

And it was free. There will be no payment collected. The one caveat to what I can do, the single thread that has bound me for my entire ancient existence, the limitation that declared I could only have what I was willing to sacrifice for . . . is no longer part of the equation.

I can do anything I want without consequence.

Enzo clears his throat. "Come on. Inside. None of us can do anything on empty stomachs."

"Unexpected wisdom from someone built like a starving Victorian orphan," Rory quips, pushing open the driver's-side door and climbing out.

Enzo looks as if he wants to argue, but just rolls his eyes and follows them toward the porch. Maybe because now's not the time. Maybe because he *does* have the body type of someone who would die from cholera.

Either way, there's something nice about the snark. It makes me feel a little more . . . here. Like maybe, if I'm lucky, my head *isn't* going to float away like a helium balloon that lost its weight.

The relief lasts for only a minute. Inside Rory's house, the unreality returns worse than before.

Joseph and Ellen Hardy are only alive right now because I had bigger problems on my *list of terrible people who need to be dealt with immediately*. With Zephyr dead, and Poppy in either the ICU or the morgue, they've been bumped to the top.

How was it less than two weeks ago that Rory told me the truth about them, and what they'd done to her? The way they'd locked her away, tortured her to force her to remember she was the Mountain? How was it only *last night* that I walked into their bathroom and found Joseph clutching one of Rory's old, used tampons, like a dog snuffling through the trash?

Hm.

I saw a video online once that said time isn't actually linear. That's just the way we process it, because otherwise our brains would break. Like Buck's. He's not seeing something special;

he's just seeing what's really there, what's hidden from most of us—that everything is actually happening all at once.

Maybe that's what's happening to me. Maybe linear time is falling away, and I can't grasp it anymore, and my brain is breaking. I'm here, in this living room, but I'm not here. And everything happening in the past and everything happening in the future both push in on either side of me, muffling the present, making my skin crawl with overstimulation.

Or maybe it's that I'm more powerful than I've ever been, and nothing matters anymore. If there are no consequences to anything I do, then nothing is real.

I blink and realize I've missed part of the conversation. Rory and Joseph are talking. I try to tune back in, catch up, but can't seem to focus through the pounding in the front of my skull.

"I don't understand," Rory is saying, the words slow and cautious, like talking to a feral animal backed into a corner.

"Your bleeding stopped about ten days ago, didn't it?" Joseph asks, and my stomach drops.

What the fuck is wrong with this guy? Outside, it starts to rain. It pounds against the tin roof, loud enough that Ellen has to raise her voice when she speaks.

"If you'll just do this every other day for the next week or so," Rory's grandmother shouts, taking a step closer to her grandchild, "you probably won't ever have to do it again. It'll probably be done."

"Done." Rory repeats. Their eyes, those beautiful, mismatched eyes, have gone cloudy. Outside, a bird screeches. "Because I'll be pregnant."

Wait, what?

My head snaps back toward Joseph. No, not Joseph, but

behind him. It isn't just the five of us in this room, there's another, a sixth, on the couch behind Rory's grandfather. A boy.
Not a boy, a man. Twenties, maybe thirties. Dark beard and a
flannel shirt. I don't recognize him. He looks uncomfortable,
glancing between all of us, hands on his knees.

I remember I'm still covered in Zephyr's blood.

"Joseph . . ." My voice doesn't sound like my own, but I don't
know what my own sounds like anymore. I tilt my head, eyes
slowly dragging toward the older man's face. "What have you
done?"

His own eyes fill with tears in response, and a fearful nerve
tics in his jaw. "You have to understand, this is the only way.
Without an heir to carry on our family, the Mountain will disappear. It is my sacred duty to protect the bloodline. I am only
doing what must be done so she can survive."

The words press into the notches of my spine like fingers
digging into a yellowing bruise, but I ignore the ache. Instead,
I look back to that man on the couch.

"You." He meets my eye. Whatever he sees, he swallows.
Outside, thunder rattles the windows. "How much did they tell
you before you came here? What did they have to say to get
you to agree?"

"I—"

"Did they ask you to fuck their granddaughter? Did they
mention she was only seventeen?"

"Look—"

"Did you know the plan was to knock her up? Did that ex-
cite you? Did they mention she wasn't human?"

"You—"

"Did they warn you about *me*?"

Harder and harder the rain pours, as if the sky has ripped

open, water flooding like blood gushing from an open wound. Birds and bugs, coyotes and gators, they scream and howl and protest, and their wails are carried on the frenzied wind that whips all around us. Lightning illuminates their shadows through the windows, casting long, eerie talons along the floor, black fangs across the walls.

The man pisses himself when I take a step closer. Gross. Maybe I'll just reach in and pluck out his bladder so that doesn't happen again.

"Creature." Enzo's voice is as calm as I've ever heard it when he speaks for the first time since entering the house. I don't realize he's right behind me until one of his finely boned hands slides from my hip to my chest, stopping me in my tracks, holding me in place with unexpected strength. "That's enough."

I want to protest. *This* is not enough; *this* has only just gotten started.

"This pathetic little man does not deserve the pleasure of your cruelty. He was nothing more than a tool in someone else's hand."

A tool. Disgust crawls up my throat, thick bile that threatens to gag me. Enzo's right. However they try to explain this to themselves, Joseph and Ellen planned to rape Rory. They were just going to use this stranger as their means to do it.

They planned to *rape* their teenage granddaughter.

To force the god of land to carry a pregnancy against their own will.

To force their own depravity on the woman I love.

"How did you ever imagine getting away with this?" I have to ask, turning my face back to Joseph's. "You had to know I would find out. You had to know what I would do to you."

A tear slips down Joseph's cheek. To his credit, he holds my gaze when he says, "I figured you'd kill me. I just hoped I'd do what had to be done first."

Ellen lets loose a sob, and her knees give out. She crashes to the floor, slumping forward at the waist, pressing her hands into the carpet. "Please. You have to understand, there was no other way. We prayed you would see the truth. You need this as much as she does—if there is no heir, you may never find the Mountain again."

Wind begins to whip *inside* the house, swirling around the living room so hard that it might take me off my feet if it wasn't my own doing. The ground rumbles underneath us. Somewhere in the distance, an animal howls.

When I speak, slow and careful so as not to be misunderstood, sparks flicker from the tip of my tongue, enunciating each word with an electric pop. "I am the god of gods. I am the beginning and end to all magic. There is *nothing* I cannot do. And the Mountain is mine. How outrageous that you would believe anything, in any life, in any world, could keep me away. What a sacrilege that is."

Ellen's body shakes with the force of her cries. Joseph's head tips forward, shoulders folding.

"You." Enzo raises the hand from my chest to flick his wrist at the man on the urine-damp couch. "Leave. Before I change my mind."

The stranger doesn't need to be told twice. He practically throws himself to his feet, fighting the indoor winds to wrench open the door and stumble down the porch steps. The violent gale slams the door behind him.

What to do now? Somehow the question is *more* difficult when the answer could be anything imaginable, not less.

In the end, it isn't up to me anyway.

Enzo steps around me, planting himself in the center of the room, his body between the humans and the gods. When he turns his head over his shoulder to meet Rory's eyes, his own have begun to glow again. They light up the space between us in shards of blue and silver and red like blood. Though my wind whips at his hair and clothes, he doesn't sway. His shadow leaps to life, a sentient being all on its own, shielding him in a cloak of darkness.

He is the god of things forbidden. And we have only seen a fraction of his power so far.

"Aurora." He says their name like an offering, and I glance to Rory's face. Her glassy eyes flick, slowly, to his. She blinks, as if unsure who or what she's seeing. "I need you to answer a question before this goes any further."

Their curls fly, wild, across their face. They don't say anything, just continue to stare.

I want to warn him that I don't think she's really here with us, but I can't make myself say it. Instead, I reach for her, my hand hovering just in front of her face. When she doesn't flinch away, I push back her curls, gathering them behind her head and using the elastic on my wrist to tie them off.

Enzo presses forward. "They want an heir for your family line. I need to know if you believe they should get exactly what they've asked for."

I frown in his direction. What the hell does that mean? This doesn't seem like the time for his mind games.

Rory seems to be considering the same thing, her thick eyebrows slanting together in confusion, a frown tugging at the corner of her mouth. Her eyes follow Enzo's shadow as it circles him. Something like recognition begins to dawn in her face.

The Mountain whispers, "Yes," and the Shade, like a knight beneath her banner, turns to see her will be done.

Tempered by my confusion, the wind inside dies down until the house is quiet again. I don't know what these two have decided without words, but I suspect I'll want to hear what happens next.

Enzo's footsteps are light as he makes his way to Ellen's side, kneeling next to her and curling one delicate finger beneath her chin. He is gentle as he tilts her face away from the carpet, forcing her to look at him. "Do you know who I am?"

"You are the devil," she sobs.

"Yes. But it's not as simple as that, is it?" He smiles, and the hand on her chin moves to her elbow, pulling her up and helping her to her feet. He rises with her, and pushes back the hair from her face when they're standing together. "I am the god-king of many kingdoms. Did you know I conquered the gift of creation?"

Realization begins to tick its way down the back of my neck in the form of rising gooseflesh. I reach for Rory and find their hand, squeezing until they squeeze back hard enough to make my knuckles pop.

Ellen and Joseph exchange a look of their own. When Joseph looks as if he might protest, Enzo's shadow slithers toward him, curling around his legs and sliding up his torso. The older man sputters, shocked, staring wide-eyed down at the black magic enveloping his body.

Enzo calls Ellen's attention back. "I can give you the heir you want. No one need touch the Mountain to carry on your line. All you have to do is ask for my help."

"But . . ." Ellen whimpers, glancing between her husband and her granddaughter and this wicked, sweet-tongued god from hell. "Why would you help me?"

"I know your legends tell you I am the villain in this story. But stories are so often forced to abandon shades of gray in favor of black and white. A parable cannot teach a lesson about good and evil if there is no evil." I've heard Enzo's practiced monologues many times, but this is different. This is not an actor putting on a performance; this is the serpent whispering in Eve's ear the succulence of the apple. "You and I both know that isn't reality. Reality is shaped by shades of gray, by people doing what they have to. That's what you and your husband have always done, isn't it? That's what I've always done. And surviving doesn't make us evil." He touches his knuckles to her cheek, so tender in his manipulation. "I am not without benevolence. I can help you because it's what you deserve. Just say the words. Tell me this is what you want, and I will consecrate your womb with the gift of life."

"Ellen," Joseph warns, cut off when the shadow claws into his throat.

His wife doesn't seem to notice. She stares, enchanted, into the mesmerizing eyes of the devil, and whispers, "Yes. This is what I want."

At my side, Rory gives a quiet groan and stumbles forward. The movement is subtle, the way the Mountain catches themself before they can fall to the ground, but I know what it means. Their world is breaking. I let go of their hand only to curl my arm around their back, pressing our bodies in a tight line. They rest their temple on the top of my head and suck in a jagged breath, like a breeze over broken glass.

Enzo's smile is cold. He tucks one hand behind Ellen's back, and places the other over her stomach. The old woman touches his shoulder as if to keep herself upright.

Power glows in his palms, as red as freshly spilled blood. The glow brightens and brightens until light encircles Ellen's pelvis and the living room is cast entirely in a red overlay. Ellen gasps, her fingers tightening on Enzo's shoulder, her eyes widening in shock.

And as quickly as it began, it ends. The light is extinguished and Enzo steps away from her, rejoining Rory and me on the other side of the room.

For a long moment, nothing much happens. Ellen reaches down to pet at her belly, confusion and hope both adorning her weathered features.

Enzo's shoulder brushes my arm as he leans in beside me, and I glance down at the top of his head, growing more and more concerned with each passing second.

Rory opens their mouth.

Before they can ask what we both must be thinking, Ellen lets out a startled little cry, eyes widening again as she clutches at her stomach. Seconds later, when something in her torso *snaps,* like a bone being broken, she doesn't scream in pain but in *delight.* Eyes practically glowing with excitement, she stares down at her stomach as it begins to *grow.*

Her torso expands like a balloon inflating, swelling up into a perfect circle cradled between her hips, slung low on her pelvis. She tugs up the hem of her floral shirt, revealing the evidence of exactly what Enzo promised. She's pregnant.

Ellen Hardy is carrying the continuation of the Mountain's lineage, a child gifted to her by the Shade. A union of the bloodlines.

It feels impossible, but so does everything else.

And then,

"What the—"

"Holy shit."

A perfect imprint of a tiny hand presses against her skin from the inside, like a palm pressed to the foggy glass of a windowpane. I lose my breath, and Rory almost loses her footing again, but somehow, we keep each other together.

Deliriously happy giggles begin streaming from Ellen's mouth as she stares down at her swollen middle. "Joseph—Joseph, are you seeing this? We did it. Oh, we did it. Everything's going to be okay now. Oh."

Lovingly, she strokes her own fingers against the tiny ones inside of her.

I tilt my attention to her husband. Joseph hasn't said a word, though the shadow has released its intangible hold on his neck. Unlike his wife, he does not look happy. He does not stare at her belly with adoration, as if this gift is the answer to all of their problems.

He looks afraid. He knows what she hasn't yet realized.

But it won't be long now.

Ellen's giggles begin to slow, quieting and growing more and more sparse until they dry up altogether. Her smile fades into a frown as she blinks down at herself. At that hand inside of her as it presses further and further out, stretching her skin more and more until nearly an entire arm is visible.

"What . . . what's happening?" She looks to Enzo for guidance. "Is this normal? Is the baby all right?"

"Oh, I have no idea." Enzo shrugs, utterly nonchalant. "I've never done this before. I'm not even certain it's a baby. Or a human. All I know for sure is that it's alive."

"Wh—" Ellen's confusion is quick to warp into fear when something else inside of her *cracks*. She gasps, this time in pain, and grabs for her hip as she falls to her knees again. "No. . . . no, this can't be right."

I can do nothing to move from the spot I'm planted in, can only watch in revulsion as her belly begins to crawl. As whatever thing has taken root inside of her starts to slither and squirm, pressing up against her insides until I can make out all of her ribs, until I can see something like a face trying to force its way through her belly button. Bones break and skin stretches, and Ellen's gasps turn to cries turn to screams.

"Make this stop!" she howls, begging Enzo for relief.

"Are you not grateful for your gift?" he asks her. "Do you no longer believe this is exactly what you deserve?"

She might've had something else to say, might've argued, might've continued to plead with him for leniency. But all that leaves her lips is a mouthful of blood, red seeping out over her teeth, down her chin, coating her shirt.

With fascination and disgust, I watch her belly as it shrinks, as the creature in her womb leaves the safe cradle of her pelvis. I can see it, see its squirming body as it snakes up her torso, punching into the cavern of her chest, breaking every bone in its path. Ellen's eyes roll back in her head, blood leaking from her open mouth, and the only sound she can make is a high-pitched, desperate whine.

No. No, that isn't Ellen. That's the *thing*, crying out from inside of her body, using her mouth as its own. When it reaches her neck, it bursts through the cords of her throat, severing the muscles and veins and the links of her spine until her head simply falls from her shoulders and hits the floor with a wet thud.

And this thing is certainly not human. It slides from the secretions of its mother's open neck, its body mushy and wet and mottled red, like an oversized clot of blood with arms and hands and a grotesque face like an unfinished Picasso. Using its tiny hands, it drags itself down her body and onto the carpet, its eyes, leaking pus and blood, moving from Enzo, to me, to Rory, before settling on Joseph.

It opens its half-formed, toothless mouth and makes that same horrific screech.

Maybe I'm going completely insane. Or maybe its scream sounded like "*Dada.*" I think I'd rather be crazy.

As it begins to drag itself across the carpet toward Joseph, leaving a trail of slimy discharge in its wake, the older man struggles against his shadowy warden, desperate to break free and get away.

"Willa Mae," he dares to say; dares to turn wild eyes on his grandchild. "Please—you know I've only ever done what I had to! Don't let them do this! The Shade will betray you! The Magician may already be lost! I am your only ally!"

"Enzo," Rory says slowly, raising one hand and giving the smallest flick of their fingers. "Let him go."

"As you wish, kitten." The shadow leaps from Joseph's feet and back to Enzo's, falling in line with his body, perfectly unremarkable.

"Thank you, thank you." Joseph scrambles toward us, reaching for Rory, and—

Lightning strikes inside the house, charring the carpet black, smoke billowing up.

It's enough to make him stop, hovering in place, frantically looking between Rory's face and the screeching thing still crawling toward him. "I knew you would understand, I knew—"

"May you never know a moment of peace." Rory's shoulders straighten. They stand up taller, reaching their full height. Outside, the birds caw and screech and swirl around the house in a cacophony of rage. "As I have not known one since the moment you stole me from my home."

"But—"

"Run."

His anguish is realized. Joseph's eyes widen and widen and he backs away, toward the front door, and that thing screams and screams and crawls faster to reach him. He flings the door open and the uncanny brightness of the afternoon sun floods in, almost cartoonish in its sharp contrast to what's happening down here. Joseph races onto the porch, yelling out in pain and shock as a frenzied flock of hummingbirds, dozens of them, peck at his wrinkled skin, as swamp bugs buzz and sting and swarm around his head, as a violent wind nearly knocks him off his feet. And still, he forces himself to run, scrambling down the porch steps and fleeing as quickly as he can into the heart of the bayou.

All the while, his crying child drags itself over carpet, and wood, and dirt, to get to him.

From the doorway, we watch until they both disappear. I have a feeling we won't see either ever again. I really hope I'm right.

3

YOU'LL KNOW AS SOON AS I DO

When the pig finishes eating Rory's grandmother's corpse, she sends it home in the same direction she summoned it from. And we're left with nothing but the stains on the carpet and a too-quiet house.

Enzo, sitting on the kitchen counter, having just watched a five-hundred-pound sow chomp her way through raw flesh, cartilage, and bone, clears his throat. "Anyone still hungry?"

Rory doesn't look at him—but a crow does fly directly into the kitchen window, making him jump. I put my head in my hands.

"A simple *no* would suffice." Enzo taps his fingers against the counter's ledge, his rings clinking against the butcher block when he does. "Should check in with my parents."

It's such a human thing to say. I look up from my palms, considering the boy on the other side of the room. This demon of unspeakable power who has existed since the dawn of creation. This teenager who loves his mom and dad.

He finds me staring and smiles, sad and apologetic. I want to kiss him. I don't think either of us can be touched right now.

"Oh. Right." I look away to pull my phone from my pocket, opening the forgotten texts from my mother.

MOTHERSHIP

I'm with your dad at the hospital. They're going to keep him for psych evaluation. If you can, could you meet us here? I don't know when he'll be allowed visitors. I'm going to stay until all of the intake is finished. Might be a while.

And then, later, only fifteen minutes ago:

MOTHERSHIP

He's been admitted. Going to head home soon. Worried about you. I know I don't know what's happening . . . but I'd like to. Please call if you need me. Want to at least know you're okay.

Am I okay?

Does she, of all people, have any right to ask if I am?

In the church, while time hung suspended like a noose in the Evergod's hand, I'd started to forgive her. I'd realized, for the first time, that she was so much like me, in her own fucked-up way. We are both always trying to make the right choices, to protect ourselves and the ones we love, and somehow we end up ruining everything anyway. I'd decided I needed to take my anger and learn to let it go; to make things right between us.

What's changed since then? Nothing. Everything. I am exactly the person I was the last time I spoke to her, and I'm not, at all. I *remember* the empathy I'd felt for my mother, but I can't seem to actually make myself *feel it* again. Maybe it's the Cyclone's power, electricity short-circuiting the pathways in my head. Maybe it's the sting of Marian's betrayal—a defense mechanism that says if I assume the worst from everyone, no one can disappoint me.

Or maybe I'm just manic and need to take a nap.

Either way, I text back with a pin for my location, followed by:

need a ride home. we should talk.

I don't have any idea what I'm going to say. I guess I'll figure it out when she gets here.

I'd half expected to find a text from Indy waiting for me, but there isn't one. No one else has reached out. I open Instagram, scroll through stories looking for any mention of Poppy or what happened at the church, but there's nothing. I can't explain why, but the quiet is more disturbing than any flood of notifications would be.

"My mom's coming to get me," I tell the room, putting my phone back in my pocket. "She has questions."

"What are you going to tell her?" Rory asks, though they don't look at me. They stare out the window overlooking the front porch, eyes in the swampy distance where their grandfather disappeared.

"You'll know as soon as I do."

There is so much more I want to say, but I can't seem to drag the words to the surface. I want to tell her how much I love her. How sorry I am that this happened. I want to ask if they're okay, even though I know they aren't, even though I know no one could possibly be okay after the things we've seen today.

She doesn't give me the chance to say anything anyway. Rory turns away from the window, eyes distant and glassy as she addresses Enzo. "I can give you a ride to your parents'."

"Oh. Yeah, okay, thanks." He clears his throat. Exchanges a look with me before looking back at her. "Thank you."

Rory shrugs one shoulder.

He killed for her today. The implications of that aren't lost on me. They don't hate each other, not anymore, not even if some part of them might want to. And now they're being awkward about it. Gods and teenagers.

"What are you gonna do after?" I finally manage to find my tongue.

She blinks, her lips parting. I can *see* the struggle play out across her expression, the way her mind reaches for something, anything. Her eyes dart to the stains on the carpet, black and brown and flecked with bright red.

"I guess I'll . . ." Clean up the blood and afterbirth? Tidy up the house that she lives in alone, now that her grandparent-kidnappers are both gone?

"Come to my place. Once you've dropped him off, just . . . come over, okay?" I swallow. "You won't even have to sneak in through the window. Probably."

Maybe, by then, my head won't feel like fresh-blown glass, stretchy and burning and more likely to crack than not. Maybe I'll actually be able to hold a conversation, to say the things I desperately want to say, to sort through my own fucked-up, muddled feelings to figure out what the hell those things even are.

"You too." I glance at Enzo. He's still perched on the edge of the kitchen counter, nervously twirling one of his decorative rings round and round between his thumb and forefinger. He raises his eyebrows at me. "Come over, whenever you're finished with your parents. I'll feed you. We can . . . come up with a plan."

Marian is going to kill all of us. At the very least, she's going to try. I don't know what to expect from Indy or Rhett. Buck and Murphy are wild cards, too, but for totally different reasons.

Maybe I fucked everything up with what I did in the church, but what other options did we have? Zephyr getting the knife, or killing Murphy and our parents? Poppy taking the Cyclone's power while Marian put a bullet in my chest?

Everything is terrible, and I have no idea how to fix any of it. But it was still our best option. I played the hand I was dealt, just like everyone else. I did nothing wrong. If I tell myself this over and over, it may start to taste like truth.

Enzo slides to the ground, feet connecting soundlessly. "You want us to wait here until your mom shows up?"

"No." I answer too fast. "Um. I'll be fine. She'll be here soon anyway."

Enzo and Rory exchange another look. Silent communication slips between them as if they're passing clandestine notes written in code, and I'm on the outside watching them conspire against me. Or maybe I'm just feeling a little raw. It's probably all in my head.

"Are you sure?" Rory asks. She takes a deep breath. "I don't know if it's a good idea for any of us to be alone right now."

"I'll be fine." Sparks flutter along the outside of my forearms, making my hair stand on end. I swallow. "There's nothing more dangerous than me out there."

"Excuse you—" Enzo begins to argue, that arrogant, infernal drawl on his tongue.

I can't listen to whatever he might want to say, so I don't give him the chance to finish. "You might be the devil. But even Lucifer was carved by the hand of his god, and we both know I could cut your wings if I wanted to."

Something wild and bright ignites in Enzo's eyes. His expression trembles with the blooming of renewed fascination. "*Oh.*"

Rory sighs. "Okay. I'll see you soon, then. Just—be careful. All-powerful Magician or not, I'm still bigger than you, and I'll beat your ass if you let yourself get hurt."

"Thanks, babe."

She brushes her shoulder against mine as she leaves, a subtle, barely there acknowledgment that we both know everything is terrible, but we're still here, still breathing, still together. The flash of her skin on mine is too quick and almost too much all at once. I take a deep breath that rattles in my lungs.

Enzo stops in front of me on his way to the door, following in their footsteps. He kisses the side of my mouth and says, "You should take a shower, darling. Your poor mother is in enough distress. And the remains of that British skid mark really don't deserve to decorate your skin a moment longer."

And then they're both gone, and the house is quiet, and I feel like crying and I don't know why. Instead of letting myself, I stand in the center of the living room, looking down at my blood-splattered clothes, and listen until I hear the roar of the old car and the sound of tires on the dirt road.

If my mother was leaving the hospital when she got my message, it'll be a half hour before she gets here. Maybe twenty minutes now. If she was on her way home already, it'll be longer. Still, I hurry to get undressed in the bathroom. I turn on the water and stand beneath the shower head like my body's moving on autopilot. Even though this isn't my house, isn't my shower, the act itself is familiar enough that I don't actually have to think, or be present in my own skin. It's a comfortable kind of dissociation.

The burn of the water, just on the wrong side of too hot to

be normal, helps bring my brain back online, but only a little. Only enough for it to really hit me how fucked everything is. How the hell was I doing this same thing just last night—washing more blood off myself in this shower before falling asleep tucked between Enzo and Rory? How was it only *this morning* that I woke up to find them drinking lavender tea on the front porch?

That can't be right, can it? That memory feels as distant as the memories of other lifetimes. It's only the thin—and ever fraying—cord of logic that keeps me tethered to its reality. It was only a few hours ago, no matter how far away it might feel.

Everything has changed since then. And nothing has changed. We are all the same people, and I don't think we'll ever be those people again.

There's fresh laundry folded on Rory's bed. Maybe Ellen did a load before—

I shudder. If I'm lucky, I will suffer some memory loss and never have to think about that *thing* ever again.

Rifling through the options, I find a pair of my own sweatpants left from one of our sleepovers and one of Rory's vintage tees, and I quickly tug both on. I carry my boots onto the front porch, wanting to get out of the house and away from the stench starting to overtake the living room. I snag them on, then snake my fingers through my wet hair. Can't pull it up, 'cause I gave Rory my hair tie. No way I'm going back inside to grab one from the bathroom.

What time is it? I check my phone screen. Not even five. The whole world has gotten flipped upside down, and people who clocked into work at their office jobs this morning haven't even started the drive home yet. How is that possible?

Overhead, the sky is a bizarre shade of blue—*too* blue, like it was rendered from a child's drawing of what the sky should look like, like it's been scribbled in with crayon. As I stare, a bubble of thunder bursts somewhere in the cloudless horizon, but it sounds wrong too. Like a slow, out-of-place kind of *hiccup*. Like nothing up there really knows what it's doing anymore.

Can't imagine why that might be.

I curl my hands, feeling that growing energy as it threads itself between my fingers. It's a living thing, and it's desperate for attention.

Sending Rory and Enzo off together wasn't just because I'm unafraid of being alone. It was also that I *wanted* to be alone. As deeply and eternally as I love them both, I still have to be a person when they're around. I have to fix myself into something that might actually have a soul. But I don't feel like a person right now. And I'm deeply disinterested in finding out about my soul.

So, there's that, but there's also *this*. For hours now, I've felt my magic rummaging beneath the surface of my skin, begging to be tended to. It wants to be touched, and cradled, and I want nothing more than to indulge it. But, like petting a stray dog and not knowing if it'll bite, there's healthy trepidation.

I've always suspected, if I were to use the Ouroboros to take someone's power for myself, the results could be catastrophic. As the god of magic, it has always been my place to counterbalance the rest of the pantheon. They each have their own limited realms, their sacred duties, their scope of power. My own power has only ever been limited by sacrifice. Willing to pay the price, and I could easily levy control of another's domain for a time. My whole existence has always been a system of checks and balances for the rest of them—and so, without them, there could be no *me*.

After all, what is a Magician without an audience?

I am not a person when no one is looking at me.

That whole system falls apart, though, if my own power goes unchecked. There can't ever be balance in a world where one person has *all* the power and no real consequences. And now I've taken the Cyclone's realm for my own. In doing so, I've tossed the rulebook out the fucking window. Because I'm not just able to *act* as the god of weather—I *am* the god of weather. And the god of weather is not bound by the Magician's obligation to sacrifice.

Since the birth of the knife, I've avoided using it, because I believed it would destroy any possibility of maintaining the balance. Because I believed it would unlock my own power in its entirety—that I would take not only the god's gifts, but their ability to use their magic without paying a price.

If my suspicions are proven true, I can do anything. I can mimic anyone's power, take hold of any domain. And there's nothing, and no one, that can stop me.

It also means there's nothing keeping the rest of the pantheon in check. If I am unbound from the balance, so are they. Their own magic will evolve, their domains expanding in a futile attempt to keep up with me—until we all destroy one another.

Or something like that.

There is another component to all this. When one god takes the power of another, those powers become warped. They shift into something new, something that fits their new deity. Like Rory's ability to root their enemies in place, a bastardization of the power of the Stillness, mingled with their own.

I have no idea how the powers of the Cyclone and the Magician will merge. And as desperate as my magic is to be touched, as desperate as I am to give in, I am not stupid enough *not* to be a little afraid. Part of me whispers that I've already gone too far to ever go back. Another part screams warnings in a language I can't understand.

I'm not sure how long I sit there on the front porch, focusing on the voices in my head until the rest of the world has slipped away, but then there are tires squelching through mud and my mom's car is parked in the grass and I've missed my opportunity to play with the magic anyway.

Maybe for the best. Maybe whatever's going to happen should wait until I've had that nap, and that meal, and I don't feel so much like a stuffed animal that lost all its stuffing.

Mom looks tired. That's what I think when I slide into the passenger seat and buckle my seat belt. In some faraway part of my brain, someone puts up a sticky note with a comment on how ridiculous it feels to be an ageless, all-powerful god in a body that has to *wear a seat belt*. Mom's knuckles are white around the steering wheel, her sharp cheekbones more gaunt than usual. Without the perfect makeup she always wears, she looks older, and sadder, and the bags under her eyes are too dark and thick to be from just one night of missed sleep.

She smiles at me, but there's nothing happy about it.

It's not until she pulls away from the log house and we're on the road, driving away, that muscles I didn't even know were tense start to relax. It's not until then that she speaks, either.

"Your dad can have visitors, by the way. We can go up to see him tomorrow if you want."

I don't know if I want that. In the last several years, I've been in a room with my dad only twice—my life was threatened both times. I wonder if she has any idea I drove out to see him in Florida. I don't think so. But I suspect my mother might surprise me with what she knows.

Realizing I haven't answered and I have no idea how long I've been stuck in my head, I say, "Maybe."

She sniffs and nods and I know she knows I mean no. At least for now.

"You left with those friends of yours, right? One of them was Enzo. The other—is her name Willa Mae?"

I know it isn't a deadname, not exactly, but it still makes me feel sick. Worse than actually hearing my own deadname does. "Her name's Rory."

"Okay." She takes a deep breath. I wonder what she's not saying. I don't think I'd actually like to know. "They were at the church. Are the two of them okay?"

"No. Yeah. I don't know."

She nods again. "Are you okay?"

It's a perfectly motherly question to ask, but it makes me grind my teeth anyway. I can't help picturing her talking to her patients at the hospital like this. It's the way she's always done with me—handling me at arm's length, always examining me with her X-ray vision for some kind of diagnosis.

There's no point saying any of this to her. It isn't going to change anything.

"I think so." I rub my hands against my thighs, feeling crackles of static as I do. "Hard to tell."

"Sure, yeah. You're probably in shock. It was—" She stops herself from saying whatever she was about to. A frown line creases between her eyebrows. Her hands tighten even harder on the wheel. Finally, she finishes with, "The boy who did this—he's dead now?"

The oceans are drying up. That's all I can see in my head. "Yeah."

"And you . . . rescued us. You were trying to help him through some crisis he was having. Some break from reality. But he had a gun. He shot your friend Poppy. And you . . . you made sure no one else got hurt. Right?"

Oh. I have the vaguest memory of talking to a cop in the church attic. The flash of their badge and Enzo's sharp-tongued replies as he spoke for me more often than not and Rory's hand, soft but firm, on my lower back and. Okay. Yeah. "Right."

She nods, a sad kind of relief drooping in her shoulders. I get the impression she's not relieved because that's what actually happened—she knows it isn't, she's just relieved that I'm playing along.

How awful it would be for her if people thought I was some kind of crazy murderer. No, this is so much better. I'm a hero. Her kid, the hero who rescued the hostages and saved their friends from getting shot.

Well, except Poppy. But even heroes don't get perfect scores all the time.

I see Marian's face, watching the ambulance drive away. I close my eyes, like that might get her to leave me alone.

"Gem . . ."

Deep breath. Eyes open. I glance over at her again. "Yeah?"

"Does all of this have anything to do with your grandparents?"

Not where I thought this was going. "Huh?"

"Your dad's parents. Is any of it . . . is it connected to them? To their death?"

My first instinct is to say no.

Well, no, my first instinct is to say "*Huh?*" again, because I still don't get the leap she's making. My second instinct is to say no.

But I guess that's not entirely true. It is about them, in its own fucked-up little way. About how different my life would have been if they'd lived. So much of what's happened over the last few months has been because I didn't have all the information I needed. They could've helped me with that.

"Sort of" is the answer I settle on. "Yeah, I guess. It's connected to them."

She makes a sound like maybe she's going to cry, like that really wasn't the answer she was hoping for. I haven't seen my mother cry very often in my life, despite plenty of reasons to. I imagine she thinks it's a waste of mascara. Of course, she's not wearing any makeup right now.

"I don't think I really understood how much the accident changed things. Not for a long time, and—and maybe I still don't understand it. I didn't know much about them, you know, I never met them. Your dad described them as . . . eccentric. I thought . . . you know, it was the seventies. They were hippies. But that's not—that's not what was going on, is it? They weren't just eccentric. Right?"

Well, I don't know. I never met them, either. Still, I take a deep breath and say, "No. I think what they had going on was bigger than just peace signs and smoking pot."

Or whatever hippies did. I missed that era.

"And I could see how much their deaths changed things. I could see the ripple effect, you know, all these years, I just—I didn't put it together. But now, it seems clear. I think their deaths broke your dad. Maybe even Paul, too."

Paul. Something about the name is a gut punch, and it makes my teeth chatter until they sear the inside of my cheek. It took my mother years to say my dad's name after they separated, but it's been even longer since she's mentioned his brother. If my dad was a ghost we talked circles around, my uncle, Paul Echols, was struck from our history book entirely. I don't remember enough about him to have any idea what she's talking about, but something—something in her tone, or the words, or the memory of his name, *something*—makes my skin itch.

"What did Paul do?" I ask, wondering what could be worse than the shit my dad put us through near the end.

She glances at me, mouth open and skin gray, unspeaking. She only looks back to the road when the tires start to screech, the textured strip warning her she's swerving too close to the ditch. "He's just . . . He's just a real piece of work."

Well, okay.

"But it's not just trauma, right? It isn't just that they lost their parents in this horrible way when they were really young. There's something more going on, there's—" She takes a deep breath, swallows, says, "That boy who did this. He could *do* things. And that's part of it too. Isn't it?"

"Yes." No more and no less than the truth she's asking for. My head hurts worse than it did before, pounding behind my eyes until there are black spots in my vision. Even if I wanted to, I couldn't hold her hand through an explanation right now.

"And you . . . Can you also do things?"

"Yes."

"Enzo, and Rory, and the other kids—"

"*Yes.*" I slump forward, the seat belt digging into my chest, and press my fingertips into my eyes, massaging them. Flashes of color flood the dark when I do, disconnected and meaningless at first, just pressure on the optic nerves. And then—faces?

I swear, I see a glimpse of faces lurking in the shadows of my mind's eye, one after the other, divided by flashes of white like lightning. Some of them I recognize. Others are shrouded in too much fog to see clearly. Several of them are me, different versions of me, different voices in my head all clamoring for attention, all trying to get me to listen.

It certainly doesn't make my headache lessen. I lower my hands and lean back in my seat again. "But it's not just my story to tell. And honestly . . . you're probably better off not knowing everything."

My mother says something. I think maybe she's arguing, pressing me for more details, but I can't hear her. Or I can, or I could, if I tried to dig past the voices suddenly growing louder and louder. Not just my own, but others, all of those faces— each with their own voice, each demanding to be heard.

"*You brought this on yourself,*" someone whispers.

Someone else screams, "*Look at what you've done!*"

They stack on top of one another, and then there are others on top of *them*, accusations and threats and warnings and I can't tune any of them out and I can't focus on a single thread, so it all just becomes noise. And the flashing lights don't go away, the darkness and the faces shrouded in that darkness and the bolts of color that reverberate through my skull, even when my eyes are open. And I can't see, and I can't hear, and I can't breathe, or think, because everything is happening all at once as time folds in on itself and I am spread paper-thin across epochs.

"Gem? Gem?"

I blink. The voices dip away. My vision returns. The clock on the dashboard reads 5:23 and my mother is staring at me from the driver's seat.

I am not spread across epochs. I am Gem Echols. I am seventeen years old. I live in Gracie, Georgia. I am totally present in my body right now.

I'm fine. I'm going to be fine.

"We're home," she says, and I think she wants to say more.

"I need to lie down," I tell her, before she can.

And I don't wait for her response, just tug open the door handle with shaking fingers and stumble my way inside, barely making it up the steps without my knees giving out under me. Hank is waiting for us, asleep in front of the door, and he whines when I step inside. The old dog frantically butts his head into my shins and licks at my knuckles, and I scrub my hand between his ears before stumbling my way down the hall.

I only manage to kick off my shoes before falling, face-first, into bed. Hank hops up next to me, curling himself into a doughnut at my waist, and I thread my fingers into the thick coils of his hair like a touchstone to whatever pitiful scrap of humanity is left in me.

I'm not even tired, not really, not physically. If time exists anymore, if I'm still bound to the rules of it, I haven't actually been awake that long, despite how it feels. I just don't know what else to do. I'm too much for my body. These bones can't hold me. But maybe, in sleep, I can let some of it go.

Yeah. Okay. Maybe sleep will help. And if it doesn't, at least Rory and Enzo will be here when I wake up.

4

LIFE FINDING A WAY, EVEN IN DARKNESS

From the eyes of Enzo Truly

It's quiet in the front seat of the old car when Aurora drives him home. She doesn't offer a reprieve by turning on the radio, and he's too uncomfortable to do it himself. Instead, he spends several minutes staring at the road but watching her in his periphery, wondering if the silence is supposed to be awkward or comfortable. Are they each meant to be lost in their own thoughts, replaying the events of the day, sitting in companionable quiet? Or does she have nothing to say to him, now that the moment's passed, now that she's had time to take what he did to her grandmother and turn it over a few times in her mind?

She reaches for the gearshift too quickly, and he jumps. And then flushes, because that's utterly humiliating.

"Your monster mask is slipping," she warns, kind enough to not actually look at him. Her hands flex over the steering wheel as she takes a left past the Circle K gas station. "That just for their benefit?"

Enzo isn't sure if the *them* in question is their boyfriend—is that gender affirming? he'll have to ask Gem later—or her grandparents. In any case, he scoffs and says, "Obviously not. It isn't a mask, kitten. I *am* a monster."

She hums considerately. His stomach hurts.

"What?" he demands of her silence. "You can't be deluding yourself into thinking I might secretly be a good person. Have you forgotten who I am?"

"Have you?" she counters.

Her tone makes him want to yell. Instead, he bites his tongue until he tastes blood.

At length, he says, "I'm just tired. Don't read too much into it. Whatever humanity you're projecting onto me, it isn't real."

"Fuck you," she startles him by biting out.

"What the hell did I do?" He sits up straighter, reinvigorated. Arguing with her might be enough to pull him out of his slump.

Aurora shakes her head, molars tensing in the back of her jaw. She glares at the road in front of them and doesn't turn her head to face him. "You don't get to do that to me anymore. You don't get to play that game where you act like nothing matters. Not after what you saw this morning. Not after what we did."

"I don't see what that—"

"You stuck your hands into the worst thing that's ever happened to me. My blood's all over you now, and I can't ever take that back." She swallows. "I've earned the right to see you bleed, Enzo."

Silence again creeps over the car, heavier this time than before. Enzo stares at his hands, unable to look at her any longer.

He understands the metaphor, but imagines himself literally covered in her blood anyway.

He asks himself if he can bleed for her.

The car crawls to a stop eventually in front of his house. The light's on in the living room, and his heart quickens. All else aside, he needs to see his parents again. He doesn't know what he'll say to them, what questions they might have ... but he needs them. They were the ones kidnapped and held hostage, but *he* needs *them*.

Pathetic.

"I am afraid," he finally tells her.

She sniffs. "Of what?"

The answer to that question might make him laugh if it weren't so earnest. "Everything."

Their eyes meet. He studies the blossom of green etched into one of hers. Life finding a way, even in darkness.

"I'm afraid of what's coming. I'm afraid of the things we've already done. I'm afraid of how much I want, and how wanting a thing gives it the power to hurt me. I'm afraid of you."

Aurora isn't so cruel as to ask him why he is afraid of her. And for that much, he's grateful. She winces but does not look away. "I'm afraid of you, too."

"I know." He swallows now. "I used to like that."

"And now?"

He hesitates—then sighs, resigned. "Now I'm just afraid of what it means that I don't."

She nods and finally looks away, studying her own hands. "And Gem?"

"Yes."

"Are you afraid for them or of them?"

His chest hurts. "*Yes.*"

"Me too." She swipes away the teardrop that rests on one cheek. "I don't know what to do next. I don't know how to help them."

"Me either." One hand on the door handle, ready to make his escape. The other hand hovers for too long before lowering, as cautiously as reaching for a wild animal, to settle over the back of one of hers. "But whatever it is, we'll do it together. You don't have to save them on your own this time."

Again, their eyes meet. Hers wet; his burning.

"I think I'm glad you're here," she admits, and it feels like blasphemy.

"I think I am, too," he answers.

When her fingers thread with his and squeeze, he worries he might actually burn. By the grace of some god or another, he doesn't.

"We're going to be okay," she tells him. Or tells herself in front of him.

Either way, he answers. "We're going to be okay. All of us."

And in that moment, with Aurora's hand like an anchor to hope in his palm, he means it.

5

A WORLD AWAY

From the ~~fractured~~ mind of ~~the Mountain~~ Rory
whoever They are right now

Later.

"Gem is dead," the Shade tells her, his blood soaking her sheets as he lies, mostly naked and flayed open, in her bed.

"Shut the fuck up," she warns, spinning toward him and holding up one shaking hand. An accusatory finger points at his bare, red-slicked chest. "That isn't true."

Gem is *alive*. It's only that they've been missing for days. Rory isn't sure how many—she hasn't slept since she last saw them.

On the bedside table, Enzo's phone dings. They both jump.

"Who is it? Who is that, who's texting you?" she demands, but doesn't let him look for himself. She snatches the phone up before he can, eyes skimming the notification.

Not Gem. Rhett Clancy. The Librarian checking in on the Shade.

It's never Gem. It's always Rhett, or Enzo's parents, or his fucking Discord server. He doesn't even like carrying it around anymore, keeps trying to leave it behind when they go out. But Rory won't let him.

Someday, it will be Gem again. It will be. Because they're not dead.

She throws the phone at his stomach, too hard. He groans when it makes contact. "Tell him to leave you alone."

"I'm not doing that."

"He was the cause of all of this!" When she screeches, a cockroach skitters from her hair and across her forehead.

It's been a long night. There are other gods just as eager to find Gem as they are. They're the reason for Enzo's bloodletting.

"A fact which he's hyperaware of," Enzo growls in retort, tossing his phone away like its presence burns him. "He's eager to make it up to me. And knowledge, now more than ever, is power."

She does not care about power. All she cares about is Gem.

Her body shakes as she stares down at Enzo and sees nothing but shadow.

"Oh, Aurora," he whispers, and it sounds a world away. She doesn't notice him moving and flinches in surprise when his bloody hands cup her throat. His breath ghosts against her mouth when he whispers, "I'm sorry. I'm sorry."

"They . . . are not . . . dead . . ." She forces the words out through trembling teeth.

"I know. I know." His forehead touches hers when his voice breaks. "Some part of me thinks it would be easier to believe that. It hurts too much, to keep thinking we're going to find them, and then . . ."

Light returns to her vision. She blinks, finding Enzo's red-rimmed gaze locked on hers. Slowly, her shaking hands rise to his biceps and squeeze until he must be in pain. "We *are* going to find them."

Because there is no other option.

Because there cannot be a future where that does not happen.

Because if that did not happen . . .

"And what if we don't?" Enzo demands.

She could hate him for the question, if he did not quiver just to ask it.

"If we don't find them . . . then you and I are going to turn the whole of this world into a tomb."

Her demon's mouth rests against her temple, eerie in its tenderness. Rory closes her eyes and imagines the carnage their union could beget.

Whichever god they worship, the world would be wise to pray for Gem's return.

Her hand curls around my throat like a collar, her mouth nestled in the crook behind my ear, and she whispers,

"You would surrender all I have to offer you for only the *possibility* of more power? Little fool—*I* am power."

There is an unruly part of me that would like to sink into her arms, but I turn instead. I don't know if I mean to hit her or kiss her, but it doesn't matter.

The dream changes before I have the chance to choose.

My feet bleed as I run barefoot up the cobblestone hill in Dorset. I don't know where I've lost my shoes, and the pain is so vicious I can hardly breathe through it. With each slice into my skin, it's harder to force myself to go on.

But I have to. I have to fight through this. I have to get away before they realize—

A mother's agonized wail cuts through the evening air, and I know. They've found the child's body.

· ·

Zephyr's mother sobs that same wail over his coffin, her other son's arms around her, her own shoes mismatched on the carpet of this terrible church.

Somewhere in the distance, thunder rumbles over the hillside as the Mountain's coffin is lowered into the ground. Sometimes, we make our leave together. When I have my way, she outlives me. This life, I will spend every new breath mourning her.

And hunting those responsible to the edge of this world.

The Shade hunts me across desert sands and forest floors and the seafoam top of the ocean, the two of us racing across the Ether. Me, always one league ahead; him, never deterred and always at my back. I am faster, but he is relentless. I am stronger, but he is more wicked. I have long feared what would happen if I succumbed to my own exhaustion and he caught me. Not because I do not want to be held in his palm but because I enjoy our chase too much. I twist my ankle in a thread of seaweed, tumble into the sand, and taste salt water when I open my mouth to scream. His arms are already snaking around me.

I don't scream at the familiar arms around me, though there is a part of me that wants to. I feel sick, nausea pressing its fingers into the back of my throat, insistent and cruel. I don't scream, though there is a part of me that wonders if I should, that knows I should, that is so tired of keeping quiet and keeping secrets and keeping myself small and soft and polite.

He kisses my neck and I imagine using my nails to peel the skin from my throat. Imagine peeling away all of the skin he's ever touched until I'm nothing but blood and exposed muscle and bone and he would never, ever want to touch me again because I would be disgusting. I want to be disgusting, I want to disgust him as much as he disgusts me.

"Happy birthday, baby."

I want to cry, but I can't, want to tell him everything I think about him, but I can't, want to run, but I can't. I don't want to hurt his feelings, I love him. I love him. It's what he does to me that I hate; it's me that I hate. This isn't how I wanted to spend my ninth birthday.

"Make a wish." My mother giggles as my cake is placed in front of me, a dozen candles lit above a thick layer of homemade frosting. My brother watches me with wide-eyed devotion, and I offer him a smile like bestowing charity on the needy.

I suck in a deep breath and let it out quickly, extinguishing every candle in one blow.

As I do, my father presses the button on our giant wooden camera to capture the moment.

There is very little that I would wish for. I have everything I want. I can hardly imagine a world where I don't.

I don't realize the boy has a camera.
This is my first high school party,
my first time having a drink,
my first time with three boys in the loft of a barn.
I'm scared, and excited,
and I can't feel my own skin,
   and I think if I just let them do whatever they want to me,
                 eventually, I'll have to feel it.

                    But I don't know one of them has a camera.
                                              I wonder
                                                 if I
                                            would've
                                                told
                                               them
                                                 no,
                                                if I
                                               knew.

"No!" I scream so forcefully that I taste blood in the back of my throat. Fire consumes everything, smoke consumes everything, and I can hardly see or breathe or think through it all. I can hear the Shade's screams, twisted up inside his laughter. I cannot hear the Inferno anymore. I don't know what that means. But for the first time, I realize we are truly going to burn this world to the ground.

· ·

The Mountain's wails are like battle cries as she falls to her knees at my side, the shell of our home burnt-out and destroyed in front of us. Everything we've loved, everything we've worked for, gone. We have never hurt anyone, and still the Lionheart will not let us know a moment of peace. Maybe peace is no longer an option; perhaps it never was.

My rage is a balm to the breaking of my heart.

"Where is your heart?" the Reaper asks as we stand in a fog-shrouded room of gray. I can see nothing but her body and my own, though neither of us looks the way I remember.

I touch a hand to my chest and frown when my fingers clutch at open air. I look down at my torso and see my skin has been carved open. There is a hole at the center of me, a cavity where my heart should live.

"Am I dead?" I ask her, fingers searching the slick, broken-rib edges of my wound, searching for where my heart may have slipped, as if I might find it hidden behind my severed sternum.

"You've always been dead," she tells me. "That's why you're afraid of me."

The Reaper is gone, but the fog remains. I stand in front of a full-length mirror and watch my own reflection. I am me, but I'm not. This hole in my chest is not mine. These mismatched eyes, one gold and one silver, are not mine. These fangs and talons and leathery wings beginning to burst free from under the surface are not mine.

"But they are yours, aren't they?" my therapist asks. I watch his hand circle my hip and undo the button on my jeans. "Gem Echols is just a performance. Nothing about *Gem* is real. Not even this body."

I slam my fist into the mirror and it shatters.

"Don't like your reflection?" the Muse whispers at my back.

I run through the halls of the museum, but they never end. It stretches farther and farther, going on forever. I will never get away from this place, and he will always be right behind me.

The paintings on the walls are of my own faces. I scream, and they all scream back at me.

A gunshot.
A bullet right between the ribs.
Pain flaring in my chest.

The last thing I see is Marian's face,
somber and sad and resigned,
as she lets me die in that church attic
to save everyone else.

Goodbye.

The End

6

GO HOME

The Evergod straddles my waist, the tip of the Ouroboros pressed into my chest. His hazel eyes glint with madness, crooked teeth warped into a Cheshire cat's vicious grin, and he tilts his head so far to one side I think it might crack right off his shoulders.

I reach for his wrist, but he predicts my move, shifting away so my fingers barely graze his arm. I reach for him again, and he does the same. He's barely moved.

It smells like hay and cow shit. The ground under me is rocky and uncomfortable, and my thin T-shirt isn't enough to protect me from the twigs digging into my skin, pinpricks of pain scattered along my neck, back, and legs.

Moooooo.

I tilt my head just enough to see a familiar brown cow with a white heart at the center of her forehead. She's lying in her paddock a few feet away, watching us. If she's disturbed by the threat to my life, she gives no indication of it. Her ears twitch with my eyes on her, and she moos again, sounding somehow indignant. Maybe she doesn't like us bringing our issues to her barn.

All at once, the weight of reality slams into me.

This is not a dream. I am in the Wheeler family barn.

And Buck is on top of me, with my knife.

Electric bolts fire in my hands and I try to scramble out from under the smaller boy. He's surprisingly dense, heavier than I would've expected, more muscle than meets the eye. And before I can actually grip him to try to hoist him away, he simply leaps to his feet, giggling as he spins like a ballerina.

My knees threaten to give out as soon as I force myself to stand, legs as wobbly as gelatin. Power surges through my arms, that electric energy I haven't been able to harness finally coming to the surface, finally given the chance to be *used*.

It should be an extremely cool moment, when I open my flat palm toward Buck's body and send a bolt of lightning, summoned straight from my skin and lurching toward his—if he didn't ruin it by sidestepping without any effort. If the lightning didn't strike wood instead of flesh, the smoke in the aftermath smelling of cedar instead of burnt meat.

He giggles again, and tosses the knife onto the barn floor between us. "You're so silly, Gem. I wasn't going to hurt you. It isn't *time* for you to be carved open. Tick, tick, tick."

"What the fuck am I doing here?" I demand, embarrassed at his utter lack of fear. I want to scream, *Do you not know who I am?* But I suspect he'd only laugh at me again.

I reach for the Ouroboros, half expecting him to stop me. He doesn't. I don't know where the knife's been. The last time I remember seeing it was when I used it on Zephyr. Have I had it on me this whole time? I don't know. I was too out of it, my head too full of cotton balls and glass.

Things are clearer now. So much clearer. I don't know if that's better or worse.

"You needed a nap," he informs me, walking over to his cow and petting her behind one ear.

"Yeah, I was taking one. In my *bed*. How did you get me here?" I want to strangle him. I imagine that might go as well as electrocuting him did.

Buck sighs, looking at me through his long eyelashes with something like pity. I get the feeling he's sorry I'm too stupid to grasp what's going on here. "You needed a *longer* nap. I helped."

One second passes. Then another. My fist tightens around the knife handle.

"How long have I been here?"

Buck smiles, slow and toothy. A breeze makes the barn windows rock and my hair flutter over my eyes, and a chill crawls across my skin. He doesn't answer.

"What have I *missed*?"

He shrugs one shoulder, obviously unbothered by the reality of kidnapping me and holding me in some kind of coma. "You found more than you lost."

I want to ask him to elaborate on that, but I'm not sure I need him to. I *did* need a nap, as much as I needed answers. Buck gave me both in those dreams that weren't exactly dreams. All I have to do is accept what I saw, and I'll know everything I need to.

Whether or not I'm willing to do that is another thing entirely.

"Go home, Gem Echols," the Evergod says with a smile and a sigh. His dirty fingernails scratch lovingly into the base of the cow's ear. "It's time for the Magician to go home."

And I don't know what else to do except exactly what he tells me. I tuck the Ouroboros into the waistband of my pants and walk, barefoot, down the dirt road from the Wheeler farm to my mother's house.

7

LET ME TAKE YOU HOME

When my family lived in the suburbs of Atlanta, we had this perfect cookie-cutter house. That's where I was born—well, that's where I lived when I came home from the hospital—and that's where I stayed until seventh grade, when my father's brain broke and my mom dragged us back to her hometown in the middle of nowhere, South Georgia. I haven't thought about that house in years, but I don't know why. It was the only home I ever knew until four years ago. It was where I became *me;* at least the version of me I was before Rory and Poppy showed up in Gracie a few months ago and everything changed again.

It was nothing special. A little split-level built in the early 2000s, tucked away in a cul-de-sac. White siding and dark, mustard-yellow shutters on the windows, and a big backyard with a chain-link fence so Hank could run around without chasing the other kids who'd ride by on their scooters. (This was back when Hank could run at all.) On the upper level was my parents' bedroom, the living room and dining room, a big kitchen with a bay window that overlooked our driveway. The lower level had the laundry room with a bathroom attached, and two more bedrooms. One of them was mine. The other was Paul's.

I don't remember when he moved in, but I know he moved out right before my tenth birthday. I don't remember why. Not why he was there or why he left.

The house my mom grew up in is nothing at all like that cookie-cutter cul-de-sac house in Atlanta. Our home in Gracie belonged to my grandparents before us, before they moved to Tampa to be closer to their family on the rez. My great-grandfather built this place in the 1920s with lumber he cut with his own ax. I don't think it's changed much in the years since.

There are no streetlights out here in the middle of nowhere, the rural part of an already rural town, and I can only make out the house from the flicker of the yellow porch light. Bugs dance around the bulb, buzzing and hissing and zapping themselves on its glass. There are two old rocking chairs, left over from when my grandparents lived here, that no one actually ever sits in.

In so many ways, this house feels like a time capsule, a footprint of someone else's life. Like even though my mom and I have lived here for four years, even though this was the first home she ever knew, we haven't really made it our own. I don't know her reasons. But it's hard for this place to feel like my home when I've always known I'm not going to stay. I wasn't meant to die in Gracie.

That's what I used to think, anyway. Now I wonder if I already have.

The car we share is parked in the grass off the dirt driveway. I have no idea what time it is, have nothing on me but the knife and the clothes I fell asleep in, but the dark tells me it's late. If

I'm lucky, Mom's asleep, and we won't have to deal with questions about where I've been until tomorrow. I still have no idea how long I've been gone.

When I pass the car and start up the porch steps, a breeze kicks in, making the limbs on the old oak by my bedroom window rattle and shake and scrape against the glass. I pause, fingers hovering over the hand-carved porch railing, and tilt my head to look at the tree. It stares back at me in silence so loud it could burst my eardrums.

Maybe I was never meant to die in Gracie, but living here hasn't always been all bad. For a while, I thought I could hear the land trying to talk to me with my ancestors' voices. For a while, I honestly believed I was connected to this place, grounded here, like the earth itself wanted me to stay, even if the people didn't.

It's been a while since I've heard the land try to speak. I don't think it wants me to stay anymore. I don't think it loves the Magician the way it loved Gem Echols.

When I notice a flash of silver beyond the tree, I frown, squinting into the dark at what looks like *another* car. It's too far away, too tucked in shadow, for me to make out any detail. It could be Rory's grandfather's. Maybe she's inside. I turn away, spurred forward by the thought.

The door is locked, which surprises me for a second. Out here in the boonies, we never lock our door. But then I think of Zephyr showing up and dragging my sleeping mother out of bed and, yeah. Okay. It wouldn't have helped anyway, if she'd had the door locked that night. But I get it.

I know there's a spare key somewhere on the porch, even if I've never used it. I lift up the mat, check on top of the doorframe, push aside the little decorative ceramic frog in a straw hat that's sitting at the top of the steps. At this rate, all my rustling around out here is gonna wake my mom up, but that might be the only way I can get in the house.

It occurs to me, when I jiggle the window, trying to pry it open and making a metal-on-glass clinking as I do, that Hank isn't barking. And that's weird. Because Hank *loves* to bark. It's one of the few things he can still enjoy, geriatric as he is. And he would definitely bark at someone trying to break in.

There's no opportunity to really get anxious about the quiet, though, because the front door opens as soon as I have the thought.

For a long moment, my mother and I just stare at each other. Her in the doorway of our home and me on the front porch, rifling around like a burglar.

I've always known my mother was beautiful, because her beauty has always been intentional. She buys the most expensive makeup she can afford, and applies it in such a way that it doesn't look like she's wearing any at all. She shops at Ross and Kohl's for clothes, inoffensive and boring but budget friendly with designer tags. She has the *vibe* of someone beautiful, if forgettable, and I've always known that's exactly the way she likes it.

See, our foundations are the same; our sharp bones and our wide, honeycomb eyes, and our thick, almost-black hair. But, just like this house we live in, neither of us has ever made a home out of our body. My mother treats hers like an art gallery, perfectly put together for the satisfaction of onlookers. I've always treated mine more like a shitty highway motel room—the kind of place where the water runs a little brown and cockroaches skitter when you turn the light on, and you know you're probably leaving with bedbugs, but no one cares how many guests you invite or how much noise you make or what gets destroyed along the way.

All of this is only important because the version of my mother standing in the doorway is *not* perfectly put together. If she were a gallery, she'd be closed for repairs. She's in nothing but a bathrobe. I know this robe. It's perfectly white and fluffy and I got it for her for Christmas a few years ago because it's the kind of thing you get for a mother who lives with you and is still a stranger. It *isn't* perfectly white and fluffy, though. Not right now. There are stains all over the front of it, its faux fur squashed and sticky, like she's been living in it for who knows how long. Her eyes are swollen and red-rimmed, her cheeks sunken like she hasn't eaten or slept or done anything but cried. Her hair is greasy and limp and pulled back in a ponytail like that might hide the tangles.

Her hands shake.

"Gem?"

"Hey. Sorry, I didn't mean—"

I've never heard my mother make a sound like the sob that comes out of her as she throws herself from the threshold and into my chest. She wraps her skinny arms around my shoulders and presses her face against mine, scattering kisses along my cheek and temple. She stinks, but in a way that feels sort of comforting, as gross and weird as that is, and I don't push her away.

She only stops kissing me to look over her shoulder and call out, "Ecke! It's them! Gem is home!"

What the hell is she—

"Oh, Gem. Oh, mvto. Mvto, Creator, for bringing them home."

And behind my mother, *her* mother, my grandmother, appears. If my mom and I have the same foundation, it's only because

Norma Tiger is the blueprint. My grandmother is the spitting image of us both, but our features are at home on her. With her dark hair in a long braid, smudged eyeliner beneath each amber eye, her features softened by wrinkles and smile lines and sun, she looks completely at peace in her own body. I haven't seen her in a long time, but she looks exactly like I remember and it makes me want to cry.

She pulls me to her when my mother backs away, petting my hair and pressing her cheek to the side of my head. She whispers words in a language I can't speak but can *almost* understand, and my eyes close. I sway on my feet, closer to her solid warmth.

"What are you doing here?" I finally ask when we pull apart.

"What do you mean?" she demands, taking my wrist and guiding me inside. Her voice is warm and gentle, rounded at the edges—but solid; unshakable. "Of course I'm here."

"I don't understand." I let myself be shuffled into a seat at the kitchen table. It smells like hominy and sweet potato and frying grease and my stomach rumbles.

"You disappear for two weeks and you thought I'd just stay home and hope for the best?" She scoffs, grabbing a big wooden spoon and stirring something in a pot on the stove.

I'm sorry—"*Two weeks?*"

My mother kneels on the kitchen floor next to my chair, putting her hands over my knees and looking up at me. It makes me feel nauseous, the way I feel like the adult in the relationship when I look down at her. The way my mother's sunken features make her eyes even bigger, like a child herself staring up at me. "Gem, baby, where were you? What happened?"

"I . . ." Two weeks. Two fucking weeks I've been taking a goddamn nap in Buck Wheeler's barn. I'm gonna kill that guy. "I lost track of time."

My grandmother makes a *noise*. My mother's eyebrows tense together. She looks like she's going to say something, to ask me to elaborate, but there's nothing more I can give her.

So, instead of letting her ask, I say, "There's stuff I shouldn't explain, and then there's stuff I really, really can't explain. Okay?"

She swallows.

I can see there's still more she wants to say, but my grandmother interjects, "Catherine, go take a shower."

"But—"

"No. You smell like rot. They're home now. I have them. You take your shower. You eat. And you get some rest. They're not going to disappear again. Are you, Gem?"

I touch the tips of my fingers to my mother's cheek, and we both jump a little at the static bolt that flares from my hand. I can't make that promise, and I think my mother knows that. There's a part of me that wishes I could, though. Any world where I could make that promise would be a whole hell of a lot simpler than the one we actually live in.

She takes my hand from her face, twisting our fingers together and bringing my knuckles to her mouth. She kisses them again, then rises to her feet, kissing the top of my head. "I'll be right back. Don't—"

"I'll be here when you get out." Maybe I shouldn't make that promise, either. But it feels cruel to give her nothing.

Moving slowly, she finally backs away. Only when the bathroom door shuts between us do her eyes finally leave me.

My grandmother slides a bowl of soup and a piece of fry bread in front of me, and only then do I realize the urgency of my hunger. Have I eaten anything in the last fourteen days? I rip the bread open, sinking half of it into the bowl, using it as a spoon to slurp up the liquid. What leaks from the bread onto my hand, I lick off without any concern for decency. When my first serving starts to dwindle, my grandmother adds a second without a word.

Only after my third bowl of soup and fifth piece of fry bread do I finally stop eating long enough to take a breath. I swipe the back of my hand over my mouth and rub my palms against the thighs of my pants, glancing up to find my grandmother watching me from the other side of the table.

I have so many questions, but I don't know if she has any answers. I need to talk to Rory and Enzo. I need to find my phone. I need to know what the hell is going on—how's Poppy?

What I actually ask my grandmother is "Where's Hank?"

She frowns, eyes glancing down the hall toward my bedroom door. "He is not well."

Panic flutters in my chest. "What do you mean? What's wrong?"

"He's old, Gem. He's tired." She sighs, rubbing her fingers into her weathered wrist. "He's in your room. Has barely left it since you did."

If guilt were enough to kill a person, I'd be a goner. I go to push myself away from the table, to check on him, to tell him I'm sorry for disappearing, but my grandmother stills me with a flick of her fingers.

"Wait. You talk with me first."

If there's nothing I can tell my mom, there's even less I can tell my grandmother. But I don't move. I wait for her questions, for the interrogation that must be coming, knowing I won't have good enough answers for either of us.

What she says isn't at all what I'm expecting. "I want you to come home with me."

My eyebrows knit together. "Huh?"

She waves her hand around the room, head shaking with something like disappointment when she does. It stings, but I don't know why. "This place was a good home for your grandfather and me for a long time. We thought it was a good home for your mother, too. And we hoped it would be one for you. But you don't want to be here, do you?"

I swallow. "I didn't—I wasn't gone because I was running away or—because I hate this house or something."

"Sure. Whatever you say. But that isn't what I'm talking about." She sighs. "Do you know why your grandfather and I moved away?"

"To be closer to the reservation."

"Yes. To be with our *people.*" She takes a deep breath, reaching across the table to place her hand over the back of mine. Her skin is soft with wrinkles, time wearing her body down until all that's left is the tender pulp of her marrow. "There can be so much good in surrounding yourself with people who aren't like you. You have proven that to me time and again, teaching me so much about the world we live in. But . . . there is just as much good in going home, Gem. Sometimes, what we need is *our* people, to remind us of who we are. To care for us in a way only our people can."

She didn't want to die in Gracie any more than I do.

My chest hurts. An image of my body flayed open, the center of me cut out and missing, flashes through my mind, but I try to push it down. She has no idea how badly I want exactly what she's talking about. To feel connected to my people again. To hear the land speak to me again. To feel grounded in my body, and my life, and time.

But she also has no idea *what* she's talking about. Her people can't be my people because I don't even know if I'm a person.

Who am I when no one is looking at me?

She squeezes my hand. "When all of this is over and you can finally rest—let me take you home. Let your people help you come back to yourself."

I only realize it's the end of the conversation when she stands up and kisses my forehead before moving back to the stove and ladling soup into an old margarine tub for leftovers. After another moment of waiting, I stand up and head to my room.

Hank is right where I left him, curled up in the center of my bed. He doesn't react at all when I enter, and my stomach drops. I freeze halfway across the floor, staring in horror at his too-still body. When I watch his chest finally rise and fall with a deep breath, I could scream. I sink onto the edge of the bed and wrap my hands around either side of his face, kissing his furry snout. He stinks worse than my mom does, and I care even less.

He finally seems to register that I'm here, his tail hitting the comforter with a thunk, his tongue flicking out to kiss my chin. But he still doesn't raise his head.

"I'm so sorry," I whisper into the tangles of his wiry fur, hand slipping up and down his spine. He's thinner, I can tell by the way the bones hit my palm. For every rib my fingers find, another part of my own body shatters. "I never wanted to leave you alone."

He whines, rolling over onto his side and pressing the top of his head against my knee. One eye cracks open, just enough to look up at my face, before he falls back asleep in my lap.

I don't know how long I sit there just petting him, telling him in ways both verbal and not how much I love him and what a good boy he's been, but eventually my bedroom door opens and my mom slips in. Freshly showered, hair still damp, with new pajamas on, she sits down at the top of my bed near the pillows and watches me with Hank. She doesn't say anything for a long moment. I watch her brush a tear from the corner of her eye.

"I'm gonna have the vet come out tomorrow. It's time."

Even if I know she's right, I want to hate her for it. I want to fight her, scream at her, ask her how she could do that to him. I want to, but I don't. Because I *do* know she's right, no matter how much it sucks, and *fuck*, it *sucks*.

"Will you be here?" Her voice is hopeful if not optimistic, wavering in the gray space between what she wants and what she's prepared for.

"I—" My fingers twist in the fur on his neck. I want to tell her yes. I want to be able to say yes for *him*. Through everything that's happened, every person I've been and every mistake I've made over the last eleven years, Hank is the only one who's loved me through all of it. He never would have left my side. How can I not be there with him at the end? What kind of monster would I be to abandon him when he needed me there to say goodbye?

But I can't make that promise. There's too much I don't know. I need to talk to the others, need to catch up on everything I've missed.

"I'll try," I finally say. It's pathetic.

"Okay." She nods, reaching down to run her knuckles against his backside. "I'll be with him. No matter what, he won't be alone."

She's talking about *his* comfort, but I know she says it for my benefit. I want to cry, or throw up, or thank her. Instead, I just keep sitting there. Pathetic.

"What have I—" I clear my throat, taking a deep breath to try to shake loose the knot in my voice. "What did I miss?"

"There's a cop, Officer Allen, who keeps coming around here asking questions. He's been looking for you. The Beauregards—I get the feeling they don't like being told their son was killed in self-defense. They're pushing for a different ending to the story, and they've got enough money to push hard." She shakes her head. "I'm not gonna lie to you, Gem. You disappearing? It doesn't make you look innocent."

I'm going to kill Buck Wheeler.

"That wasn't exactly my choice," I bite out.

"Yeah. I had a feeling. So did your friends—uh, your ... people." She waves a hand toward the door. "Rory and Enzo have been here every day."

"Oh?"

"Mm. They don't seem to like me very much." She sniffs. "But I get the feeling they love you a lot. So, that's something."

I don't know if that's true. It seems more likely that they just know too much—too much about her, too much about me, too much about our secrets and shadows and the places where hurts overlap. My mother has probably screwed me up beyond belief, but she's still my mother.

She's not *theirs*, though.

"They do. They love me a lot." They love me so much that they cannot truly hate, and will never, ever forgive, the woman at the root of my life. I swallow, brushing the back of my hand over Hank's jaw.

"Your other friend, Rhett, he's been by here the last few days with them."

"Huh?"

"Rhett Clancy? Big boy with the red hair and—"

"No, I know who he is. But Rhett is not my friend." In fact, that weasel's on my list. Right after Buck. Zephyr couldn't have done anything he did without the Librarian's help.

"Well, he seems to think he is." She shrugs. "He's been helping them try and find you."

That doesn't make any sense. I really need to talk to Rory and Enzo.

I rub my hand over Hank's neck and say, "I'm tired. I think I'm gonna try and get some sleep. You should, too."

I'm not tired, not even a little. I've been asleep for too long, and now I have shit to do. But I need to get her out of this room, and she's looking at me like she's worried if she takes her eyes off me, I'm going to disappear again. Her worry isn't misplaced, which makes it worse.

She studies me, eyes narrowed, for a long moment before she nods. "Okay. I'll come check on you in the morning."

"Okay."

I watch her stand and move toward the door before something else occurs to me. Something Rory and Enzo can't help me with. Something I think only my mom can.

And I don't want to ask. There is a part of me—a big part—that's screaming louder than all the other voices right now, warning me not to open my mouth, not to open this can of worms. But now that the question is alive in my throat, I don't know how not to ask. I think, if I let it sit there for too long, I'm going to choke on it.

"Hey, Mom?"

She pauses at the door, fingers on the handle, and looks at me over her shoulder. "Hmm?"

"Why did Uncle Paul move out?"

That ball in my throat shifts. I don't realize I'm in pain until it lessens a fraction.

My mother's face falls, her body tensing so tautly that it makes her look smaller. Her, the child. Me, the adult. Her molars grind, knuckles whitening as her hand tightens over the doorknob. "Gem . . . are you sure you want to get into that right now?"

"I want to know." That is a lie. I don't realize it until I've already said it and my mouth goes dry. I try again. "I need to know."

She considers me, like she's gauging the truth of that. Or maybe she's weighing my need to hear this story against her own need to never talk about it again. I'm not totally sure what conclusion she comes to, but eventually she asks, "What do you remember?"

"I—" That's a loaded question. Maybe it wouldn't have been, two weeks ago, but it is now, thanks to Buck Wheeler and his dreams. There are memories that weren't there before, memories dancing at the outskirts of my mind, right in the periphery of conscious thought. I don't want to look at them, though. I can't seem to bring myself to look directly at them and see them for what they are. "I'm not sure."

She swallows. "We never had any proof . . . that he'd done anything. I still don't know. Not really. You have to know, if we'd ever caught him, if we'd actually seen anything, if you'd ever said something, it would've been different. I would have killed him myself."

"If I'd said something?"

"Oh—that's not—I didn't mean it like that. It wasn't your fault." She winces, trying desperately to undo the knot she's tied in her own tongue. "I just meant we would've believed you."

My heart knocks inside my chest, clamoring at the doorway of my bones, begging to be let loose. It doesn't want to be trapped in this body any more than I do.

"Where is your heart?" the Reaper asks.

"But I started to . . . worry. I had this weird feeling. I didn't . . . I couldn't shake it. There weren't any signs. There was no reason to be afraid. Maybe I was the crazy one. Or maybe I wasn't. I still don't . . . I don't really know. I told your dad about this weight in my gut. I told him I didn't have any reason to be suspicious, I told him I hadn't seen anything, but he was . . . the idea that something might be happening to you, right under his nose . . . I'd never seen him like that before. He confronted his brother, and . . ." Her eyes have gone glassy, lips parted. She's here, but she isn't. "Like I said, I still don't know exactly what happened. But Paul packed his bags and left the next day. They never spoke again. And we stopped saying his name."

That would've been just a few weeks before my tenth birthday.

Which was right before my dad started losing reality, his mind breaking slowly, slowly, until the night he started seeing ghosts in our home. Ghosts who wanted to hurt us. Right under his nose.

Which was right before my mother and I ran away, hiding out in *her* childhood home so that *mine* couldn't ever touch us again.

Which was right before she started pushing me toward therapy and meds. I always thought it was because she was afraid I would turn out like my dad. All her watching me, second-guessing me, attaching some kind of diagnosis to everything I said and felt and did, I always thought it was her comparing me to him.

But maybe it was something else entirely.

I watch my hands shake over Hank's fur. I can't feel my own skin. How many times in my life have I been unable to feel my own skin? How many times has my body not felt like my own?

It feels like admitting to a crime when I say, "I think something really bad happened to me."

"Gem—"

"I don't wanna talk about it anymore." Another lie. I *can't* talk about it anymore. My heart has clawed its way up and out of my chest, into the cradle of my throat. It's even bigger than the question was, and it hurts even worse. If I keep talking about this, I think it's going to kill me.

She hesitates. I can feel the tension bubbling off her body when she tries again. "Gem, he got married a few years ago. I looked them up on Facebook once. His wife already had kids when they got married. One of them is a little girl. Her name is Hannah. If—if you know—"

"Please." I wince. "I hear what you're saying. I'm just . . . I can't do this right now. Okay? Just not tonight. Please don't make me do this *tonight*. I'm so tired."

I can't make myself look at her, but, eventually, I hear the click of the door that tells me she's left. Some time after that, I manage to get out of bed, and find my phone waiting for me on top of my dresser.

There are still no notifications. No texts, no calls. Nothing. It makes my body feel cold. If no one is looking for me, am I already dead?

"You've always been dead," says the Reaper.

I open the Find My app and click Enzo's contact name, pulling up his location. He's out in the bayou, at Rory's house. They're still together. I need to get to them.

My hand brushes over the top of Hank's head one last time. "I'm gonna try to be here tomorrow. Okay?"

His tail smacks against the comforter.

"I'm sorry," I whisper to him, and my grandmother, and my mother, before my body disappears.

8

YOU DIDN'T THINK I WAS ME

When my body materializes in the empty living room of Rory's (not grandparents', 'cause they're dead, so just Rory's) house, the first thing I notice is Enzo's phone, abandoned on the coffee table, but no Enzo in sight.

The second thing I notice is how much my magic has changed. And also, how much it hasn't.

I remember the first time I came here with them, the way they led me to the swampy backyard behind the log home and *stole my shoes* for the alligator. I remember their taunting, bright-eyed and so irritating—especially then, when I *wanted* to keep wanting to hurt them, but I *also* really wanted to kiss them.

That was my first real taste of magic in this lifetime. It was like a flood beneath my skin, power surging through every inch of me, pressing against the confines of my body until it could break free. It was as if the center of gravity shifted. Like I was tethered, not to the earth, but to *Rory* themself. They were all I could see, or hear, or think about; the only thing in the world that mattered. Everything else just fell away.

This magic, this *new* magic, this version of magic where I can do anything I want without sacrifice . . . is not like that.

My memories from the day Zephyr kidnapped my parents are hazy. Everything between the Ouroboros slotting between his ribs and waking up in Buck's barn feels like a fever dream, more nightmare than reality, blending in with the rest of the strange visions from the two weeks I spent passed out in the Evergod's care. But I remember the feeling of this new magic in my body. The way it pressed up against me, slithering around and trying to break free, just like that *thing* trying to claw its way out of Ellen's—

Nope. Uh-uh.

I glance over at the stain, still on the carpet, and shudder. I've seen a lot of fucked-up shit in my lifetimes. That was still near the top of the list.

Anyway. The pressure in my head is gone, the thrum inside my bones quieted, like the magic has settled down. Like it's just another part of me now, there to be used when I reach for it, but not so desperate to escape. I don't know when it happened. Maybe while I was unconscious. Maybe when I used it in the barn, trying—and failing—to electrocute Buck Wheeler's ass.

(And I won't fail next time. He's as good as dead. He might be the god of time, but I am the god of gods. I will break him.)

Now reaching for my magic feels as natural and easy as breathing. I test the theory, raising my hand to the stain on the carpet and flicking my fingers. Inch by inch, the mess crawls out of existence until there's nothing left.

I look up at the fireplace and reach for a framed picture on the mantel. Without hesitation, the frame soars across the room, landing directly in my palm. I glance down at the photo of Ellen and Joseph and a little girl I don't recognize—not

Rory—and toss it onto the floor without reverence. They don't deserve it.

This feels right. This ability to call for my magic whenever I want it, to do whatever I want, to make anything happen without fear or reluctance or even know-how. What I can do is limited only by my imagination. And I've always had a *wild* imagination.

I swear, this is the way things were always supposed to be. I should've gutted that little weather boy a long time ago.

There are similarities, still, to the way it felt when I used my magic before. The rush of it is the same. The pulses of electricity shooting through my nerves, the way my heartbeat races just a little faster, the whisper of power as it blows through my body like a gust of wind. It's heady, and intoxicating, and I want to do it again.

I'm here for a reason, though. And I only realize I'm standing there in the middle of the room, static and silent and reveling in the feeling of my own skin, when the front door opens.

Rory freezes. The expression on her face doesn't look like excitement or relief or anything else I might've counted on. If anything, she looks . . . afraid.

"What's the problem?" Enzo's voice cracks through the door from behind her.

I don't understand why she's looking at me that way. I want to go to her, want to touch her, want to touch him, but something is wrong.

Her shoulders are too broad for Enzo to see around her, and one of his hands squeezes past her arm, bloody knuckles—why are his knuckles *bloody?*—tightening in her shirt as he tries to shove her away. It is completely ineffective, but, after a long moment, Rory steps inside and Enzo wiggles in after her.

Unlike Rory, Enzo doesn't look afraid when his eyes light on me.

Like her, he also really doesn't look happy to see me.

"Do you think this is funny?" His voice is like a laceration, the sharp tip of a whip as it collides with my skin. From the waistband of his jeans, he produces a *handgun* in a flash of metal, pointing it at my face from across the room. "Do I look like I'm laughing?"

"Uh . . ." Something in my brain apparently short-circuits and all I can think to say is "Bitch, why are you *strapped* right now?"

Enzo blinks, the fury evaporating out of him, the moment broken. "Gem?"

"Well, I'm not the fucking Kool-Aid Man." I open my palm and twist my wrist, and the gun flies from Enzo's hand onto the couch. "Not exactly the welcome wagon I was hoping for. Why do people keep trying to shoot me?"

Rory's feet pound across the floor so loud the walls rattle. They barrel toward me, face contorted in an expression I can't read, and I back up without wanting or meaning to. It doesn't do much good, though. They grab me, hands gripping my waist so tight there's a pop of pain, and they yank me off my feet and—

And they're hugging me. Their arms wrap around my middle, their face falling into my chest, and they breathe deep, like they might be able to just suck me right into their lungs. Instantly, my body goes warm and soft, and I wrap my legs around their hips, my own face nuzzling into their unruly curls. My hands slide over their shoulders to grip their thick biceps.

Everything about Rory is familiar to me. The smell of them, like edible flowers dipped in burnt sugar. The warmth of them, like a sun-drenched hillside on a perfect afternoon. The feel of them, like the softest wool ever spun.

When they tip their head back to look up at me, my hungry eyes drink in their face. Those perfect, mismatched eyes. The tattoos on their chin, marks from their tribe in Alaska. Their wide nose and full lips and—

"What happened to you?" I touch the cut on the side of their face, a jagged slice raking from the corner of their eye down to the apple of their cheek.

They frown, lowering me to my feet. I want to protest and insist I keep being held, but I manage to contain myself. My thighs still miss the feel of them.

"Me?" they demand. "What happened to *you*? Where have you *been*?"

"The Wheeler family barn," I deadpan. "Quite literally taking a dirt nap. Buck had me in some kind of time paralysis this whole time. I had no idea until it was over. I'm *so* sorry."

Rory exchanges a look with Enzo, who's come around to stand at their side. Neither of them looks happy with my answer.

"What?"

"We've been to the Wheeler barn, Gem," Rory answers slowly.

"Twice since you disappeared. You might have woken up there," Enzo explains. "But you weren't kept there."

Well, that's delightfully revolting. My skins crawls, the sloshing liquid in my stomach curdling at the thought of Buck Wheeler moving my lifeless body around like some kind of doll.

I'm not *just* going to kill that little freak. I'm going to savor it.

Enzo touches his knuckles to my cheek, and the cool feel of his skin on mine helps me remember to breathe. I find his eyes, like two stained-glass windows of red and gold, and hold his gaze as my hand reaches up to take his. When I kiss his knuckles, we both shiver.

With a groan, he slides his other hand around the back of my neck and pulls me to him, his arm falling down to wrap around my waist as he buries his head in my chest. He smells of rich spices and freshly welded metal and things forgotten by time. The sharp lines of his body press into mine like knifepoints marking their territory.

Eventually, he, too, pulls away. I want to claw at his skin, could rip his face free of his skull for the crime of the space between us. Somehow, I manage self-control.

If only because I have a lot of questions.

"Who the hell did you two think I was when you walked in here? Not me, clearly. And—a gun?" I raise my eyebrows at Rory. "Why does the *Shade* have a *gun*?"

Asked in the same tone one might use for "Why is the baby driving the school bus" or "Why is that rat making an omelet?"

Rory puts a hand on Enzo's shoulder and he winces. It takes me a moment to realize they're . . . comforting him? That doesn't seem right. I've missed a lot.

"Things have been weird."

"Elaborate."

Enzo rubs his palms into his eye sockets and Rory watches him with concern as they explain, slowly, "We knew someone had you, we just couldn't figure out *who* or *where*. Things have gotten . . . bad. When Poppy got out of the hospital—"

"Poppy's alive?!" I don't know if I'm relieved or disappointed. *"You've always been dead."*

No, I do, definitely disappointed.

"Poppy's worse than alive." I have no idea what that means,

but Enzo sounds exhausted about it. He reaches for me again, blessedly, and our fingers tighten together like we're trying to see who can squeeze harder. One of our hands might break, but it's fine, it'd be well worth it.

Rory sighs, shaking their head. "When Poppy got out of the hospital, we confronted her and Marian. They're out for blood. They want to find you as much as we did. We thought it might be an act, like they were trying to throw us off their trail, but . . ."

They run their fingers against my jaw, touching me with a kind of reverence like they still aren't sure I'm standing in front of them.

I reach up to take their hand, but don't pull it away from my face, enjoying the warmth of their skin on mine. Still, I say, "That doesn't explain the gun."

"Right." They clear their throat, glancing at Enzo, then back to me. "You know how you said you couldn't take another god's power 'cause it would throw off the balance?"

I have a feeling I'm not gonna like this. "Uh-huh."

"So, you know how you went and did it anyway?"

I resist the urge to defend myself and instead say, through my teeth, "Yes."

"Right. Well, the balance?" they ask.

"Thrown," Enzo offers. "Fucked, one might even say."

"One might," Rory agrees.

"What the hell does that mean?" I want to make out with both of them at the same time, and I'm starting to want to punch them both in the face.

"Our magic's been a little . . . unpredictable." Rory swallows. "Everything's sort of . . . I don't know. It's like someone tilted the table and now all the pieces are scattered across the board.

Things don't work the way they're supposed to. Some things we should be able to do, suddenly we can't. Other things we've never been able to do . . . things we shouldn't be able to do . . . now we can."

I'd seen this coming. Their magic is evolving to meet mine. But it doesn't actually explain: "So . . . the gun?"

Enzo shrugs. Rory squeezes his shoulder. "Magic's a bit unreliable at the moment. Bullets are more predictable. And we all know how the Lionheart loves her weapons."

Huh. My thumb brushes against the back of Rory's, and my nails dig into the soft, breakable skin over Enzo's knuckles. "That still doesn't answer the question of why you didn't think I was me."

"Right. Uh."

Again, the two of them exchange a *look*. This never proves good for me.

Slowly picking out their words, Rory explains, "Indy . . . has occasionally been wearing other people's faces."

That is one of the worst sentences I've ever heard.

"Pardon me?"

"The Muse is a mirror." Enzo does not sound impressed. "Apparently, now that power is a bit more literal."

"You thought I was . . . Indy. Wearing a Gem costume." I'm going to throw up.

"Yeah, and it was really upsetting, actually, because we just came to a cease-fire." Rory huffs, rolling their eyes. "We dropped Rhett off at his house right before we came back here."

"Rhett." Right. I suddenly remember what my mother said, about Rhett hanging around with them. "What are you two doing with him?"

"Oh, darling, talk about things being thrown off balance. The Librarian is on the verge of collapse." Enzo tsks.

"It's Alexandria all over again," Rory sighs.

I can only guess what the expression on my face is, because Enzo elaborates, "The poor boy is eaten up with guilt. Blames himself for handing Zephyr all the information he needed."

"As he should," Rory snaps. "It was his fault. That's not the only thing, though. He's really not handling his shit. Getting in other people's heads, taking all their thoughts? It's too much for him. He's cracking."

Enzo shakes his head, clicking his tongue. "I hate to say it—I've warmed up to him more than I intended—but I fear we'll have one less player on the board soon. I give it twenty-four hours. Forty-eight, if Indigo's exceptionally adept at suicide watch."

That's . . . grim. And certainly something to think about.

None of us seems to know what to say next, and the house grows quiet and still, each of us touching the other, nothing but our breath occupying the space between our bodies.

Finally, Rory says, "I'm exhausted, and I want to hold you."

And I say, "Yes," even though I'm not tired at all.

And Enzo says nothing but takes both our hands and leads us out of the living room and down the hall and into the back bedroom where we all slept together on the last night I still sort of felt like myself. An older version of myself, who was a younger version of myself.

Rory kicks off her mud-caked boots and balls up her socks, tossing both to the corner of the room. She has to peel herself out of her jeans, soaked through with maybe sweat or maybe swamp water or maybe even blood, I don't know. Her shirt comes last, and she falls into bed in her cotton underwear and sports bra, watching me from under a sheet of curls.

I expect a different level of clothes-etiquette from Enzo, but he's just as careless with kicking off his own shoes and yanking his jeans down his legs. He is careful, at least, to unbutton each button on his shirt without tearing any, so I know the world isn't *actually* ending yet, probably. He crawls onto her mattress without hesitation, like he owns the place, settling onto his side of the bed and balancing himself on his elbows.

Both of them watching me. Waiting. I hesitate to undress for only a moment and only because I'm struck by how *different* they seem. There's a level of familiarity between their bodies that didn't exist the last time we were together. Something has shifted here, between the two of them, and I don't know what it is. I didn't get to watch it happen because I was taking a fucking nap.

Buck. Dead. First thing in the morning, seriously.

As quickly as I can shake myself out of it, I pull the Ouro-boros from my waistband and set it silently on Rory's dresser. I don't miss the way both of their eyes dart to it, bodies tensing, though neither moves to retrieve it. I'm not sure what I would do if they did.

With that taken care of, I make quick work of tugging off my sweats and yanking Rory's shirt over my head. It's the same outfit I put on the last time I was here, the last time I showered, the last time I felt human. I wonder if I smell as bad as my mom—or worse, Hank. And then I try not to think about that. Stripped to my underwear, I move to Enzo's side of the bed, the closest to the dresser, and hook my leg over his hips to hoist myself up and into the center of the mattress.

As present in my body as I'm feeling compared to recent

memory, I'm still not levelheaded enough to be sure who moves first. Maybe I grab for both of them as soon as I'm in bed. Maybe Enzo dives like a wolf on a fresh carcass. Maybe Rory's arms are already pulling me into her like quicksand. Maybe the answer is just *yes,* all of us moving at once, all of us desperate.

It doesn't matter, really. Enzo's teeth are on my lips until I taste blood, and Rory's thigh slips between mine like warm honey spilling over the center of me. And then Rory's mouth is on mine, her bubblegum tongue licking the blood from my teeth, and Enzo's hands find the peaks on my chest. And every whispered "I missed you" and "I love you" and "I need you" blends together until the three of us may as well be speaking with one voice. It's loud enough to drown out the chorus in my head.

She is soft and warm and strong where he is sharp and cool and lithe and there is nothing I could ever need that doesn't exist here, just me and them; God and the devil and Eden itself.

I watch as their faces brush over my shoulder, my eyelids heavy, heart beating across every inch of my skin. His nose ghosts over hers. Her lips part. I think they might kiss, as un-believable as that seems, but they don't. The almost-moment ends as quickly as it started, both of their mouths falling on my neck instead. And I want to ask them, *need* to know what's happened here that's changed the way they look at each other, but *both of their mouths are on my neck.* I can hardly catch my breath. There's no hope of coherent questions.

Enzo shifts forward. His teeth sting a path down my chest, my stomach, past the waistline of my underwear as he tugs them over my hips and down my thighs. I gasp when his tongue flat-tens against me, head rolling back against Rory's chest. When I open my lips to moan, she swallows the sound with her own mouth over mine.

This wasn't where I expected this night to go. It feels good, feels too good, almost too much, it just wasn't what I'd planned. But everything is too much, and all the time, and I think we might die soon, and I don't want to die before we get a chance to do this.

I want this, I do. I roll my hips to meet Enzo's mouth, and my hand grips Rory's as tightly as I can so she can ground me into her body, and I want this. I do.

It's just.

This isn't where I thought this would happen. The last time we were here—

The man sitting on the couch. Rory's grandparents waiting for her. That thing and its stain on the carpet.

No worse than what they deserved. How could they do that to her? They were supposed to protect her, and they tried to force her to—

For a split second, the arms around me don't feel like Rory's and I can't breathe.

"Stop." The word tumbles out so quietly, I don't think Enzo even hears me.

Rory does, though. She doesn't let go of my hand, but reaches down with her other to tangle her fingers in Enzo's hair. With a yank, she pulls him up, drags his mouth off me.

Neck exposed, lips glinting in the glow from the window, Enzo looks like he might snap at her. But whatever he sees on my face quiets him.

"Gem?" Rory asks.

"I'm okay," I tell her. I meet Enzo's worried eyes. "I'm okay. I just—not tonight. I'm sorry."

"You have no reason to be sorry," Rory says at the same moment Enzo replies, "*I'm* the one who's sorry."

I swallow. "Just—just lie with me, okay? Both of you? Please? Don't stop touching me."

"Okay." Enzo nods slowly. His hands find my waist, slide up my back. He presses in, tucks himself against my chest, presses his nose into my collarbone.

Rory's fingers tug the elastic of my underwear until they're back on my body. It's so tender, I could cry, and I know that's stupid, but I could cry anyway. She kisses the back of my head and rests her cheek against mine.

Eventually, they both fall asleep. Rory first, then Enzo. And I lie awake long after sunrise, listening to the sounds of their breathing and the bayou outside and thinking about how much has changed and how much really hasn't.

9

AND NEW ONES HAVE TAKEN THEIR PLACE

I'm only just beginning to fall asleep, Enzo's breath on my shoulder and Rory's on the back of my neck, birds chirping outside the bedroom window and sunlight spilling across our bodies on the mattress, when I hear tires on dirt. Anywhere else, it could be a neighbor leaving for work, or someone driving past on their commute. Out here, in the sticks, if someone's close enough to hear, they're *too* close.

I tug my arm from under Enzo's rib cage, shifting on my hips to slide out from between them. They don't seem to notice the loss of me. Enzo's head tips further forward until it lands on Rory's arm. Her cheek nuzzles into the top of his head. They keep sleeping.

I wish I could take a moment to study them, to enjoy the sight of the people I love most in the world *not* trying to kill each other. But a car door slams. I yank on the same pants I've been wearing for two weeks and head toward the porch.

Before I even get outside, I spot a flash of pastel pink from the living room window, and my stomach rolls.

Well, I guess there was no avoiding this forever. Here we go.

Poppy's car is the most obnoxious one in Gracie, I'm sure. I don't know enough about cars to know anything about the brand, but I know that the long hood and dramatic curve of the roof mean it's a sports car, and that means it's probably expensive. The Pepto-inspired paint job is underscored by accents of sunflower yellow, and there's a naked troll doll hanging from a string on the rearview mirror.

The car spins when it tries to stop, whizzing past the porch when I step outside in my sweats and sports bra. It finally halts a few feet too far in the swamp, mud slicking up the sides, a distinct thump inside as the passengers are tossed around.

Marian is the first person to get out of the car, the passenger-side door popping open and her shaved head peeking out over the roof. She turns to me, meeting my stare from across the yard, an icy resolve in her dark eyes.

The last time I saw Marian, she was incoherent. She'd thought her girlfriend was dead—and maybe *big dead* this time, since no one can be sure Poppy will survive her own death curse to wake up again in another lifetime. She'd been too out of it, too distraught, to notice or care that I was alive at all.

She doesn't look incoherent anymore. Her expression is as sharp as a knife.

There's someone else climbing out of the back seat, pushing up the passenger seat to crawl through the door, but I don't yet recognize who it is. My attention is pulled to the driver's side when Poppy emerges.

Poppy White always veers dangerously close to *too much* to look at. It's kind of her thing. I think maybe it's a defense mechanism, like a bird that makes itself so colorful and fluffy that predators don't realize it's a snack. In Poppy's case, she's like, on the verge of death, but she wears a lot of neon about it.

This fit, however, really is too much. My brain actually fritzes out a little when I look at her, because I'm not sure where to start.

She only has one eye now. Her dress is made entirely of worms on a string. Her eye patch is Hello Kitty themed and covered in rhinestones. The worms seem to be tied together at the ends, stretching over her thin torso and down to her knees, just a long, rainbow tube of fuzz with tiny googly eyes to indicate where the faces are. The side of her head is shaved, and she's got a long line of stitches stretched across that part of her skull. Her pink cowgirl boots match neither the dress nor the eye patch, but they do match the giant pink bow she's put over that side of her head, like it'll hide her new scar.

I can only blink at her as she slams the car door and starts toward me, those pink boots squelching in the mud under her.

"You should've stayed gone, Magician."

"Sorry to disappoint." I glance to Marian, tilting my head. "Stings, doesn't it? When people don't do what they should?"

The Lionheart rolls her eyes at me and steps aside to let Murphy out of the back seat.

Wait—pause.

Murphy is not friends with Poppy and Marian in the same way that *Rhett* is not friends with Rory and Enzo. The Siren has never wanted anything to do with the rest of us. She went out of her way to forget her power during our very first lifetime together, abandoning the pantheon and who she used to be in search of blissful human ignorance. Even when the wall was knocked down between lifetimes, when Murphy's perfect cheerleader persona was shattered by the revelation that she was the god of water from another world, she didn't want anything to do with it.

Why would she be hanging around with these two? The ones who started *all* of this?

She takes in the swampy lot and sniffs with an air of pretension that makes me defensive on Rory's behalf.

"Where've you been, Gemothy?" Poppy demands, and one foot lands on the bottom porch step. Her fingers—creepily thin, bone white, too long for her tiny hands—wrap around the railing. She tries to hide the way she sways just before they do, but I catch it.

The Reaper might not be dead, but she's still good and fucked up. Guess her mom shouldn't have shot her in the head, then.

Instead of answering, I ask, "How'd you know I was back?"

"A little stag told me."

If time is not actually linear, and that's just the way we perceive it, then Buck Wheeler is *already* dead.

"What do you want?" I cross my arms and lean back against the doorframe. I'm not sure if this is an act of bravado or if I'm really and truly unafraid of them. The Reaper is terrifying when she's in her element. The Lionheart is the worst enemy a person could have.

And yet . . . I think . . . I search my feelings, looking for any hint of concern and . . . No. These three are nothing. They're so small, compared to me.

I can do anything.

"We came to ask you that same question," Murphy snaps, drawing my attention back to her. She tugs her braids up into a bun, as if worried a bug might fly into her hair or something, and places her hand in Marian's. The other god helps her cross the yard without getting her shoes muddy, and Murphy moves past Poppy to climb up the steps toward me.

"Well, I could use a shower and maybe some breakfast. Are you offering?"

Murphy's palm connects with my face so hard my neck twists. The aftermath of her slap is a burn that spreads from my cheekbone to my jaw and nose, into my throat and sinuses. I blink stars from my vision before looking back to her.

"That was bitchy." Why is she mad at me, anyway? "Why are you mad at me, anyway? I saved your life. Remember?"

"You *destroyed* my life," she seethes. "Your cruelty brought us to this world in the first place, and your *incompetence* gave Zephyr back his memories. Everything that has happened comes back to you."

That doesn't seem fair. I never intended to hurt her, or anyone else. I rub my fingertips against my cheek. Whatever. I don't care if Murphy hates me. She can get in line.

"Are we having a salon?" drawls Enzo from behind me, voice sleep-raspy, crackling around the edges. "My invitation must have been lost in the mail."

I step aside, and the Shade and the Mountain move through the doorway together, onto the porch. Rory takes my chin between her fingers, tilting my head to examine what must be an ugly red handprint on my skin.

She raises her eyebrows.

"Your sister was a little too excited to see me," I explain.

She scowls, hand falling away.

"We've earned answers, Gem." Marian speaks at last, the timbre of her voice solid and unwavering. She is as unyielding as her girlfriend is brittle. "You've gone and turned it all upside down. You betrayed everyone—"

"*I* betrayed everyone?" If I sound condescending, it's because I am. "You tried to have me killed."

"Because you were going to kill Poppy! The two of you were swayed by the Librarian. It was clear on your faces. We were not all leaving that church alive."

"But we did," I remind her.

"All but one of us," Murphy amends.

"God save the king." Poppy makes the sign of the cross over her chest with her middle finger.

"The only reason Poppy isn't dead is *luck,*" Marian snarls.

"Is it?" I raise an eyebrow. "Or am I just that good?"

It's a bluff, sure, but they don't need to know that. Marian and Murphy exchange a look, but Poppy just snarls, fists clenching, and I notice the plastic My Little Pony rings on her fingers. Like the ones you'd find topping cupcakes at a kid's birthday party.

"Even if I was going to forgive you for almost killing her— and I'm not—there's another problem." Marian's upper lip curls over her teeth. "You've upended the balance of magic."

Right. The *balance.* Everyone's power being topsy-turvy. Cut to Enzo carrying around a gun because the (second) scariest god to ever walk the earth can't get his magic up the way he used to.

"We want to know your goal here." Murphy juts out her chin. "Why'd you do it? What are you planning?"

I realize it isn't just Murphy and Marian and Poppy watching me expectantly. It's Rory and Enzo too. Everyone's staring at me, like they're waiting for an answer. Like they need to know.

What am I planning? *Why* did I kill Zephyr and throw the

balance out of whack? What's going to happen now that everything is upside down and nothing makes any sense?

Well, this is awkward.

"I'm not planning anything."

"Bullshit—" Marian begins.

"I did it because I could." I know I should be embarrassed by that answer. And maybe there's a part of me that still has some shame, some shred of humanity, that is. But it isn't enough to make me stop talking. "I did it because none of you could stop me, and he was going to die anyway, and I wanted to know what would happen. That's all the reason there is. It's not that deep."

"It's not ... that ... deep," Poppy repeats slowly, like the words are breaking her brain.

I pretend I don't see the disappointment on Rory's face, or the flash of anger on Enzo's.

For as long as I can remember, I've struggled with my impulsivity. The future is a difficult thing to conceptualize for someone who can't ever be convinced they're going to live past the moment they're standing in. And if the future doesn't exist, there are no consequences.

But I don't know that any of my do-it-yourself facial piercings or ill-advised hookups or any of the times I took something someone gave me without *really* knowing what it was ... were ever quite as bad as this.

And if time isn't linear, I am both currently making the biggest impulsive mistake of my life, *and* facing the consequences, all at once. Which sucks. But it's not like I can undo it.

Well. I guess I could. I'm the god of magic, and I can do anything I want. What's a little time hopping, really?

It's an exciting idea, but I tuck it away. If I've learned anything from literally any piece of media ever made about time travel, that shit's more likely to cause a bunch of new problems than it is to fix anything.

"Do they know?" Murphy finally tears her eyes away from me to look at Rory. "Do they have any idea how bad this is?"

"They haven't seen . . ." Rory's voice trails off, and she glances to Enzo.

"Haven't seen what?" I demand. A newborn surge of panic, like the legs of a centipede, skitters around in my chest.

"You want to know how deep this is?" Poppy's voice lilts, taking on a hysterical edge. I think she might start laughing soon. "Let me show you."

The Reaper steps away, stumbling backward down the porch steps, but she never takes her eyes off my face. She careens deeper into the swampy water at the edge of the property, muck sloshing up toward the top of her boots, no doubt splashing inside and soaking her feet.

Murphy turns to watch her. Enzo and Rory, too. Marian's eyes don't leave me. I wonder if she's too afraid to look away, or if she just wants to see my own fear at whatever is about to be unveiled. Or maybe she just can't stomach the sight of her girlfriend like this.

Poppy holds her arms out on either side of her skeletal frame. I'm struck by the image of Christ on the Cross, that stained-glass window, the last thing I saw before passing out in the church attic. Her crown of thorns is just a giant fucking bow.

She raises her arms slowly, and I don't know what's happening at first. Her face is twisted in a grimace of a smile, teeth bared, eyes wild. Clearly, something must be happening, but I don't—

And then dead bodies begin to rise from the swamp.

Dead animal bodies, that is. Half-eaten carcasses of birds

and possums and raccoons, the bloated and white-eyed corpses of fish, a couple of partially decayed gators ripped from their watery rest. Among the animals are a severed human arm and the disconnected bones of what might've been someone's skeleton once.

In unison, they all rise from the mud and crawl or slither or roll onto the grass, and start moving, an army of the dead, toward the porch.

I feel like I'm gonna throw up. "What the hell are you doing?"

"Oh, this?" Poppy cackles. "I've reanimated corpses. Duh! It's, like, totally a dream come true. This is exactly how I wanted to spend today."

"Powers they were in control of have started to disappear," Murphy tells me, looking away from the revolting show of guts and gore on the lawn. "And new ones have taken their place. Ones they can't control at all."

First of all, fuck.

Second of all, maybe that explains their newfound kinship with Murphy. She hasn't touched her power in a thousand years. She had very little control over it even before the balance was thrown off. Naturally, she would empathize with this.

When the bodies begin to breach the bottom step, Rory sighs from next to me. She doesn't look excited when she raises her hands, waving them toward the approaching army.

Again, at first, it doesn't look like much. But then I hear . . .

Wait. What am I hearing?

A swarm of hornets burst out from under the porch, flying in unison to attack the already dead creatures, biting and stinging in a choreographed flight. They're joined moments later by another swarm, this time bees. Together, buzzing and flitting and working in groups, the little bugs manage to pick up body parts many times their own size, *tossing them* back into the swamp from where they came.

That isn't the weird part. No, actually, that's perfectly on par with what Rory has always been able to do. And if that were all it was, I might think maybe her magic had been unaffected.

But it's the buzzing itself that's different. It's so *loud*. And when everything else is silent and still in the front yard, when all I can hear is the sound of the hornets and the bees buzzing louder than I've ever heard before, I realize . . .

They're talking.

No. They're *screaming*.

"IT HURTS!"

"PLEASE STOP!"

"WE DON'T WANT THIS!"

"PLEASE LET US GO!"

Screaming in unison the same way they move, these little buzzing bugs are pleading, with human voices, to be cut free from the Mountain's control. My mouth floods with saliva, tongue thick against the roof of my mouth. I might be sick.

Marian, still watching my face, must realize the moment I put it together. She explains, "The god of land has always been able to commune with fauna. Now she forces that on the rest of us."

When the yard is clear of dismembered bodies, the swarms go their separate ways. Hornets back beneath the house, and bees back to their hive. My stomach doesn't settle.

Rory's face doesn't look much happier.

Poppy finally lowers her arms, pressing her hands into the waist of her wormy dress. Her expression is purely smug when she asks, "And what about your boyfriend? Hm? Ask him about his power."

I turn to Enzo, but he doesn't look back at me. His face is

ashen; his hands are clenched into fists. A tremor threads along his shoulders.

"What's she talking about?"

"As far as we can tell—the Shade has been neutered. He can't do *shit*." Poppy sounds as horrified as she is delighted delivering that news.

"No." I shake my head, blood gone cold. I won't believe that; she can't make me believe it. "That doesn't make any sense. I saw you that night, with Ellen—"

"And that was the last time I could do anything," he snaps. He still doesn't look at me. "Everything went haywire *after* you disappeared."

"Why would that happen? How could that happen?" Panic builds and builds inside me, ricocheting around like a pinball in an arcade game.

"My best guess?" Marian says, but I'm not looking at her. "Without the balance, there can't be a god of things forbidden. Because *nothing* is forbidden anymore."

What is the point of the devil if hell is here, on Earth?

The Shade is as useless in this world as the keeper of the scales.

No. No, that can't be what's happening here. Enzo is . . . he's *him*. He's a tiny little twink with a small-dog complex, but he's not actually weak. He's terrifying; he's . . .

He finally turns to look at me. I wish he hadn't. His stare is hollowed out. My heart stops.

"Where is your heart?"

I did this to him. To all of them. I broke everything.

And I broke it on purpose.

"Well. I think we've made our point." Poppy stomps out of the muck and heads toward her car. "I need to get home anyway. Gotta get ready. I'm a shoo-in for prom queen tonight. Getting shot in the head really locked that down."

Prom. For fuck's sake, that can't be real.

But it is. All of this is real. This is my life. I designed it myself.

"You're welcome." I hope she doesn't notice the way my voice catches on my teeth.

Murphy follows after Poppy. Marian hesitates, still watching me.

"What?" I snarl. I want to hurt her. This is *her* fault, actually. I wouldn't have done anything, would have stuck to our plan, if she hadn't been preparing to betray me the entire time. *She* did this. Why should I take the blame when *she did this*?

"If you don't have a plan, Magician"—she shakes her head—"I suggest you get one. Fast."

It's a threat, but I don't know how I know. I watch her leave down the steps, watch her get into the passenger seat of Poppy's car, and watch them drive away. The chorus of Taylor Swift's "Karma" starts to blare when they're halfway off the property.

"Enzo," I start, but he cuts me off.

"Don't. It's not your fault. And I don't believe Marian, anyway." He shrugs, turning to head back inside. "I'm not *neutered*. I just don't know what my power looks like yet. We'll figure it out."

Rory and I look from his back to each other, and I know we're thinking the same thing. He doesn't believe what he's saying. I don't know if either of us does.

Back inside, while Enzo rifles through the fridge and Rory disappears into the bathroom, I go back to the bedroom to grab my phone.

A missed call from my mom, and one text.

At first, I think it's something about Hank, and adrenaline

makes my blood bounce. *Shit.* Shit, I said I was going to try to be there. Is he already gone? Did I miss it because of *Poppy*?

That's not what it is, though.

MOTHERSHIP

Officer Allen came back to the house today.

They've got a warrant for your arrest.

I throw my phone at the wall and watch it clatter to the floor, not nearly as satisfying as I'd hoped it would be.

Marian's right. I need a plan. I need to know how to fix this mess before it's too late.

There is one person who might know where to start. Someone who knows too much for his own good.

As long as he's still alive.

10

DON'T POKE THIS BEAR

I've never been to Indy's house. The one time I planned to go, we were supposed to be having sex—and instead, I had a flashback in a dollar store, before running away to call the boy I was actually in love with. Something, something, queer culture, et cetera.

It's about what I might've expected, though: simple but charming. The Ramirez trailer is a double-wide in a park of doubles and singles, distinguishable from its neighbors only because of the yellow picket fence wrapped around the side yard. The yard itself is overflowing with raised garden beds, broken up by walkways marked with paving stones. The stones themselves are shaped like frogs, or dragonflies, or hummingbirds, or other creatures you might find out here. And they're painted, clearly not by a professional. It's cute. I wonder if it was Indy's doing, or one of his parents'.

"You're sure he's here?" I ask, leaning over the center console, shoulders brushing Rory's and Enzo's on either side.

Rory shrugs, the motion knocking me closer to Enzo's side. "We dropped him off here yesterday."

Not Indy. Rhett. The Librarian is the only one who might

have answers for me—and if he doesn't, he's the one who might be able to get them.

"Let's hope he's still feeling guilty." I slide out of the car, slamming the door behind me, and head toward Indy's front door without waiting for the others.

Just . . . not so guilty that Enzo was right about his expiration date, and all we're gonna find is his body.

Indy's truck is parked in the driveway, but no one else's is, which at least gives me hope we aren't gonna run into his parents or something. I don't know what the Ramirez family knows. The Muse's power is different than the rest of ours. He's always been able to collect his memories without help from his bloodline because he can see himself, and the rest of us, for who we *really* are. Like Buck, he would've grown up knowing the truth.

Buck's parents think *he's* Jesus. I wonder what the Ramirezes think about Indy. And at the same moment, I realize I don't actually care. Any interest I feel is like an echo of itself—like remembering when I used to feel something instead of really feeling it in full.

The front porch is less of a porch and more of a step stool. Obviously homemade, just a few pieces of wood nailed together and propped up against the metal exterior. I step onto it and rap my knuckles against the door. There's one big window a couple feet down, and the blinds are drawn. I try to get a look inside anyway, to see if I can catch a hint of something inside, but there's nothing.

I *hear* something, though. There's music playing . . . I think. It's quiet enough that I can't actually make out what it sounds like, just barely loud enough that I know it's playing at all. I find myself leaning in, closer and closer to the window, trying to make out the rhythm, or the lyrics, or—

The door opens so quickly that I almost fall face-first into Indy's chest. I manage to catch myself at the last millisecond, palms braced in the doorframe, staring up at him from this stupid little step stool like a clumsy child.

"Um."

I don't know what Indy's been up to the last couple of weeks, but the balance isn't the only thing that's gotten a make-over. Ever the artist, *this* Indy is wearing an almost full face of makeup, complete with winged eyeliner and red lip liner without any lipstick. It goes not-well-at-all with his black sweatpants and crop top, but it does match the bandages on all of his fingers. Hm.

When I stare a moment too long, he raises an eyebrow at me, not moving and still not saying anything himself. Like he can't even grant me the courtesy of being surprised to see me here. I'm really starting to *hate* how predictable he makes me feel.

Well. I guess he didn't find me so predictable when I killed the Cyclone.

"You look like someone who uses pronouns." The statement comes out of my mouth without permission, completely detached from whatever is left of my brain.

Indy doesn't look like he found that joke funny at all, which is a shame. I'm done paying attention to him, though. He's not why I'm here. And while Rory and Enzo come up behind me and start talking to him—something, something, time, day, something, I don't know, I'm not listening—I duck under his arm and invite myself into the trailer.

Rhett's nowhere to be seen, at least not in the living room or kitchen, the part of the house directly off the front door. I can make out the music, though, now that I'm inside. And it is fucking abysmal.

"*This* is what you listen to?" I ask Indy, looking at the back of his head.

I don't actually know what it is, but it sounds like a metal cover of an anime intro, and I *hate it*. And to think, I'd once entertained a future where Indy and I could listen to my playlists together. How naïve I'd been.

He turns to say something in retort, but I've already started off in the direction of the sound, assuming that I'll find his bedroom and, inside it, the Librarian. Louder and louder the music gets as I stomp down the single, long hallway, amplified by the metal walls crouching in on me, making the space feel even tighter. It's claustrophobic, actually. It's darker, too, here at the end of the hall, away from the front of the house, where I realize the only light is coming from the open door, where Enzo and Rory are still standing.

The music is coming from the last door in the hallway. There's a single piece of notebook paper pushpinned to the outside, a stick-figure drawing and a child's handwriting that reads *keep out*. Curious.

"He's not here," Indy calls at my back. He sounds, more than anything, bored. When I look back at him, he's watching me— they're all watching me—with his hands in the pockets of those sweats, the waistband low on his hips, his expression somehow both blank and dour. "He left a couple hours ago. We had a disagreement."

"Oh?"

Apparently, my prompt isn't clear enough, because Indy doesn't supply any more information than that.

I look back at the bedroom door. The music playing inside. That sign.

Everything about the moment says, *Don't poke this bear.*

But I know I won't be able to think about anything else, at all, until I've poked it.

Indy sighs from behind me when I put my hand on the doorknob and push it open, sighs like he's disappointed, or tired, or maybe he's just tired of being disappointed in me. He wouldn't be the first.

In any case ... as it turns out, I really *shouldn't* have poked this bear.

I scramble backward, but there's not much room for me to run in this cramped hallway, and I slam back against the other wall, hitting my head. Black and white starbursts pop in my vision, and I can only barely hear myself when I scream, "What the FUCK is that?"

That is a doll. It's stitched together from what looks like old scraps of clothing, with eyes made of mismatched buttons and gloves sewn on to make hands. It's the size of a small child, maybe three feet tall. And it's sitting on Indy's bed.

And it's crying.

Not with tears, because it's a *doll*, but it's shaking and whimpering and moaning and when I open the door it *looks at me*. It looks up at me with those fucked-up buttons for eyes, and when I ask what it is, it starts crying harder.

Enzo and Rory have joined me in the hallway. They move in front of me.

I hear Rory say, "Oh my god."

Enzo sucks in a breath between his teeth.

All of us turn to look at Indy.

The Muse shrugs. "*That* is art. I won't apologize for making you uncomfortable. Meaningful art does that."

"Meaningful," Enzo repeats, slowly turning his head back. "And what exactly is the meaning here, Geppetto?"

"Well, if you don't get it, you aren't the intended audience." He sighs again. "You should be grateful. I am the god of creation. This way, at least *one* of us can still breathe life into something."

"What are you *doing* with them?" Rory demands, before Enzo has a chance to have any kind of response to that statement.

I peer around them, back into the room, to the sobbing doll. And I realize they're not humanizing this thing, calling it a "them." No, they're referring to the *pile of other dolls* next to the bed. Each one of them is made similarly to the crying doll above them, made from scrap fabric, cobbled together. But these dolls are . . . dead? They've had their seams ripped open, stuffing spilling out onto the floor. They aren't awake, at least.

Don't think I could handle a bunch of dolls screaming in agony about their guts hanging out of them.

"Trial and error." Indy leans back against the still-open door. "No concern of yours."

"Oh, no, I'm deeply concerned," I snap.

He smiles. "Then I guess you shouldn't have abandoned the scales, *keeper*. It's not my problem if you don't like my new trick."

"This is why Rhett bailed, isn't it?" I wave my hand into the room, and shoot Enzo an *oh my god, what are you doing, please stop* look as he walks inside, as if to examine the weeping doll closer.

Indy's smile goes sharp. "Creative differences."

I jump at the sound of a gunshot.

My heart leaps to the tip of my tongue, blood gone cold. Rory scoops an arm around my waist and drag me to their side.

In the bedroom, Enzo stands over the now-silent doll, and lets off another shot into its head for good measure. Stuffing flies everywhere. A piece clings to a strand of his hair, not letting go even when he turns around and heads back into the hall.

As he makes his way toward the door, shoving that gun into his waistband, he says, "You are the god of finger-painting and viral dances. Don't get cocky."

Indy watches him leave, watches his back as he no doubt heads for the car.

And I watch Indy, fascinated, as he reaches up to touch his fingers to the corner of his eye. To that immaculately winged eyeliner. And he *pulls it* from his skin. Like a perfectly sharpened razor, it glints in the sun coming through the door, and Indy raises his hand and lets it fly at the back of Enzo's neck.

I don't think. I lift my own hand, letting magic bubble up and out of me without knowing exactly what's going to happen.

And, because I am the god of magic, that *wing* of eyeliner turns into a *bird*. It falls to the ground, unsteady on its fledgling wings, feathers patchy and dull, beak chipped. It squawks, pitifully, but at least it doesn't talk to me in English.

Rory's chest brushes against my back, and Enzo stops at the gate, both of them turning to see what I've done.

Indy shakes his head.

No, Indy shakes *my* head. Rory and I flee from the house as the god of art shows me my own face, the image of him flickering like a dying bulb—him, then me, then him, then me.

In my voice, he calls after us, "I should have listened when I had the chance!"

Rhett's house is walking distance from Indy's. Rory moves the car, anyway, so we don't have to come back here. Enzo and I make the walk from one side of the park to the other, knuckles brushing with our every step. Mostly silent.

It's only when Rhett's house finally comes into view, Rory parked outside waiting for us, that I make myself ask, "Do you hate me?"

Enzo pulls up short, shooting me a stern look. "Why would you ask that?"

"I broke you."

"Don't give yourself too much credit, darling." He shrugs one shoulder, then reaches up to press the tips of his fingers to my jaw. I wonder if he feels my pulse quicken when he does. "The only thing that could break me is losing you."

"That's . . ." I huff. "Like, *so* fruity."

He laughs, dropping his hand. "And you are *so* emotionally damaged."

"Yeah, well." I take a deep breath, looking back to Rory. She raises her eyebrows, waving toward Rhett's house. I take Enzo's hand and start tugging him up the road. "What are we gonna do if he doesn't have an answer for me?"

"Honestly?" Enzo sniffs. "I think we get out of here."

"Leave Gracie?"

"Leave Earth."

He says it just as we're getting to Rory's car, and she groans, putting a hand to her forehead. "Not this shit again."

"It's not shit. It's a valid point. It's the whole reason I came to this god-infested shithole." He drops my hand and shoves both of his in his pockets. "The three of us could return to the Ether. We could rule."

"And what would there be for me to rule, exactly?" Rory curls her hand around the ledge of the driver's-side window. "In your kingdom of ash?"

"Now, kitten, let's not fight . . ."

I get the feeling I'm witnessing the continuation of an argument whose beginning I missed. Not wanting to feel left out, I change the direction: "I have no idea how to get back there. And even if I did, the whole pantheon is tethered to each other. You might wanna go back—you wanna take the Reaper and the Lionheart with you?"

"It's a price—"

"And what if your powers were just as upside down once we got there? You wanna go back to the *Ether*, as a *human*?"

Enzo's cheeks pale. He clears his throat. "Well. Perhaps we find a way to restore the balance first, then."

"Perhaps." Rory snickers. "Thought you didn't wanna face off with the Heartkeeper again anyway. You know she's gonna hand you your ass if you ever walk back in there."

And Enzo answers her, but I don't hear what he's saying. They're talking, bantering, chirping back and forth and rolling their eyes at each other but I'm not here and I don't know what they're talking about.

The Heartkeeper.

"I know your heart, Magician."

Is this the faceless woman haunting my unconscious mind? The last time I heard her name, I couldn't summon a single memory. Unlike every other god on the list, I had no recollection of her, and I couldn't understand how that was possible. It was like I hadn't forgotten, but she'd been *erased*.

Now, she tangles at the edge of my memory. I can feel her taunting, daring me to walk toward her, to look closer. My throat threatens to close.

"Gem?"

I don't know how many times Rory says my name before I hear her. I jolt, blinking back into the present. "Sorry."

"You okay?" She frowns, reaching up to tuck back a strand

of my hair. When the pads of her fingers brush the tip of my ear, a shiver races down my spine.

Short answer: No.

But the short answer really just begs for a whole conversation attached to it, and we don't have time for that. We need answers, which means we need Rhett. And then we need to get the hell out of here.

I swallow. "Oh, yeah, totally. I'm definitely mentally stable."

"Oh, good." Rory rolls her eyes and lets her hand fall.

Unlike Indy, Rhett does not live in a home where people bother to garden. The trailer is older, with rust patches along the side, and plywood nailed down to fix leaky spots on the roof. The yard is overgrown, grass halfway up my calves, and littered with kids' yard toys—a kiddie pool that's been chewed on and turned upside down, a plastic lawnmower, a naked baby doll that reminds me of Indy's and makes me shudder.

And when Enzo knocks, it isn't Rhett who answers the door.

Well, maybe answering the door is a generous take. It's more like the door flings open, and a tornado of children—I can't even count how many there are—go rolling around in front of us. There is so much red hair happening, so many freckles, and it all just blends into one giant kid as they wrestle each other to be the mouthpiece.

"What d'ya want!"

"Ain't nobody buyin' nothin'!"

"My mama's *home*. She's sleepin' right now but she got a shotgun under her bed and it is *always* loaded."

Um. Enzo and I exchange a look.

Rory leans against the doorframe, smiling down at the flea circus. "We're looking for your brother, Rhett. He home?"

"Ooooh, he's sick."

"No he ain't!"

"Yeah he is!"

"Quit lyin'!"

Rory clears her throat, drawing their attention back to her. "Hi. Hey. We know he's sick. We're here to check on him. Can we come in?"

"Yeah!"

"No!"

"Don't be rude!"

"Don't be stupid!"

"Hey." Enzo smiles. "Do you like money?"

Twenty dollars for each child—that's a hundred bucks; apparently there's five of these things—later, and we're headed to the bedroom Rhett Clancy no doubt shares with at least two of his siblings.

"I swear, if I find one more horror-movie monster behind this door," Rory growls, hand tightening around the doorknob. We glance back at the kids, double-check they're all properly distracted, before letting ourselves in.

At first glance, there don't appear to be any sentient puppets or inhuman worm-babies or screaming wasps. The room is actually not at all what I was expecting, though I'm not sure *what* I was expecting. There's a bunk bed in one corner and a full bed across from it, a simple wooden dresser shoved against the wall between them. A single window with a view of the white siding of someone else's trailer and nothing else.

It's a little messy, clothes and empty, dirty dishes left abandoned on the floor or any flat surface. But not so bad you might wanna call the *Hoarders* team or something. My own room's definitely been worse. There's nothing on the walls. No picture or posters or art or anything that might indicate someone actually *lives* here, instead of just sleeping here. I guess it feels more like a college dorm than a childhood bedroom.

Rhett's sitting on the full bed, his head in his hands. He doesn't even bother looking up when we enter, like he knows who's here and he doesn't care that much. And maybe that's true.

Enzo whisks into the room, sidestepping dirty laundry to drop down at the foot of Rhett's bed. He leans back against the wall, sliding his hands into his pockets. "So, Indigo has a thing for dolls . . ."

"*Ugh.*" Rhett grunts.

"Sorry it ended like that. Sucks." Enzo runs his teeth along his lower lip. He raises his foot to set it next to Rhett's leg, gently toeing him with his shoe. I raise an eyebrow, trying my best to quell any judgmental bitchiness that threatens to bubble up. "But we need your help again."

"I can't help."

"That's not true," Rory chides. They lean against the foot of his bed, crossing their arms. Their bear tattoo shifts on their muscled biceps, as if tensing to pounce. "You're the only one who can help."

Rhett presses his fingers into his eyes, pressing them so deep and so tight that I wonder if he might just push them right back into his brain. "Well, sorry it ended like that. Sucks."

"Don't be rude, Librarian." I roll my eyes. "Just answer a few questions and we'll be on our way."

Rhett jumps, which is hilarious, considering he's built like a lumberjack and he's in a child's bed. The whole frame squeaks underneath him. Enzo grips the footboard so he doesn't get tossed to the floor.

"You're . . . here?"

"Apparently."

"You ain't in jail."

"Not yet. Though, that is what I wanted to talk to you about."
I fold my hands over my waist, fingers lacing. "The Gracie PD
and Zephyr's parents. I need to know how to make that nui-
sance go away. Show me their weak spots so I can move on to
real problems. Like restoring the balance."

Rhett looks at me like he's thinking about picking me up by
the ankles and throwing me off the side of a cliff. Which is fine.
He can hate me. Everyone else does. He's not actually gonna do
anything about it.

What would he do, anyway? Read my thoughts? Remind
me that I'm the asshole? Yeah, okay.

"I *gave you* your solution already," he growls out. "You ain't
want nothin' to do with it. Watn't Zephyr you shoulda plugged
with that knife. And now we're all fucked."

"Yeah, yeah. Okay. Mistakes were made. We're not here to
dwell on those. We're here for solutions." My elbow bumps Rory's when I curl my hands around the footboard and lean in,
closer to Enzo, closer to Rhett on his other side. "It's okay if
you don't know. We can take you to the police station. See how
long it takes before you find out."

"Good luck," Rhett snaps. "Power's on the fritz, ain't that
right? Not pickin' up shit when I touch people now—just gotta
live with what's already in my damn head."

"Hm." I frown, cocking my head at him. "So, what can you
do, Librarian?"

"Ain't no use to you; can promise ya that."

I run my tongue against my teeth, hands tightening, frustration firing off in every cell. Power races through me, bubbles in
my hands, demands to be excised. Somehow, I barely keep myself from starting a lightning storm in this guy's lower intestine.
"If a human cop tries to arrest the god of magic, what do you

think happens? You think you get rid of me? That I go quietly? No. This becomes an us problem—*all* of us. I know you know more than you're letting on. Tell me how I get the department off my ass, before—"

"Like I fuckin' said, Mage. I *gave you* your solution." He sneers the words, eyes lighting up when he looks at me, something like a dare in his expression.

Next to me, Rory frowns. "What do you mean?"

"Who do you think *told* Zephyr's parents to start sniffin' around you? They ain't the only rich family who stands to gain from your ass bein' the one pinned for this."

I raise an eyebrow.

Rhett rolls his eyes at me. I know he thinks I'm stupid. "Mrs. White ain't exactly keen on explainin' why she shot her own kid in the head."

A moment passes. My teeth grind so hard I taste my own blood.

Poppy.

Enzo and Rory must come to the realization at the same time. Rory snaps, "Fucking bitch," while Enzo just shakes his head, running his palm over his face.

"What are you saying?" he asks, while I struggle to find my tongue past the rage begging to spew out of me. "*Of course* the Reaper's the one pushing for Gem's arrest behind the scenes. But if we were to make her disappear, doesn't that only make them look more guilty?"

"Depends on how good an actor you are, Slim Shady. Y'all spin a story. Make it convincin'." Rhett shrugs. "'Sides, boys in blue answer to whoever's wavin' the most cash around. Poppy *and* her bank account disappear? They ain't gon' care 'bout shit no more."

This was always the way it was going to end, I realize. I sealed this fate a long time ago, when I cut the Caretaker's heart out.

"*May death evade you forever.*" That was what she'd whispered to me as she'd died. I'd thought it a plea for her sister's safety. Maybe a threat that I would live forever with the weight of what I'd done.

But death hasn't evaded me.

"*You've always been dead.*"

I was always going to take on Death's curse, the one that's been sucking the Reaper dry for lifetimes now.

The difference between Poppy and me is that I can do anything I want. Dead or alive. The curse won't be *my* undoing.

"Tonight's the night we kill the Reaper." I stand straight, feeling pulses of magic threading their way down my arms, down my sides, flooding into every inch of me. "And I know exactly where she's gonna be."

"Okay. Yeah. I guess we're doing this." Rory takes a deep breath, and one of her hands curls over mine. "But Gem, there's something we need you to do first."

Enzo clears his throat, reaching over to pat gently at the back of my wrist. "If you're taking us to prom, darling . . . you have *got* to change clothes."

11

HVTVM CEHĒCARES

It's a fair enough request, considering I haven't showered or changed or done anything remotely human—other than stuffing my face with food that my grandmother made—since I woke up from the Evergod's . . . whatever the hell he did to me. (It doesn't matter what he did, because he's next. Poppy. Then Buck. Then I'll deal with the balance.) Rory takes Enzo home, and we make a plan to meet up at the school. I don't need a ride.

My grandmother's sitting on the front porch, in one of those never-used rocking chairs, when I appear in my bedroom. I can see the back of her head through the window, as she rocks herself gently back and forth, singing quietly. I can't make out the words, can't make sense of any snippet I *can* make out, but some part of me knows the song, anyway. I wish I knew it better than I do, though. I wish I could sing along with her.

Everything about her feels like a reminder of the person I'll never really be. I think I could hate her for this, for holding up a mirror and showing me what I'm not. I know it isn't fair. And I don't actually hate her, I don't think. But I do wish she would go home.

"Gem?"

Oh, shit.

Slowly, I turn away from the window, and find my mother lying in my bed, with Hank tucked up against her chest. Her eyes are huge, her lips parted, cheeks pale gray.

Because she just saw me teleport. Right in front of her.

"Hey, Mom."

She doesn't say anything else, just keeps staring at me. I swallow, rubbing a hand over my chest, and point to Hank.

"Is . . ."

It takes her a moment to say anything. When she does, finally gathering herself up, it's clear she's decided to pretend she did not see what she just saw. Probably for the best. "The vet'll be here in a couple of hours. I was worried you wouldn't make it."

"I . . ." My throat hurts. "I won't. I can't, I have to . . ."

Go and kill someone else. Not exactly something I can share with her. I wonder, is my mom a *call the police on her own kid* kind of mom? Or a *help her kid hide the body* kind of mom? I always would have thought the former. But that was before I realized she's maybe been helping me bury corpses this whole time, and I didn't even notice.

"I have to leave again" is what I finally settle on, even as my eyes burn and my hands shake with how badly I don't want that to be true.

She doesn't say anything. She doesn't reassure me that it's okay, the way I hoped she might. She doesn't try to convince me to stay, either, the way I might've expected her to. Instead, she just nods, resigned, like she knows she can't do anything about it, and bends her neck down to kiss the top of my dog's head.

I can't look at either of them anymore without being sick. I gather up a change of clothes in my fists and make my way to the bathroom, locking myself in.

Under the spray of too-hot water, sobbing until I'm gagging, I think about how this is worse than just never coming back at all. I shouldn't have come here. Here I am, stopping by two hours before Hank dies, letting him get his hopes up in whatever part of his mind is still there, that I'm gonna see him to the end of the road. Just to up and leave him again. And my mom—fuck, my mom. I'm dragging her through this, all of this, with no explanation and no sign of slowing. If I just disappeared, if I never came home again, maybe she'd be able to heal.

That's what they deserve. For me to disappear.

I towel-dry off, and my hands move quickly, of their own accord, throwing my hair into a long braid. My grandmother was the one who taught me how to braid. I wonder if she would have bothered, if she'd known the truth. That I'm not her people. That I'm not even human.

I'm only vaguely aware of the clothes I picked out. Black pants, black shirt, black boots. I linger in the hallway, debating going back to my room, debating saying goodbye to my mom and Hank. Giving him one last kiss, one last belly rub. I don't know how long I stand there before I decide to leave them be.

That's the only decent thing I can do—just disappear and leave my human life be. Let it rest. Let it move on without me. I'm not Gem Echols anymore. Maybe I haven't been for a long time. Maybe I never was to begin with.

My grandmother steps inside seconds before I would have disappeared. She doesn't seem surprised to see me there, like she thought I was here, sleeping, this whole time.

"Gem." She nods, toddling from the front door to the

kitchen stove. "Was just about to get dinner started. You wanna help me?"

"Sorry. I can't." I swallow. "I'm, um. Going to prom."

"Oh." She turns, nailing me with a heavy, heavy look. I don't know what she sees. "Well . . . what time you gonna be back?"

"I'm not sure." I sniff. "How long are you staying? I mean . . . when are you going back to Tampa?"

"I'll be here as long as I'm needed." She goes back to the stove, setting a pot down over one burner and turning the heat on. "You do what you gotta do, baby."

There's so much neither of us is saying, and I know it's not getting said. Maybe ever. Probably ever. I don't think I'm ever going to see her again. I linger for a second longer before turning for the door, to make my escape.

Just before I step onto the porch, she says, "Hvtvm cehē-cares."

I don't have any idea what that means, but it makes me want to start crying all over again.

It would be so much easier to hate her.

"Hey."

"AH!"

Rory nearly drives head-on into a tree when I appear in the passenger seat next to them. They swerve, frantically righting the car, while drivers on either side blare their horns at them.

"What the fuck, Gem! You can't just do that!" They rub a hand over their flushed face, struggling to take in a deep breath, swatting my hand away when I try to comfortingly pat at their thigh.

I huff. "Sorry. I told you I'd meet up with you."

"I—" They glower. "Right, sure."

"I didn't mean to scare you."

Rory scoffs, rolling their eyes. "I was not *scared*. That's not what that was."

"Oh . . . okay." Not going to argue. Not worth it. "You look really good."

And they really, really do. Clearly, Rory took the same opportunity to shower and change. Their curls are pulled up into two space buns, the only hairstyle I've seen them wear so far that might actually keep their hair out of their face. Which means I actually get to *look* at their face. Their perfect eyes, framed by long, dark lashes. The strong slope of their nose. Their round, full cheeks. That perfect mouth. And those incredible tattoos, the three lines on their chin, markings they *earned* before they were stolen away by their grandparents.

They've dressed themself in a moss-green boiler suit, unbuttoned far enough down their chest as to probably be against the high school's dress code, paired with brown leather boots and a leather jacket so soft it must have been worn a thousand times before this.

The sunset through the car window glints behind them, the world cast in orange and pink, and I wonder how the hell I pulled this off. Not for the first time, I wonder how I ever got so lucky that someone like them could look at me, and see me, and *love* me.

A nagging, vicious part of me whispers that they *don't* see me. Not really. I've hidden so many pieces of myself, tucked away parts too ugly to share. Even the Mountain doesn't know who I really am.

Who am I when no one is looking? Definitely not someone worth knowing.

"Gem?" I realize they've said something a moment too late to catch it. "Did you hear me?"

"Sorry." I shift in my seat, turning my head away. I warn the voices in my head to knock it off and shut up. "Sorry, just staring at my incredibly hot girlfriend. What's up?"

"You have the Ouroboros?"

I pull up the hem of my shirt, revealing the silver handle of the knife tucked into my belt.

"Maybe you should let me do it." She takes a deep breath. "I can be the one to kill her."

"No, absolutely not. The curse—"

"You are the god of magic and you can do anything and you will not let me waste away." She shoots me a leveling kind of look. Like an avalanche on a hillside. "But we don't know what'll happen if you take *another* god's power. Maybe the balance can't get any more screwed up than it is. And maybe it can."

I don't want her to have a point. I don't know why. Maybe because I feel responsible, feel like I should be the one cleaning up my own mess here. Maybe because I don't want to risk her life, even if I know she's right, and I would never let Death's curse do to her what it's done to Poppy. And maybe because I just don't want to hand the knife over. I want to be the one to use it. I want to be the one to watch the Reaper's smile finally fade for good.

It doesn't matter, though. We pull up in front of Enzo's house and I slide the knife out of my belt and across her lap. She tucks it into the inside of her jacket.

"I love you," she reminds me.

"I love you," I answer, and I don't say *too*, because maybe that part feels like a lie in a way I can't examine too closely right now.

"You—" Whatever else Rory had to say shrivels up when the front door opens and instead she guffaws, "What *is* that?"

And, god, in spite of everything else happening today, I crack a smile. "Oh, you two haven't met? That's Enzo."

I've wondered a few times, in an absent, back-of-my-mind, between-life-or-death-battles kind of way, where his wardrobe went. When he came back to himself as the Shade, when he mind-fucked his parents into moving from their apartment in Brooklyn to this nothing-special one-story on the edge of Gracie's downtown, he was *still* my best friend. Still the annoying acting school student, the pretentious antiques snob, the over-the-top twink. But he was also the (second) most powerful monster to ever walk the earth. The demon I'd once left behind. And his more statement pieces disappeared in favor of *practical wear*. For all the murders we were plotting.

Maybe it's because it's prom, or maybe because he doesn't feel like the (second) most powerful monster to ever walk the earth anymore, or maybe because he just wants to dress for the occasion of finally offing the Reaper—but this is not practical wear.

Enzo steps out onto his front porch in black velvet pants and a tight-fitting red shirt, cinched at the waist and ruffled at the throat. I recognize the textile of the red, the *mola* art of his mother's people, decorated with impossibly intricate yellow and pink and blue thread, stitched together to create a scene of a dragon sitting at the edge of a lake, the image stretched out across Enzo's torso, and ribs, and onto his back. The shirt might've been made by his mother herself, for the son she adores. Or maybe the *mola* was passed down to him from his family outside of the U.S. and he turned it into a shirt. The beaded earring dangling from one of his ears was definitely made by his mother. The ten gaudy rings on his fingers were probably picked up from ten different hole-in-the-wall thrift stores in Brooklyn.

When he sets eyes on us through the glare of the headlights, he grins.

Next to me, Rory smiles and leans back in the driver's seat. They are so good. I can't believe I deserve this.

My heart pings a hurt I try to ignore. I actually can't believe I deserve this.

Prom is in full swing by the time we park the car. There are no spots left in the lot—which doesn't make any sense, you'd think more students would be parking here on a regular-ass day than on prom night, but this place is overflowing, like the student body of all the surrounding counties also showed up—so we park down the street and walk along the ditches until we get where we're going. Which is, in this case, the football field. The whole field's been turned into an outdoor dance floor and stage. The bleachers are flooded with kids who don't wanna dance or haven't had anyone ask them. Music—boring, unimportant Top 40 radio—plays from the announcers' speaker. The concession stands are open, selling the same dry pretzels and wet hot dogs you can get at any Friday-night football game.

Clearly, the decoration budget was low, since almost nothing about the field would indicate that it's prom night, if it weren't for the people in dresses and suits, and the occasional random string of glittery garland. Or maybe the budget was fine, but they blew it all on the giant picture of Zeke King's face—literally his Twitter profile photo, blown up to be ten feet by ten feet, stretched out between two poles in the center of the field, with badly added text reading GONE, BUT NEVER FORGOT-TEN across the bottom.

"You have got to be shitting me." I can't look at it for more than thirty seconds, immediately turning away and rubbing a hand over my face.

Why are we even here? We could have waited to kill Poppy tomorrow. I could be at home, with my dog, instead of at *prom*, with the ghost of a guy my boyfriend murdered.

And that isn't our only issue.

I realize Enzo and Rory aren't looking at me or at the larger-than-life picture of Zeke. They're looking around at the people in the bleachers who are staring at *us*. And there are a lot of them. Pointing. Whispering. Harsh glares.

Shit. Poppy has these people wrapped around her finger. Of course she's told them something heinous about what happened that day in the church. God, shit, fuck, why am I here?

I open my mouth to ask if this was a terrible idea, if we should just book it back home and wait for our next opportunity. Maybe we jumped the gun. It's not like everyone doesn't already know I have an issue with impulse control.

But I don't actually get the question out. Someone on the makeshift stage says, "Can I have everyone's attention, please? It's time for the announcing of Prom Court."

What the hell is Prom Court?

"Our prom prince is . . ."

And they definitely go on to say who that person is, but I'm turning to Enzo and Rory and demanding, "There's a prince? And a princess, I'm gonna guess? Of prom?"

I thought it was just a king and a queen. And honestly, that was too much.

Rory makes a face like they're thinking of sending an earthquake to eliminate this entire event. Enzo looks . . . wistful.

"I always wanted to be prom king," he tells me, as if that

isn't the most ridiculous thing I've ever heard. "But we didn't have one at my school. Instead, we had an award ceremony and handed out little plastic Oscar knockoffs. I think I could've won Best Costuming this year, if I hadn't left."

Rory blinks at him. Then blinks at me. And all I can do is shrug, because I have no idea.

"*Aaanyway.* Gem, are you—" They stop short, eyes on something above my head. I go to turn, to look in the direction they're facing, but they grab my shoulder and stop me. Hand painfully firm, they steer me deeper beneath the bleachers, ducking us into shadow.

It smells like pee and root beer under here, and I'm pretty sure the couple over our heads are in the middle of breaking up, but okay.

Enzo trails after us, blending into the shadows as if he were born in their fold.

"That cop's here," Rory explains, before I can ask them what the issue is.

I finally get the chance to follow their line of vision, eyes hunting through the crowd until I spot him. He's nothing special. A white guy with a buzz cut and a blue uniform. He's got one hand on the gun strapped to his hip, while he talks to a group of freshman girls in skintight dresses. I feel five hundred years old, wondering how their parents let them leave the house in those outfits—but I'm older than that, really.

"Officer Allen?" I ask.

"In the flesh," Enzo sighs. "This is going to get messy, isn't it?"

Trying to convince him otherwise would be a lie. So, I don't. I stare at Officer Allen from my hiding place under the bleachers, watching as he moves from one group to the next, his hand never leaving his gun. I watch until I hear the announcer yell,

"Poppy White!"

I've never heard the stadium scream like this before. As soon as Death's name is called, applause and cheers break out so loud I worry about my eardrums. Even with my hands clapped over the sides of my face, the screaming is enough to be painful. Everyone in the bleachers overhead stomps their feet, until I think the seats might just fall down on top of us.

Through a slit in the metal, I watch the stage as Poppy slowly walks up to accept her crown. She's not wearing the kind of costume I would've expected. Her dress is all black, made of lace and tulle, with a big round skirt; she's like some kind of gothic Disney princess. When the crown is lowered on her head, she smiles so wide I wonder if it hurts her face.

She seems . . . happy. Actually happy, which doesn't make any sense.

My stomach clenches.

I'm glad she got to wear the crown. Enzo can take it for his costume closet when I cut her head off.

It takes an hour of lurking in the dark under the bleachers before an opportunity arises to lure Poppy and Marian away. They've been dancing ever since the crowning, in the middle of the field, soaking up everyone's attention. Plus, Officer Allen's been out, questioning different groups of promgoers, some of them twice.

Finally, though, there's no more cop in sight. He must've gotten bored, decided I wasn't here. And finally, enough eyes are off the Reaper and the Lionheart that the two of them clasp hands and slip away, away from the field, toward the parking lot. If anyone else notices them, they don't follow, probably assuming they're on their way to celebrate the big win by making out against Poppy's car or something.

But the Shade, the Mountain, and I slither after them like serpents.

This parking lot is the same place I first saw Poppy White. Where she tried to kill me, before I had any idea who I was, before I had any chance at defending myself. Before *Gem Echols* had ever done a thing to her or anyone else, she'd tried to snuff me out. That's what I'm thinking as the music grows fainter and the lights grow dimmer and we creep between parked cars, following the sound of Marian's laughter and Poppy's squeals.

She started this. *They* started this, the two of them, *not* me. I won't feel bad.

"Did you know a trans girl has never won prom queen in this county?" Poppy asks, from out of sight.

"Uh." Marian chuckles. "I guess I didn't know that. But I feel like I did. You know?"

How different they sound when they don't know they're being overheard. How human.

I don't like it.

"I am a legend." Poppy giggles.

"You know, Pops, I hear legends can't be killed." I slide out from around the bumper of someone's ancient minivan. "You wanna help me test that theory?"

They're exactly where I expected them, leaning up against that stupid pink sports car. Marian pulls back immediately, face twisting into a scowl, putting her body between mine and her girlfriend's. Poppy leans back on her elbows, tilting her head to get a better look at me—but not so far that the crown falls off her head.

"What do you want, peaches?" She sounds bored. Except she doesn't. She sounds like she wants to sound bored, but there's a flash hint of fear underneath it. The Reaper's afraid of me, which means she isn't as dumb as I've suspected.

"What I *want* is for your mother to have had better aim so we wouldn't need to have this conversation at all." I shrug. "Unfortunately, that's not a possibility. And now you've gone and gotten a *cop* involved?"

Her jaw tics, but it's Marian who speaks. "For all *we* knew, you were never even coming back. Blaming you didn't have any consequences if you'd already disappeared."

I won't entertain the possibility of that being true. If I'm going to do what has to be done tonight, I can't let Marian get in my head. So, I scoff. "You thought I'd abandoned the Mountain and the Shade? Run off to save myself?"

"What?" she sneers. "Like loyalty's your strong suit?"

My stomach tightens and tightens and tightens. I desperately want her to be wrong. My head pounds, a beat louder than the terrible music back at the football field.

"You have always known it would end this way, Battle," I snap. "You can't protect her anymore."

"I will protect her until my death."

The drama of it all. I sigh. "Fine. Then die."

Lightning breaks from the sky and connects square with the Lionheart's chest.

The Reaper screams.

The fresh smoke in the air smells of singed flesh.

But Marian doesn't sway under the bolt, I realize. Instead, she cups her hand around it, and I watch, horror creeping in, as she curls her fist, lightning morphing into a ball in her palm before disappearing past the surface of her skin. Her veins light up, making her glow from the inside, the whites of her eyes luminescent when she turns her face back to mine.

"Do you know that another name for Battle is War?" Her

voice doesn't sound like her own. "Do you know why humans invented war? *Resources.* It always comes down to fear that there won't be enough. To one side . . . stealing power . . . from another."

It hits me, the realization of what she's about to do, right before she actually does it. "No—"

Marian lifts one hand, and curls her fist toward herself, and I feel my own magic start to *rip out of my skin.* I hear my own scream as she drags the power from my body, and it sizzles and cracks and burns as it slices its way through me, trying to get to her.

This is the god of battle out of balance.

I did this, and I'm going to die for it.

"I'd stop if I were you, *War,*" Rory warns, and I realize she isn't next to me anymore. "Unless you think you can do it faster than I can slit her throat."

At some point, my feet must have left the ground, because I go clattering back to the pavement when Marian releases me, wheeling toward the sound of Rory's voice. Enzo scoops me up, wrapping an arm around me from behind, dragging me to his chest. My power sinks back into my body—but I swear it does so resentfully.

Across the way, still leaning against the pink metal, Poppy has the Ouroboros to her bared neck. Rory has her other hand on the girl's stomach, holding her in place as she watches Marian.

"Just let her do it," Poppy drawls. "Let her wither away to nothing. See how she likes it."

"Mountain," Marian bites out. "You know this ends badly for you."

"Gem won't let that happen to me."

"Gem isn't *Gem* anymore," Marian snaps. "And the Magician will save no one but themself. They proved as much when they ripped us all out of balance."

Does Rory hesitate, like she's listening, like a part of her believes what Marian is saying? Or does that only happen in my head? I blink, push away from Enzo—

Why does everything suddenly feel so fuzzy around the edges?

"Hey! Put down the knife!" a voice calls. My head shoots up, and I see Officer Allen running toward us from the other side of the parking lot. He lifts his receiver to his mouth. "I need backup! Gem Echols is at GHS. There is a weapon."

I can't breathe. I try to, try to make my lungs inflate, try to remind my body that it's human and it needs air, but it doesn't come. Maybe that's why my vision is foggy, everything blurred, everything wrong.

Upside down, broken. I did this.

I did this. I broke everything, I always break everything.

My hands shake and it spreads to the rest of me, like my bones want to leave my *body* behind, like even my body can't stand to be a part of me. My magic wanted to stay with the Lionheart. I don't deserve it. I don't deserve any of this.

I can't breathe.

What am I supposed to do?

Rory kills Poppy. The cop sees it. I kill the whole police department? The whole town? How many people do I have to murder just so I can live?

Rory doesn't kill Poppy. Marian kills me eventually, probably Rory, too. I still go to jail, in the meantime.

Because everyone wants to see me punished, because everyone hates me, because everyone would be better off I weren't here, if I'd never been here, if I didn't exist and never had.

I can't breathe.

And Enzo's just standing there, doing *nothing,* the (second) most powerful monster to ever walk the earth, and he's not doing anything, because I *broke* him. I killed Enzo, and all of his dreams of end-of-school award shows and growing up and seeing his mom's hometown; I killed that version of him when I knocked the wall down. And now I've as good as killed the Shade. I've taken away everything that made either of them *them,* and of course he hates me. How could he not?

And my mother is mourning me while I'm still alive. And I think I broke my dad. It was me; it was what happened to me that broke his brain, and ruined his marriage, and destroyed his whole life, and my mom's, too. I never should have been born.

I can't breathe.

I don't know how to fix this. I don't know how to undo what I did the day I killed Zephyr. I don't know how to unbreak the scales.

What I need is to be wiped from existence entirely. And maybe I *do* know a way to do that.

My hand ghosts against my waistband. My fingers curl around cool metal. I pull the Ouroboros free from its hiding spot.

"Gem? What is that?" Rory's voice. "No. No, no, no, you *gave me* the knife; what is that?"

I didn't give them the knife, though. I let them think I did. Because I am selfish and cruel and impulsive, and I am the god of magic, and I can do anything I want without consequences. Or so I thought.

And if I take my own life with this blade, will it mean my power blinks from existence? Will the scales be righted? Will I never be able to break anything ever again?

Buck's voice in my head. "*It isn't* time *for you to be carved open. Tick, tick, tick.*"

I can't breathe.

Enzo's hands are on me and he's trying to pull the knife from my grip, and I hear him begging me to put it down, but he isn't strong enough, and he can't make me, and I did that to him.

"*Tick, tick, tick.*"

"I'm sorry."

Steel slots between my ribs.

And though I don't deserve it, either, the pain is fleeting.

12

IT'S NOT THAT I ACTUALLY WANTED TO DIE

It's just that I had no idea how to fix the mess I'd made of living.

13

I DON'T KNOW ABOUT THIS

I'm back in the fog where the Reaper showed me the hole in my chest.

I don't think this room is real, but I guess that doesn't matter when I'm standing in it. Everything is gray, and everything is happening from very far away, and there are no sounds, and no mirrors, and I search my body for open wounds and only find my hands.

This isn't what I thought death would be like. It's silly, thinking I'd go to hell when I don't even *believe* in hell, but I'm still surprised everything's not covered in sulfur. Maybe I do believe. Or maybe I just assumed, while hell doesn't exist for *most* people, there would be some kind of special hell, just for me, the one person who should suffer for an eternity.

How arrogant, to hate myself that much. To think I mattered that much.

At my feet comes a *bark!*

I look down—relative, in this room that doesn't exist, where gravity and space and time can't possibly hold any weight—and,

"Hank?"

At my feet, the old mutt wags his tail, the entire lower half of his body wiggling when he does. Except he isn't old. Not here, not in this room. This version of Hank is one I remember from years ago, from playing fetch in the yard and running up and down the stairs and chasing his own tail. He jumps up, paws on my knees, and licks at my hands, and barks again, happier than I've seen him in so long.

"Buddy, how are you—"

Oh.

Okay. I see.

Hank is here with me because we're both dead.

I flatten my palm over the top of his head, scrub into his fur. The good news here is that I can't be headed to hell if Hank is with me. What does that make this place? Some kind of limbo?

As soon as I think it, the light appears, a streak of white breaking through the fog like sunlight through storm clouds. It seems far away, but when I lift my fingers toward it, the light shines against my knuckles. I marvel at the absence of blood on my hands.

The light stretches out wider in front of us, soaking up the fog, making it disappear. This is ridiculous. I glance over my shoulder, like I might find something else waiting for me—like I might see Rory and Enzo in the school parking lot, holding my dead body and screaming.

I don't actually wanna see that.

"I don't know about this, bud." Isn't there a whole thing about not going toward the light? I turn to Hank, to ask the rhetorical question of what we do next, just in time to see him slip away from me and into whatever is beyond. "Hank! *Hank!* Come back!"

A moment passes—or doesn't. There is no time in the room. I hope he'll come back, and wait for the sound of his paws on the floor, his panting, wait to see his tail pop up, wagging high in the air. Nothing. Shit.

I don't know where I'm going, but I'm not gonna let my *dog* go there by himself. Certain this isn't gonna be good, I head into the light.

14

MY NAME IS CLOVER AMARITH

*From the eyes of . . . Okay, seriously,
who the hell is Clover Amarith?*

Today is Clover's seventeenth birthday, which means she is to go to the garden of the gods and ask for the gift of magic. And she does *not* want to.

As far as most people in the Ether are concerned, the old gods abandoned them long ago. Nearly a millennium has passed since the eve that saw the pantheon wiped away, the makers of this world disappearing and leaving their people like sacrificial lambs for the Shade. Any who still hold devotion for the old gods do so in secret, in clandestine rituals and the preservation of ancient, sacred texts.

Clover's family belongs to one such group, the most important of them all, the only ones in the Ether who know the truth of the gods' disappearance—for they are the keepers of the Magician's kingdom.

While the Shade, an unfeeling god whose cruelty was without compare, ruled for one thousand years, the keepers of the kingdom remained unwavering in their belief. For one thousand years, despite the threat it posed to their own lives, despite the violence they faced if they were caught, the keepers tended to the grounds of the palace and nurtured the whispers of magic still left in this world.

Because they believed—and still do—that one day, the Magician would return.

At the heart of that faith is the garden of the gods. In the palace's center, safeguarded by all measures magical and mundane that the keepers have at their disposal, is the very place where the gods disappeared all those generations ago. And the keepers know this—Clover's family knows this—because they're still *right there*.

She exchanges a courteous nod with the guard at the garden's entrance. He beams at her, too excited, stepping out of her way to let her in.

You'd think, at this point, the keepers would stop caring so much about seventeenth birthdays. A thousand years of them, and it hasn't worked yet. Clover has been dreading this day for as far back as she can remember. She doesn't want to sit with the gods, and she certainly doesn't want to go back to her fathers and tell them she failed, just like everyone before her.

The guard closes the door at her back, and her stomach drops. She takes a deep breath, clenches her teeth, and keeps moving.

While the keepers have done their best to maintain the palace, there aren't enough of them to constitute the fleet of caretakers a castle would typically require. Beyond that, they took care for many hundreds of years not to maintain things *too* well, lest they garner the suspicion of outsiders who believed the palace to be uninhabited since the Magician's fall. The outer walls are thick with grime and overgrown weeds, and there is always something in need of repair inside.

But the garden is kept perfectly manicured at all times. It

is ardently tended by the hands of those who have come before her, each flower loved into bloom, each herb thanked when it is snipped. And the statues are cleaned with reverence that could only ever be bestowed upon . . . a god.

Ugh. The statues.

Clover shivers as she approaches the center of the garden, her footfalls light on the stone path beneath her, yet still uncannily loud in the echo chamber of the garden. She sees the Shade before the others, and her heart gives a lurch. It always does when she looks at him.

Years ago, only days before Clover herself came into this world, the Shade stormed the palace. The keepers believed he was there to smite them, that they would finally face punishment for their forbidden idolatry. It was not them he'd come for, though. He ignored their screams and pleas for mercy, moving through the palace walls until he reached its heart, the garden itself. And there, he'd come face-to-face with the other statues.

No one knows what really happened next. But ever since, the Shade, too, has vanished from the Ether. The only remnant of him is his own porcelain sculpture, posed in a kneel, eternally submitting at the Magician's feet. And the only ones who know of his existence are the keepers.

Clover's family—and most of their ilk—believe the Magician, somehow, even in their slumber, punished the Shade. That they protected their people, even from the beyond, from wherever it is that they've disappeared to. *Clover* doesn't believe that, though she also doesn't have any better guesses.

The rest of the gods are here, too. *Most* of the rest of them. The Magician stands over the Shade's kneeling body. The Evergod hovers just behind them. The Lionheart and the Reaper have their stone fingers twined in a permanent embrace. The

Hammer and the Cyclone are poised to attack, while the Stillness holds out their hands in an attempt to quell the rage of the others. The Siren is frozen at the back of the garden, turned as if she thought to leave this place, forever imprisoned before she could. Her sister, the Mountain, stands just behind her, a wyvern draped over her shoulders.

The Muse is nowhere to be found. Neither is the Heartkeeper, though that's because *that* god still walks the Ether's surface. And she does so more freely, now that the Shade has been banished, and this world is hers alone.

Perhaps that's why Clover can't bring herself to feel as strongly about this as her parents do. She's a keeper because that's how she's been raised, but she wouldn't have *chosen* this life for herself. Maybe because the Shade was gone before she ever drew her first breath, she doesn't understand the weight of what the world was truly like under his rule. She doesn't understand why they keep begging the Magician to return, and to bring their magic with them, instead of just . . . learning to be happy in the world the way it is.

She's dreading that conversation. When this fails, and she has to go back and tell her dads that nothing happened, she knows they'll be disappointed. But they'll be even more disappointed when she tells them she wants to leave. She doesn't want to waste the rest of her life locked in this palace, frozen in time, devoting every moment to a *piece of rock*.

Clover sighs, and drops down onto a bench, staring up at the Magician's statue.

"Hi." Immediately, this is deeply uncomfortable. "Uh—my name is Clover Amarith."

The statue, of course, does not respond.

"Um . . . It has been seventeen years since I entered your

kingdom." *And I've never left! Not once!* "And after this lifetime of piety, I would humbly ask that you bless me with the gift of your magic."

The word "humbly" catches on her tongue a little, but she pushes past it.

And still, of course, the statue does not respond.

"This is so fucking stupid." Clover puts her head in her hands.

How long does she have to sit in here and pretend she's having a conversation with no one? How long does she have to act like she's meditating, or praying, or whatever it is that the other keepers do when they come in here?

She stands, pacing along the edge of one rosebush, trailing her finger over a bramble until it gets caught on a thorn. With a wince, she brings her fingertip to her mouth, nursing a drop of scarlet from her skin.

Behind her, something shatters.

Clover wheels around and nearly chokes on her own blood.

The clean white stone of the Magician's statue has begun to break apart. And beneath the dust and rubble, there is *flesh*.

15

THE DESPERATION WITH WHICH I'VE MOURNED

I immediately regret following after Hank.

On the other side of the light is total darkness, with no indication that anything lies beyond it. I feel entombed. If my body is still there, I can't feel it, or move it, and certainly can't see it. There is no sound, no feeling, nothing but pitch black and me, and I would get claustrophobic and stop breathing if I were breathing to begin with. Which I'm not.

It's like my awareness, my consciousness, whatever *thing* this is that narrates my stupid little thoughts—maybe some people would call it a soul—is still kicking around, but everything else is . . . nothing. Is this what it means to be dead? Just me and my thoughts forever? Maybe I really am in hell.

There's no sense of time because I don't think time exists anymore. Maybe I'm suspended there for seconds, maybe another thousand years, before anything changes. And when it does, I'm so grateful to feel *anything*, it doesn't even matter what's coming next.

My face is first. I feel air on my cheek, which means there

is air and I have a cheek. Then on my forehead, something like dust. When I realize my ear is still there, it's because I hear something cracking over it, something falling away with the sound of shattering . . . glass? Stone?

I hear someone whisper, "Holy shit," but I don't recognize the voice of the speaker.

It also isn't *English* they're speaking. Somehow, I understand them anyway.

My hands are freed next. I feel my fingers, and they twitch when I try to move them. Little bolts of power flicker to life, sparking up through the rest of me. So, I have hands, and I have magic. Good. Okay. We're getting somewhere.

Maybe because of the magic's return, or maybe because I'm becoming more and more aware of time, the rest of me comes into focus more quickly. My mouth, my legs, my stomach, my eyes. And with my eyes comes my *sight,* and everything, all at once, shifts into a new kind of focus, dragging me out of the dark.

I know *exactly* where I am, though I can't really be here. I blink, taking in the sight of my garden, the heart of my home, the home I have not set foot in for one thousand years. It has changed as much as I have, growing and warping with time, but we are still who we have always been.

Dust crumbles from my body, and my neck falls forward, my eyes widening. My *body.* The body I have only seen in dreams for so long. Taller and stronger and more powerful than any meager meat ship I've piloted in the lifetimes since.

But I can't actually be here. This can't *really* be happening.

When I visit, in my dreams, it does not feel like this. In my dreams, haunted by visions of a time long past, I am not in control. I am subjected to the whims of a version of me who is no more, only able to watch their decisions, to sit back and relive their mistakes. Never am I actually back in my body. Never am I really *here*.

Except I am here. Now. Somehow.

I take a step forward and can *hear* the groaning of my bones as they shift and move with me. It aches, like sore muscles and fresh bruises, and I wince at the pain of it.

But I can move. I can walk on these legs, in this body, my body.

I am home, in the garden at the heart of my kingdom.

And the Shade is kneeling before me.

Or not the *Shade*, per se, but a version of him made from stone, frozen on his knees, forever staring up and into my own lifeless eyes. My hand falls to the crest of his smooth, cold cheek, thumb brushing. This is the demon who's lived in my head all these years, the monster of sharpened teeth and forked tongue, the creature of nightmares who never walked the earth. But he's here. Sort of.

What have I done? Is this really death? To go home again, to be alone here? Is that what's happening to me? My heart races at the thought—dread and excitement interlocked. I don't want to be alone, but . . . could I really be back in the Ether? And what does it mean for my magic, if I am?

Behind me comes the sound of stone cracking, and I let my hand fall from my demon's face to turn toward it. The sight of the other gods, frozen just like the Shade, immortalized in stone, makes me start with surprise. A creeping discomfort, nausea at the pit of me, thickens. They're as uncanny as wax figures and just as off-putting. I don't like this.

The sound of breaking draws my attention again, to the

back of the room. Each step is a quiet kind of agony, but I force my old-new body to move, to amble across the floor toward the sound.

My investigation leads me to the Mountain.

Oh, my Mountain. Strange tenderness coils its arms around my insides, reminding my body how it feels to be warm and soft after an eternity spent stoic and untouchable. The uncanniness of being carved from rock is even more wrong on *her*, a god who embodies so much life, left like a gravestone in this garden. And still, her beauty is unmistakable, even withstanding its perversion. Even through the stone's surface, the strength and softness of her is so clear that it calls to me, making my claws itch for the feel of her flesh beneath mine.

It isn't the Mountain the noise is coming from, though. I realize this when another *crack!* echoes off the garden walls. It's coming from the beast on her shoulders.

At first, it did not strike me as odd to find a wyvern draped over the Mountain, a familiar locked into forever at her side. The Mountain has always had familiars. To see her without one would be more eerie than the alternative.

But this creature is not frozen like its master. Under my scrutiny, the stone trapping its body begins to flake away, revealing a line of glittering green and gold scales beneath. The wyvern, fully formed at no more than four feet in length, kicks its two legs back and shatters half of the stone casing in one go, like an eager hatchling finally freed from its egg. Its wings begin to flutter, shaking off the rest of the debris until it drags itself up and up, flying into the air over my head.

I tilt back my neck to consider it and our eyes meet. I'm certain I've met this creature before, but so much time has passed, and it was of such little importance to me at that time. It makes no sense, then, the cord of familiarity that knots around my neck.

Except ... no. No, it couldn't be. But ...

"Hank?"

My voice is my own—*not* the voice of Gem Echols. And therefore, if my suspicions are proven true, not the voice of this creature's master.

And yet, the wyvern makes a pleased humming sound, almost like a purr, and buzzes through the air, butting up against my shoulder. His tongue flicks my cheek.

As good as a yes, as far as I'm concerned.

Gem's dog—my dog, I suppose, whatever part of me still houses that lifetime—followed through the echelons of reality to see his master to the end of their journey. And some ridiculous emotion bubbles up in me at the thought.

If I were still Gem Echols, I might cry.

From behind a tree in the garden, someone whimpers. I spin toward the sound and take a long stride toward it. Unbothered and disinterested, Hank flutters to the ground, bouncing on his legs to sniff at the stone casing the other gods.

"Who is there?" I demand, bristling my own nerves at the depth of my voice, the ferocity with which it echoes throughout the garden. It's been so long since I've used these vocal cords, I've nearly forgotten what they're capable of.

A moment later, a girl appears. The child is so plain as to be striking, as if some being was told to demonstrate an example of "human" and this was what they came up with. Perfectly average in stature, with beach-sand skin that is neither perfectly smooth nor horribly blemished. Her hair is cropped at her ears, her eyes the color of muddy water. Even her clothes are so utilitarian as to be invisible, fabric swaths in shades of beige draped around her until she blends into a single amorphous blob.

She stares up at me with wonder, and fear, and reverence, and I could moan at the memory of this. Too long I've been without the true gift of humanity's adoration.

"What is your name?" I take care not to let my voice sound too brutal this time, lest it crack the very walls surrounding us.

"C-C-Clover Amarith." She sucks in a deep breath, as if the act of speaking her own name nearly took everything out of her. "My family have been keepers in this p-p-palace for forty generations. Today is my seventeenth birthday."

I raise an eyebrow at her explanation. When Hank makes a delighted squealing buzz, I glance toward him. Utterly unconcerned with the stranger's presence, he's taken to frolicking in the flowers before stuffing one in his mouth. And immediately spitting it out upon realizing it doesn't taste good.

Hm. I almost crack a smile but think better of it. No showing signs of benevolence until I know who this girl *truly* is. And what she's after.

My attention returns to her, and she winces under the weight of it.

"None of that means anything to me, child." I tilt my head. "Why are you here?"

This girl, this Clover, glances toward the door, as if she thinks to bolt from the room and abandon our conversation. Bold, even to consider it. But terribly foolish, if she were to try.

"When you disappeared from the Ether, keepers dedicated their lives to protecting your legacy," she says, proving she is not so foolish after all, and looking back to me. "We have kept this palace safe, waiting for your return."

Ah, not foolish at all. Now she's trying to endear herself to me. Is it working?

Not yet. Maybe if she keeps going.

"I was the one who summoned you back," she tells me then. "Because it's my birthday—my seventeenth birthday, my transition from *child* to adult. And on a keeper's seventeenth birthday, they come to the garden of the gods, and they ask you to bring magic back to the Ether. Because—because you took magic with you when you left. Most of it, anyway. And you never answer. You never answer. But you answered me. You're here. You . . . you chose me."

Her eyes get big and then bigger. To herself, she whispers, with complete seriousness, "I'm the Chosen One."

It is impossible for me *not* to laugh at her when she says this. It cracks out of me, gone as quickly as it appeared, and the sting of it is clear in the flush on her skin.

"I did not choose you," I tell her. "If what you're saying is true, the timing is a coincidence. I am not here to grant your wish for magic's return to the Ether. I'm here . . ."

Why am I here?

What will I do now? I'd entertained the idea of coming home, but I never imagined I would have to do it alone. What waits for me in this world? This beloved world of my own creation, left to its torture for an epoch. Can it even still be called my home when I know nothing of it? When its people know so little of *me*?

I look down at my hands. Familiar and not. Long and elegant and tipped with black claws. And still unmarred with blood.

Hank hisses at his own spiked tail, flying in circles to chase it.

"But . . . but you *did* choose me. I—" Clover shakes her head.

"Um. You should come with me. I can take you to the others. There's a whole community inside who'll want to see you. My parents can tell you more about us than I can—they can help you catch up on what you've missed."

"What I've missed?"

Pain flares, like someone picking at a nerve in my chest as if it were a string on an instrument, as if my agony were a song to be played for the pleasure of an audience.

How dare this insignificant child speak to me this way. How dare she thoughtlessly mock my loss, pointing out that this world has spun through history without me.

I step forward and she steps back, but it doesn't matter. I am God, and she is nothing. And though I don't move faster or farther than she does, I am on her in that single step, my claws sinking into her skin as I grip her chin in my hand. Her blood pools over my fingertips, those mud-water eyes wetting and widening.

"You think to bestow instruction upon your god? You believe your kind could ever know more than *me*? Without me, you do not exist. Without me, this world would blink from time." I lean forward, mouth closing in on her ear. "This is a decadent hymn you've spun, casting yourself in the role of apostle, Clover Amarith. But you will sing it with *respect*, or I will eat your tongue."

Her tears leak over her cheeks, and she struggles to explain herself. Or perhaps she intends to apologize. Either way, she can't seem to get the words out.

Some buried thing inside me whispers that she could not have known. She did not mean to offend me. This girl had no way of knowing the desperation with which I've mourned this world, and the fear I've felt at every step that I will never really feel at home—not here, and not on Earth, and not anywhere.

She is devout, and she wants to help me, and I should let her. But my rage is a wild thing in my gut, so much bigger than the anger I've held in a human's body, and I will have to relearn to control it.

Behind me, the sound of crumbling rock begins to fill the chamber once more. I release Clover, her blood dripping from my hand and splashing along the stone floor when I turn away.

And before my eyes, the porcelain prisons holding captive the Shade *and* the Mountain begin to fall. The white casings shiver and splinter, turning to ash and falling away, like the melting of glaciers over a cliffside. Bit by bit, and then all at once, they are revealed to me.

They are alive and they are *here*.

I am not alone. This is not my damnation.

The Mountain twists around, body making the air around her immense hips *swish* as she does. The wild curls of Rory have disappeared, replaced by silky rings of a black that seem to change color each time she moves. With the shifting of light against her body, I can make out the deepest greens and warmest browns and most vibrant reds, all tucked in the strands of her hair, like a magic itself. Her warm brown skin is decorated with new-old markings—not the tattoos of her human life, but the hand-poked patterns in magicked ink that tell the story of her vast creations, her entire body an homage to her kingdom.

Here, in this world, nothing about her is forced to become smaller or more human for the palatability of others. She need not blend in to avoid the attention of others, to protect herself from the scrutiny of those who should be so blessed as to ever set eyes on her in the first place. Here, when onlookers stare at the strange chimera of her existence, it is because they are in awe of who she is and what she can do. Enormous in height and breadth, with two sharp tusks resting over her upper lip, she stares at me with the golden eyes of a big cat.

"Gem?" she whispers, in a voice dripping with such affection that it threatens to make my knees buckle.

"Oh, my," whispers the velvet midnight voice of the Shade, and my eyes dart to him.

I am certain that the sharpness of Enzo Truly was a holdover from the god of things forbidden, for my demon is all sharpness. His body, tall and slender, is like the blade of a knife, his jaw and cheeks and hands and mouth all perfectly formed so that one might cut themself if they dared get too close. And who would not risk it, anyway? Who, for the promise of his mouth, would not risk slicing themself open on his rows of razor-sharp teeth?

The Shade smiles, looking at me with those eyes of pure pitch, twin black holes glinting with the dying light of swallowed stars.

"You did it." The pride in his voice should not make my chest swell the way it does. The flick of his forked tongue against the corner of his mouth should not make me shiver. And yet. "*You did it.*"

We move together as one unit, the three of us. Our ancient, aching bodies force our dusty joints to walk, to gather in the center of the garden. One of the Mountain's hands spans my back. I touch a curious claw tip to one of her tusks. The Shade runs his fingertip against the shell of my ear. I trail my freshly bloodied hand beneath his jaw.

There is so much I want to say to them, but speaking feels like an impossible task. I'd thought, before, that human bodies were never meant to love as deeply as I loved them. That loving them the way I did might be enough to kill me. But I had no idea what I was talking about.

If my rage has been diluted to fit in a human's body, then so has how much I've loved them. It is agonizing in its weight, burrowing into every atom of me. I can feel them like roots buried in the soil of my body, can feel them scattered across time and space like they are the very grains that tie this world together. My heart *hurts*, it loves them so much.

And I just forced them to watch me kill myself.

"I am so s—"

There is no opportunity for the thought to find its footing in my mouth.

All of us turn in unison, as the Lionheart begins to break free from her statue.

16

NOT MY PROBLEM

I could kill them all right now.

Right now, while the rest of the pantheon struggles to break their bodies free, while flesh and bone force their way through cocoons of fossil, I could use a single spell to wipe all of them from existence. They wouldn't have the chance to defend themselves, wouldn't be able to fight back at all. It would be easy, and then it would be over.

My hand tingles as if magic asks the question, *Are we doing this?*

Hesitation wavers in a trail along my skin, keeping the magic in check. There's only one reason for my reluctance, but it's reason enough.

I have *no idea* what my magic is going to look like here.

"We are powerless!" the Hammer rages, slamming his fist into a tree so hard that bark explodes. He howls with pain, ripping back his hand to examine his knuckles for injury. He's not used to this new human body. He has yet to learn its limits.

"We are not *powerless*," I chastise, waving my hand at the scene he's just caused, the destruction he's just wrought. "We are stronger than any other creature who walks this world."

But I understand his frustrations. It does not matter that we are stronger than ants. They are still ants, and we used to be gods.

• •

"I feel powerless," I tell my therapist. I don't want to be here, talking to this woman in her cardigan and cross necklace, but my mother insists.

"Why do you think that is?" She asks, and I get the impression she's watching the clock as closely as I am, counting down the minutes until she no longer has to sit with the sight of me.

I swallow. "So much has changed. I thought my life would be different. I don't know. Lately, it's like everything is happening to me. And I'm just watching it."

On Earth, we'd been forced into echoes of ourselves, remnants of the gods we used to be. I haven't touched the *full* extent of my power since the last day I stood in this world. And that was before I killed the Cyclone—before the balance was thrown off kilter, before everything changed, again.

Now we're back where we belong, and we have a whole new arsenal of power at our disposal, every one of us. But what does that mean? What does that mean if we're still out of balance?

Are we still out of balance? It isn't as if I have a physical scale to check in with, and I'm not confident enough to vibe-check my way into certainty. Maybe what I did with the Ouroboros, giving myself up to the blade, was enough to bring things back, full circle. Maybe everything is fixed, and we're just ... here, now. Maybe that *was* the fix.

Or maybe not.

Either way, I don't know what would happen if I reached for the full weight of my magic. I don't know that I have any more control than I did when Gem Echols first tried to harness it. And I won't risk the Shade and the Mountain by unleashing a bloodbath that might catch them in its waves.

The door to the garden clatters as Clover Amarith runs away, and I tilt my head to watch her go. So much for devotion. But I can hardly blame her, just the same. Probably for the best that the girl make herself scarce.

A man in an equally boring beige outfit, with an automatic rifle strapped to his back, looks through the door as it swings shut behind her. He screams, pointing into the garden, calling for someone else over his shoulder.

"They're here! The Magician has returned!"

I don't want to deal with these people. Any excitement I might've felt at that first brush of worship has faded into irritation that they might get in the way of what I actually want to do. Which is to say, anything I want. Like kissing. Or forming a new world from the ash of this one, cradling the fresh beating heart of a new empire in the palms of my hands. Or taking a nap.

The Reaper's shell is the first to shatter completely, disintegrating around her body, becoming a pile of ash on the floor. In her human form, Poppy White begat attention because she looked so close to death. In her true form, she *is* Death. Her body is skeletal, only a memory of flesh. She is bones stitched together with a cloak of shadow.

This is camp. The thought invades without my consent,

pestering at the edge of my mind like a buzzing insect. Mentally, I swat it away.

The eyeless sockets in her skull turn toward me, then the Lionheart, as her lover breaks free of her own cage.

The god of battle grips her shield in one hand, her lover's bones in the other. She tosses her head back, freeing herself from the last of the stone, the long, long braid of her hair like a whip through the garden. She looks to the Reaper. Then to me.

A moment hovers between us.

Lionheart's eyes brighten until they mock the color of blood. The hair on the back of my neck rises in response, my palms tingling with knowledge of the inevitable. The Reaper's laughter spills from her bones like a thousand children in an early grave.

When Magic and Battle collide, we are no longer in the garden at all. Her shield swings toward me, a roar rolling from her chest that rouses the earth itself, like a clap of thunder heard in every corner of our world. And in that moment, I watch the cosmos unfold around her, the Ether and the other gods all slipping away beneath us.

This is what it means to be a god.

Her shield misses me, slamming into a comet that races past our heads. It explodes on impact, shards scattering across the vastness of space. The responding *hiss* that slithers from between my teeth is both familiar and not, and the stars tremble in answer.

"We have no fight anymore," I remind her. "All you wanted was to return—I've given that to you. Should you not be thanking me, Lionheart?"

Perhaps I imagine the pain in her expression. She shakes her head and the whip of her hair cracks, reverberating through time and splitting the universe wide open. "You do not see how far you have fallen, Magician. Our fight is no longer the issue. Some people just have to die."

"You are confused." My claws skim the fog of eternity before plucking loose a splinter of infinite possibility. It's so hot it feels cold in my hand. "I am not a person."

The splinter flies from between my fingers, spinning over itself, aimed at her throat. It shatters on impact, turning to cosmic dust. She sighs as if disappointed.

Her whip lashes around my neck. I sink my claws into the fine strands of her leathery hair, trying to pry myself free as she drags me into her orbit.

"You are so much more human than you know."

My scream is a black hole that devours us both.

How dare she.

Blink.

Lionheart watches me from across the garden. At her side, the Reaper still holds her hand—she radiates a tremendous amount of smugness for someone with no face.

No one has moved.

Did that all happen in my head?

"This is far from over," the Lionheart finally warns. "But for this moment . . . we are going home."

I barely manage not to shudder as I watch them leave, the Reaper still giggling all the while. Good riddance, then. Let them be a problem for the so-called keepers. Despite my strange daydream, it's *true* that the Lionheart and I have no fight, not anymore.

The light catches on glittering smudges along my fingertips. I stare in confusion at my own hands. I tell myself it is not stardust on my skin.

It wouldn't matter if it were; I'm not given time to process the thought. The Siren bursts free of her shell at the same moment the Librarian falls to his knees as the stone around him breaks.

Here, in the Ether, the Siren's body is made of *scale*, not skin. It glimmers in shades of blue and green as she turns on web-toed feet, staring in horror down at herself. Her mouth is a row of fangs, her neck sliced with gills, her head bald but for a thin layer of golden fur. She turns glowing, iridescent eyes on me, pupils so small they may as well not be there. "*What have you done?!*"

Her supersonic scream is enough to make my teeth chatter. A long fracture slices its way across the garden's ceiling, threatening to rain glass down on our heads.

Hank flies to my shoulder, talons digging deep into skin and muscle.

The Librarian is a wisp of his human self, more the impression of a man than a man in true standing. He might be altogether too mousy, too unremarkable, to pass for a god at all, if it weren't for the extra eyes. They appear over his skin as if intentionally placed—the center of his forehead, the back of his neck, dotted on certain knuckles but not on others. Always seeing *everything*.

"My head . . ." he whispers, touching the tips of his fingers to his scalp. "Everything is . . . clear."

You're welcome. The last time I saw the Librarian, he was verging on a serious psychotic break, consumed and being destroyed by all the thoughts he'd taken in from the people around him. His human body was never meant to handle the pressure of that many minds at once. Not the way this body was.

A little gratitude would be nice.

"Send us back!" the Siren screeches, and I feel a trickle of blood from my ear.

She moves in closer, leaving a wet trail behind her as her bare feet slide against the stone floor. Hank's talons dig and dig. The Mountain *growls* at my side, though I could not begin to guess if it's directed at me or her sister. The Shade's shadow sways against the far wall of the room, growing bigger and bigger, a monster who can only exist by a trick of the light.

"I NEED TO GO HOME!"

"Fine!" I raise my hands, uncertain even as I do if I mean to protect myself or attack her. "Go!"

And the Siren is no more.

No statue. No body. The Siren simply . . . disappears from the room. It is as if she was never there to begin with. There is only the vaguest echo of her memory, and a stale wrongness in the air that makes a nerve in my jaw tic.

Silence slips like the temptation of a knife between myself and my partners. Well, almost silence. From elsewhere in the castle, I hear screaming. But that's not *my* problem.

"Did you . . . send her back to Earth?" the Shade asks, in a tone that implies he already knows the answer.

I clear my throat. "I have no idea where I sent her."

"For fuck's sake." The Mountain touches a paw-like hand to the center of her forehead. "Well, obviously, we have to find her."

"She's still here," the Librarian tells us softly. Half his eyes look toward us. The other half drink in the rest of the room. "In this world, I mean."

I don't bother to ask how he knows this.

The statues of the Stillness, the Hammer, and the Cyclone do not move.

Curious. If I'm as dead as they are, killed with the same weapon in the same world apart from this one, how am I here, and they aren't?

And where is the Muse's statue? And where—

"Hello."

I blink. Has the Evergod been free this entire time?

No, that can't be right. I would have noticed.

My nose crinkles with distaste.

As far as appearances are concerned, the Evergod's true form is as human as we come. Nothing about him indicates he is one of the most powerful of the pantheon. He's just . . . old.

A little old man hunched over and smiling, gray hair in wisps on his head, skin wrinkled so deep that the folds nearly cover his eyes. He keeps on smiling at me.

"Well, what happens now?" the Mountain asks. She may be asking me, or maybe she's inquiring of the god of time.

It's the Shade who answers, though. He tilts his head toward the door as footsteps approach, an army racing through the palace to get to the garden.

When he smiles, it isn't nearly as genial as the Evergod. It makes my claws throb, like a toothache begging to be tongued.

What I want his answer to be is that now we can finally take a moment to be together. We disappear, the three of us, into this world we built and get to rebuild. We relearn each other, in these new-old bodies, and we let the luxury of godhood sink in.

Instead, he says, "I think *now* we deal with Gem's fan club."

Ugh.

17

IT SUITS ME TO IGNORE
THE CONTRADICTION

We always knew you would return to us. Others—they call us a cult, you know. But they won't anymore. Oh, no. Never again. You'll set them all straight."

Rune Amarith is a little man with big glasses and even bigger greed. He rubs his palms together, pacing back and forth in the garden in his brown tweed jacket, fantasizing about the vengeance I will (apparently) mete out on his behalf.

He's one of the small cluster of this group who call themselves the keepers. If I am (or was) the keeper of the scales, they are the keepers of the keeper. And after bursting into the garden, they've all gathered around me as if I were an exhibit in the zoo and they'd paid weekend prices for tickets.

Rune is the only one who dares get close. The others hover at the edge of the garden. They watch me—but they watch the others in my party more closely. The Shade draws the most attention. None of it appears particularly positive.

"I've never endeavored to set anyone straight." I tilt my head at the aggressive little man, curious in the way a child examining a bug might be. "And you *are* a cult. Are you not?"

"Well, I—" Rune seems to debate whether or not he wants to argue semantics with his god, and ultimately decides against it. Clearing his throat, he motions behind him, to the others. "I am Clover's father. I always knew she was special. Her dad and I—well, you don't need to know the whole story—"

"Certainly not," I agree. It does not escape me that I'm having this conversation instead of exploring my kingdom. My patience is dwindling. "And what exactly were you all hoping I might do, upon my return?"

Rune blinks at me. He glances anxiously over his shoulder at the rest of his cult.

"Do you not have an answer for me?" I raise an eyebrow, boredom inching ever closer to irritation. "You've waited with bated breath for an eon and you've no lore on what the Magician might do when they came to collect their world?"

A middle-aged man the size of a tree steps forward from where he'd been fastened to Clover's side. "Your Holiness, my name is Briareus Amarith. I believe my husband is faltering because he does not know how to convey the gravity of our hope."

I consider Briareus. Then Rune, who barely comes up to his elbow. Shaking my head, I ask, "Is someone going to attempt conveyance, or shall the Librarian divest you of every thought in your heads?"

"We hoped you would save the world," Clover snaps. Every eye turns to her. More than half of the keepers look horrified at her tone. "You were supposed to come back and save the world."

"Save the world . . ." It's such a bizarre thing to say, I nearly laugh at her again. "Save the world from what, exactly?"

"Well." Rune coughs, and glances behind me.

At the Shade.

"Naturally," the Mountain chuffs, rubbing her clawed hands over her face. She looks exhausted. I know she fears for the Siren. I know there is still so much to be said between us, now that we're here. How badly I want to get my lovers away from this conversation, so we might speak freely among ourselves.

Soon. And even sooner, if the keepers aren't quick to prove this dialogue valuable.

"That is not a very polite thing to imply," the Shade drawls, clicking his tongue at the gathered group in a *tsk*.

"How can you let him live?" Clover demands of me, throwing out an arm demonstratively, a fresh fire burning in her boring eyes. Someone older and smarter than her curls an arm around her middle and tries to hush her, but the poor fool can't seem to be stopped. "He stole your weapon and destroyed our world! He wrought havoc for a thousand years!"

"This weapon?" I slide the Ouroboros from the inner pocket of my cloak with ease. The silver tip glints in the light pouring through from the low sun overhead.

A whispered hush falls over the keepers. Briareus takes a step back, dragging his husband with him by one of his elbow patches.

"This was a gift. I gave it to him freely."

"And then took it back, quite impolitely," the Shade reminds me.

"And yet here we are, demon. After all this time."

"Because I found it in my heart to forgive you, creature."

"Oh, get a fucking room," the Mountain snarls.

"I don't understand." Clover, somehow still talking despite all evidence that she should shut up, shakes her head. "You two are . . . allies?"

"Historians will call us allies," the Shade sighs. The drama of it borders on excess. "And right to our faces, at that."

He's making jokes. I wonder if anyone but me can tell he's putting on an act.

Likely not. I'd only ever known the *Shade,* I might think this performance was genuine. But I've seen Enzo's acting. And I know it still when I see it now.

I need to be alone with *both* of my gods.

"You were supposed to save us. You—you were supposed to reclaim this world and—and obliterate the tyranny of the Shade and—and—" Rune's hands shake as he wrings his fingers.

I take a step forward and the man whimpers. Tilting my head closer to his, I soften my voice as best I can, though I cannot seem to excise the mockery from my tone. "It is almost always bad practice for a human to assume they know the will of their god. Now . . . tell me. What awful things has the wicked shadow done that you so hoped I'd set you free from?"

"Come on, now, that's hardly fair. I've been gone for ages." The Shade sighs.

"Ages," the Evergod chimes up. He's across the garden, sitting on a bench. Hank has dozed off at his feet. "One, two, three, four, five, six, seven, ten, thirteen, sixteen, four billion five hundred forty-three million six hundred seventy-one thousand eight hundred twenty-two."

"Mm-hmm." The Librarian nods, blinking half his eyes, rubbing his hand over his chin.

Wonderful. Anyway.

"His . . . his kind are monsters!" Rune sputters, wincing at his own words like he expects to be struck with lightning.

I would not do that, of course. The Shade would never be

offended at the accusation he was a monster. Nor would anyone try to deny it.

"And they *ruled* this world. Our numbers are not only so low because outsiders believe we are mad—for generations, his followers castigated any who refused to fall in line behind them! They stomped out any good that dared to stand up against them!"

"Things hidden are not the opposition of that which is good." The Shade sighs again. "It was a bleak period for me, too, you know. I was working through a breakup."

The Mountain steps forward, easing me aside so she can stoop down to face the keepers herself. "What is the land like? Tell me what is left of the Ether beyond the walls of this palace."

I am not the mind reader of the gods, but I imagine the *look* shared between Rune and Briareus cannot mean anything good.

The Mountain looks to the Shade with a low snarl, teeth bared.

He holds up his hands. "As I said . . . I was working through it."

"And he has not been here for years," I remind these humans. It suits me to ignore the contradiction of a thousand years passing as a *bleak period,* while the lifetime of Enzo Truly feels like a forever. So, I do. "Is your world even still in need of saving?"

Clover pipes up. "The Heartkeeper is the only god left who walks this world. I mean, she was. Until today."

At my back, the Shade *hisses.* His hatred, at least, is not part of the performance. "Miserable, evil—you want to damn the wicked? Let us sentence the god of love."

Even hearing her name makes my skin itch, my chest tightening as if a vise has been wrapped over my rib cage. I do not press at the feeling. I do not think I want to know what lies beneath it.

"But she is not a ruler," Clover continues. "If we hadn't heard firsthand accounts of those who've seen her, we wouldn't even know she was here. Meanwhile, the Ether still crawls with the Shade's army."

"They survived my departure?" He claps his hands. "Oh, excellent. I'd worried they would turn to dust. This is great news for us. Did you hear that, darling? We have our own *army*."

Clover blinks at him. I sigh.

Slowly, the girl turns to look at me. "It was as if the Ether had been abandoned by any god at all."

"Until today," I repeat.

The keepers shift, whispering again among themselves.

"If what you hoped to gain from my return was a god to fall before, by all means, hit your knees." I shrug, only feigning boredom now, confident no human could see through the ruse to guess at the tremor of uncertainty beneath. "You have been wise to fall in line behind my name. I am the god of gods, and I have returned to my world. I will extend you the gratitude you deserve for looking after my home while I've been away. Take care not to overwhelm that with resentment at your misplaced disappointment."

A single moment hangs, quiet and thick, in the garden. And when it bursts, every keeper in my company hits their knees. Even Clover, the last to lower herself to the ground, face robed in hesitance, finally submits.

"We are so sorry, Your Holiness," Briareus whispers. "Whatever your plans, we will follow you. We are your dedicated servants eternal."

Power.

It is not *unfamiliar*, the rush that pumps from every blood vessel in my body, pounding through my veins until I can hear it whooshing in my ears, taste it in my mouth, feel it crackling in the palms of my hands. But this power is so very different from my magic. My magic is what I can do all on my own. It is who I am, what I am capable of, something drawn from within that cannot be stolen or squashed.

This power is a different kind of intoxicant, because it stems from a different source altogether. This power is one I haven't felt in so long. One that can only come from being . . .

Their god.

The Shade's mouth against my ear, the hint of his awful teeth on my skin as he whispers, "Look at the way they offer themselves to you. Like sacrificial lambs."

The Mountain's eyes on mine, her expression guarded and impossible to discern. Whatever she sees in my expression, she gives a small shake of her head.

For her, I manage to claw my way back down so I can speak again. "My plan is . . ."

Ah. Well, I don't actually have one of those, do I?

Luckily, the Mountain seems to. "We are traveling to the Shade's kingdom."

"Oh?" The Shade perks up, raising his eyebrows at her.

"The Reaper and the Lionheart will be back, and there is much about this world we need to understand before we are ready to face them." This is what the Mountain says, but I hear the words she isn't speaking.

She needs to see the world beyond this palace.

She needs to find her sister.

And we need to determine if the balance has been righted— or if all of our powers are still unhinged.

She continues, "In the Shade's palace, we will have an *army* to stand guard."

I wonder if the humans hear the mockery that I do, if they have any idea she's taunting him.

Their wide-eyed faces give no indication, one way or another.

"Is this your plan, O Mage?" Rune whispers.

I very nearly answer "Uh, yep" but bite my tongue at the last second. Instead, I incline my head. "Yes. I will travel with my companions to the kingdom of things forbidden."

Something like a sick excitement skitters with a spider's legs along my skin. It feels fitting to return there now, the kingdom that's haunted the dreams of my human existence for so long. In a strange way, it feels as if that is the place where everything began. That kingdom of secrets. How appropriate, now, that this is where we would take our final stand.

"And your companions are . . ." Rune motions around the room, a frown tugging at his lips.

I look to the Librarian.

A few of his eyes are watching me. Enough that he knows when he's been pulled back into the conversation. "I go in search of the Muse. His kingdom borders the Shade's. We'll travel in the same direction, until we don't."

Fine. I glance at the Evergod, and—oh, he's napping. The god in the body of an old man has fallen asleep with his head tipped back and his mouth open. As comfortable and unbothered as the dozing wyvern at his feet.

I suppose it doesn't matter, anyway. The god of time will do whatever he pleases, whenever it suits him.

"We will accompany you," Briareus offers quickly. "Much has changed since your disappearance. We offer our service as guide—and our flesh as shield, should you need it."

I wonder if he knows his daughter just full-body flinched behind him. I don't think she believes in me the way her daddies do. Poor thing.

"Your offer is generous, and I accept." I smile, meeting Clover's eye. "I look forward to your dying for me, should the occasion arise."

The girl looks like she wants to punch me. I really could giggle.

"My companions and I have traveled far. We require rest before the journey." I look back to Rune and Briareus, narrowing my eyes. "You will prepare for our departure and leave us be."

"Yes, Your Holiness."

"Of course, we will see to everything."

"Good." Hoping the Librarian and the Evergod can take care of themselves for a few hours, I take the Shade's hand in one of mine, the Mountain's in the other. "Now . . . let me show you to my bedroom."

18

THIS IS ONLY GOING TO GET WORSE

The moment the door clicks shut behind us, the Shade's mask falls away.

I almost don't take note of it, delighted as I am by the sight of my bedchamber. It appears as though the keepers have done their diligence to keep it as pristine as possible over the millennium. It looks almost exactly as I left it. A massive bed at the center of the room. Huge, windowed doors leading out to a balcony that overlooks the grounds. A fireplace, unlit but not abandoned, as if it's just been waiting for me to return, to breathe life into it once more. And my altar, a stone table carved with runic equations, covered in relics of a time when I stood before it and practiced my craft. The herbs and tonics have disappeared, no doubt turning to dust with time, but the glass and bones and blades remain.

When I do realize what's happened, it's only because the Mountain says, "Enzo, are you all right?"

I turn to look at him and frown, panic puncturing my heart like a thread pulled by a needle.

He's leaning against the wall next to the door, halfway crouched, head tilted back. His hands grip his thighs, little tremors rippling across the surface of his body. He breathes deep through those too-sharp teeth.

Finally, seeming to catch the air in his lungs and hold on to it, he pushes himself from the wall and turns to us. "Fine, kitten. Just . . . it's strange to be home, isn't it?"

"This is what you wanted," I remind him, trying—and perhaps failing—to keep the defensive note from coating my tongue. "You always planned to come back here."

"Of course, yes." He nods in agreement, at odds with the way he seems to fray at the very edges of himself. "It's just . . . I wasn't expecting it to feel this way."

I don't understand. I open my mouth as if to ask for an explanation but close it just as quickly. There is a part of me, dull and aching and as heavy as a rock in my stomach, that suspects I wouldn't *like* the answer if I heard it out loud.

One thing is perfectly clear, though. This *is* Enzo. The Shade, yes, but Enzo just the same. The humanity he found on Earth wasn't stripped away when he returned to the Ether.

I glance beside me, where Rory stands, face screwed up as they watch him. It's clear on them, too. They are the ancient god of the land *and* they are my high school girlfriend.

These are new, old bodies they're inhabiting, but the souls inside them haven't changed any since that moment in the Gracie High School parking lot. They are exactly the people they were when I left them there.

So, why do *I* feel so different? Why is it that Gem Echols is only a memory now?

Could it be because I killed them?

"Things will get easier," Rory assures him, and perhaps this is the correct thing to say, because Enzo's face softens when he turns an appreciative look toward them.

Jealousy, cold and cruel, strikes me in the stomach. And on its heels comes anger, razing along my periphery, begging me to meet its stare.

It should make me happy, shouldn't it? The two of them finally setting aside their ancient grudges and finding something like kinship. I cannot live without either, do not wish to ever be apart from them again, so I should feel *gratitude* they can do more than stomach the other's company.

But when jealousy and anger are cut open, the gooey organs of fear spill out.

If they come to *like* each other—hells forbid even *love* each other—then what would they need *me* for?

Pathetic—and I realize this, even as I cannot stop myself—I shrug off the layer of my cloak, letting the thick fabric pool at my feet. The Ouroboros, tucked within its folds, clatters against the stone floor, the impact dulled by the weight of the garment. I can only hope, with something like acidic desperation clotting in my mouth, that it does not distract my companions from the show of my body.

"Come to bed, demon," I encourage, stepping backward toward the bed, now dressed only in the gauzy undergarments I once preferred. "Allow me to kiss it better."

His enchanting eyes, black pits as they are, alight once more. Enzo's lips part, showing off the tips of those teeth. His forked tongue slides across his lower lip.

Seeming to come to a decision within himself, he pushes the lapel of his black silk jacket from his shoulders, allowing it to join the cloak on the floor. He stalks like a shadow across my chamber, until he reaches the foot of my bed. His hands find the buttons on his shirt as he begins to undress fully.

I could soak in the sight of him like this forever. Even if humanity clings to the recesses of his consciousness, there is nothing human about this body. This ancient monster is closer to a weapon than he'll ever be to a man. With every button undone, he reveals another sharp pane of muscle, covered in thick black tattoos and not a single scar.

Scars ... My eyes flit over his chest, at the spot where Enzo's top-surgery scars once were. How strange, the *cisness* of this body, compared to the boy I'd come to love.

As soon as the thought occurs to me, I have to suppress the urge to roll my eyes at my own idiocy. Cisness. What a ridiculous human concept, and one that has no bearing here. The Shade is not *cis;* he's demonic. He isn't a *man;* he's a god.

My thoughts are pulled away by the sound of Rory's clothes hitting the floor. My eyes shoot toward them, widening at the sight of their bare chest suddenly revealed, their body stripped down to only a swath of black around their hips.

If the Shade's true form is that of a monster, the Mountain's is that of a beast. They move like a predator, like an animal stalking its kill, shoulders rolling with lethal grace, hips swaying with mesmerizing power as they make their way toward the bed. I note the way their ears twitch at sounds I cannot make out, no doubt hearing things lurking around the palace, communing with every spore and rodent that hides in its walls.

When their hands encircle my waist, palms big enough to fit around me entirely, I cannot help groaning.

When the Shade's mouth brushes my throat, those rows of

razors tucked behind deceptively soft lips, I arch *into* the threat, not away.

How addictive it is, to be shown tenderness by those whose power could so easily give brutality instead. What might it say about me that I cannot imagine anything more exciting than handing my body to those who could ruin it, knowing they won't? And better still—knowing I am stronger than either of them, even if they tried.

Like cartographers, their hands explore the topography of my body, mapping the miles of my skin until every slope bears their names. I want to lay claim to every part of them, want to know the way they feel from the inside out, want to show them the soft wound of my body's center and let them press it like a healing bruise.

But there are things we still cannot do, things we are still not ready for, boundaries that have to be drawn and redrawn and keys to doors still not found or carved anew. And so, instead, I worship at the altar of these new-old bodies, whispering my gratitude to their bones for giving them homes to come back to.

And eventually, when we have made and unmade the worlds between us, the gods rest.

> The Mountain and I have to escape this place. We have been on Earth for only days now, in these new bodies, and I fear it won't be long before the other gods see us dead. They will never forgive me for bringing them here without their consent. They believe I've ruined everything, forever, and perhaps they're right.
>
> The night we run, I wait for the Mountain at the edge of the sea as she bids goodbye to her new human family.

I stare out at the water, watching my ship rock with each wave that lurches beneath it. I know the Reaper and the Lionheart lie on that ship. I know they will try to find me. I pray to the gods of this new world, the gods these Vikings worship, that they never will.

I cannot explain my choices to them. They did not know my demon as I knew him. They did not see the way he sank beneath the burden of his own heart. If they had, I wonder if they would have followed the same path—or if I am simply weak.

The Mountain joins me, touching the braid against my skull. "Are you ready?"

"Yes," I whisper, turning away from the sleeping boat.

Despite my prayers, there is a part of me, deep in my gut, that knows this is only going to get worse.

....

Marvel's Loki begins an obsession with Norse mythology that will later lead to my overly identifying with the Greek Icarus. Even later, I will accredit the son of Daedalus for my gender crisis. In that way, I suppose the MCU made me trans. But that hasn't happened yet.

Today, I'm ten years old, and it's the day of my birthday party, and I've forced my parents to indulge a Viking theme. They've constructed a fake ship in our backyard, and the kids from my class run up and down its plastic deck, waving swords and axes made of balloons.

Face painted, hair in tight braids, I hide under the ship, watching my parents from the other side of the yard. They don't know anyone's got eyes on them, arguing quietly as they are. My mother waves a hand, tears in her eyes. My father rolls his own, turning away from her. All they ever do lately is argue.

It's my fault. And I know it's my fault, somewhere, deep in my gut, but I can't handle the truth of it. So, I pretend I don't. And they love me, so they pretend they don't. And we have a birthday party in the backyard and none of us have a good time and none of us mention Paul's absence and none of us know this is only going to get worse.

I know morning has arrived when sunlight dapples over my eyelids and drags me unceremoniously from my dreams.

It's for the best. These memories, flashbacks of humanity squashed together, lifetimes becoming sticky and indecipherable from one another, are altogether unpleasant. I blink myself back to the Ether, back to godhood, and bark out a laugh when wyvern-Hank licks my face.

"When did you get here?"

"He must've spent the night with Buck," Rory tells me. She's sitting on a chaise made of emerald velvet, watching the balcony from where the sun pours in. "The Evergod dropped him off on his way to breakfast."

"Hm." I rub my palm over the little dragon's skull before rising from the sheets. He makes a whizzing little purr, flying up toward my head and bouncing through the air to follow me across the room. When I settle at the Mountain's side, he falls into her lap.

I realize, only then, that we're not staring at the balcony at all. We're staring at Enzo *on* the balcony. Fully dressed in new clothes—I can only assume the keepers jumped to fulfill any request the Shade threw at them—he stands at the railing, hands curled tight over the stone border, eyes glassy as he considers the ground below.

"Why . . . does he look as if he's planning to jump?" I ask Rory finally, though I don't look away from my boyfriend when I do.

"You're one to talk."

Well, I certainly look away at that, attention snapping to her face, trying to decipher the tone behind those words. She doesn't look at me, though. I can't tell if she's angry, or just stating facts. I suppose we should eventually talk about it, about prom night in the parking lot, Officer Allen and Poppy and the Ouroboros and—

I tricked her so I could kill myself. I lied to her, and then she had to watch me die. And it all worked out okay in the end, I guess, but I still did that and I didn't even really think twice about it. I just *did it*. Because I *could*.

My tongue is heavy.

When I don't have anything to say in response, Rory moves on. "He tried using his power again."

"Oh!" I whip back toward Enzo. I take in the sight of his glassy eyes and white knuckles on the railing. "Oh . . ."

If Enzo's powers are still unreachable, it must mean two things to be true.

The first—going under the Ouroboros myself did not restore the balance. Everyone's powers are going to be a shitshow. But I probably don't have to worry about making a sacrifice anytime I reach for my magic. And that would be plenty of reason to be grateful, considering I'm not sure what's really waiting for us outside of this palace, out in the rest of the Ether, except:

The second—the Shade is practically human, in a world full of gods and other monsters who want him dead.

He doesn't even have his gun anymore.

"Enzo . . ." I start, though I'm not entirely sure what I'm going to say. I rise and take a step forward, hands reaching out as if to offer some slice of comfort.

He turns to me, and I freeze. He's wearing another mask. This one isn't even his charming, irreverent villain persona. This one is carved from ice.

"Could you do me a favor, darling?" he asks, in a tone so clipped the request sounds like an accusation.

"Oh—of course. Anything."

"Good." He closes the windowed doors to the balcony and draws the drapes. The sun disappears, flinging us into darkness. Hank rises into the air, flying to the nearest candelabra and blowing it aflame. "I need you to perform a scrying spell."

That isn't at all what I was expecting. I frown, looking to my altar. A scrying spell is simple enough. All I'll need is a bowl and some water. There's a bowl on the altar already. I'm sure someone around here has a pitcher they could bring.

"Okay. Yes, of course. What is it you're wanting to see?"

"Earth."

"Hmm?" I think I must have misheard him. Right? But when seconds tick and Rory turns her face away from mine and Enzo doesn't waver or correct himself, I can no longer pretend I did. "You want to see . . . Earth."

"I want to see Enzo Truly." He raises his dark eyebrows, challenging me. "Is that going to be a problem, Magician?"

"Well, yes." When I said I would do anything, I wasn't imagining he would ask for the impossible. "I can't show you an entirely different world."

"Of course you can." Is his smile truly cruel, or am I imagining it? "You're the god of gods. There is *nothing* you can't do. Not anymore."

Oh, fuck me.

I can't explain why I don't want to do this. No one asks me to—likely because no one cares about what I want in this moment—but I can't even explain it to myself. The idea of looking back, looking down on who we used to be, makes my skin crawl, my stomach hurt, my eyes sting. Ridiculous. Doesn't make any sense at all.

And still, here I am, standing at my altar, a pitcher of water in one hand, about to perform the first spell this room has seen in one thousand years.

Enzo and Rory stand on the other side of the table. Nerves make Enzo's muscles tic, and he tilts his head back, trying to convey the lie that is his complete lack of fear. Rory looks on curiously, leaning too close to the stone slab, eyes intent on the bowl like they don't want to miss a drop of what's to come.

"You might not like it," I warn him, for the last time.

"I don't anticipate I will," he brushes me off, for the last time.

Resolved, I pour the water.

At first, nothing happens. I wonder, naïvely hopeful, if Enzo was wrong. If there are limitations on my magic, still, despite what he'd like to believe, and it really is impossible to show someone another world.

That would be nice. I would accept a limitation if it were that.

And yet, as soon as I've had the thought, the image on the surface of the water bowl, my own reflection peering back at me, begins to morph. Ripples form in the liquid like waves, shudders sending shocks along the surface. New colors begin to appear, new shapes forming.

When the water goes still once more, Enzo Truly is lying in a hospital bed.

I recognize the hospital immediately. I've been there many times, in my stint as Gem Echols, because that's where their mother works. Gracie Community Hospital. The only one in that tiny town.

Enzo's body looks so small in the bed. I'm not sure if it's because of his actual size, or because the Shade is so much taller, and the difference between the two is even more profound when seeing them at the same time. He's hooked up to an IV, and a heart monitor, and other machines telling the doctors and nurses what's happening inside his body.

His mother is asleep in the chair next to him, her hand wrapped over his, her face against the hard plastic edge of the bed.

His father sits in another chair next to her. When a nurse walks in, Mr. Truly straightens his spine. In a tone soft enough so as not to wake his wife, he asks, "Any updates on the others?"

"No, sir," the young man in scrubs whispers back. He checks Enzo's vitals, frowning all the while. "They're all doing the same as our boy. No change."

When Mr. Truly looks as if he might cry, the nurse adds, "Hey. No change means no bad change, either. They could start waking up at any time. We're not giving up on Enzo. Okay?"

I thrust my fingers into the water bowl, disrupting the image, sending it away. My body shakes. My mouth tastes like bile.

"Hey!" Enzo snaps. "What the hell was that?"

"I think we all saw what we needed to see." Why do I sound

hoarse, as if I were fighting back tears? Why would *I* be about to cry? That doesn't make any sense.

"No, but really. What the hell was that?" Rory asks, stepping back from the altar, her eyebrows creasing over the bridge of her nose. She looks between Enzo and me and asks, "Are our human bodies . . . still alive? In *comas*?"

"Maybe yours." I shrug. "Definitely not mine."

If time isn't linear, of course we can be here, as powerful and alive as we've ever been, *and* in the hospital in Gracie, Georgia, at the same time. If time isn't linear, then right now, Enzo Truly and Gem Echols could be meeting for the first time, while the Shade and I hunt the rest of the pantheon across the Ether. The Mountain and I might be tending to our hillside home in eighteenth-century Scotland, all while Rory first learns to walk in her parents' home in rural Alaska.

If time isn't linear, then of course I'm already dead.

I feel like I'm going to be sick.

CHAPTER 19

THE WALKING DEAD

The caravan the keepers found for us is impressive, admittedly, given they had one night's notice. They've gotten their hands on an RV, the sides coated in thick, protective metal, with a bedroom and a bathroom and two extra bunk beds.

I remember Enzo telling me that the Ether followed a lot of the same patterns as Earth. So, it shouldn't surprise me to see an RV pull up outside the palace's front steps, instead of a horse-drawn carriage or something. But it somehow makes everything feel both unfamiliar and too familiar, in ways that don't at all help to settle my stomach, still knotted from the vision in the scrying bowl.

If someone tries to show me an evil Tom Hanks movie, I think I might lose it.

The bizarre disconnect between my memory of this world and the reality of it does not end there, though. I got my hands on a map of the Ether earlier in the morning, intending to plan out our route, only to be left with a sour taste in my mouth. How is it possible that our world is so . . . small?

I really don't remember it feeling *small* here. Why, in my memory, were the reaches of this world beyond compare? Especially when, actually compared to the vastness of Earth, the Ether in its entirety is smaller than a single continent.

It shouldn't matter. And it doesn't matter, I guess. But it sets me on edge, for reasons I can't yet put my claw tip to.

The one bright spot in my morning is getting to annoy the shit out of Clover Amarith. Her family, against their daughter's obvious wishes, will be accompanying us on our trek. I've overheard her arguing with her fathers twice already, while the keepers load up the RV with supplies we'll need for the coming days.

"You are the Chosen One, handpicked by the Magician themself. Of course you're coming with us."

"I don't think I was chosen for anything, Papa. I'm—"

"What? What is it?"

"I'm not even convinced that's the real *Magician in there."*

The last line was stage-whispered, and followed by a long flurry of panic at her blasphemy. I think of smiting her. Striking her dead where she stands, chest cracking open from the force of lightning. I could make an example of her. And really, what Chosen One wouldn't want to die for their god? Isn't that what religious cults are all about? She could be a martyr.

I don't, though. Not because I would care if I killed her; obviously I wouldn't. That would be ridiculous. But because I'm not done messing with her yet. It's funny, getting under her skin.

Rory stares out at the wall surrounding the palace's grounds. In only minutes now, we'll load into the RV and drive through the gate, the rest of the Ether finally revealed to us. I know she's anxious for what she's going to find. I wish I could offer her anything that might be a comfort, but Enzo's cryptic silence on the matter tells me she's right to worry.

It might be better for all of us if I just tried for teleportation. I could zip us all across the world to Enzo's palace, saving the days of travel. As everyone is keen to remind me, I can do anything without consequence now.

But this body still feels new and foreign, and I'm not convinced enough that I've control over my magic to risk it. The worst-case scenario involves leaving chunks of their bodies behind, and the visual is enough to make me shudder.

I don't have to admit my fear, because Rory has no interest in skipping the travel. She needs this, for better or worse. She needs to see what's become of the world we made together.

Enzo, too, is inclined to take the long way. This army of his—the only power he's got left, for the time being—is supposedly crawling all over the Ether, like mindless soldiers left without a leader. He isn't sure how many are left behind at his grim castle, or even what the Heartkeeper might have done to his palace since he's been gone. Traveling gives him the chance to collect his soldiers along the way, building up a defense before we run into his bogeyman. The infamous god of love.

And these soldiers aren't the only stragglers we're expected to contend with. The Librarian has as good as invited himself along, having already claimed one of the bottom bunk beds in the RV. The Evergod, I can only assume, will be coming, too. The two of them are currently sitting on the palace steps, talking in whispers. That probably bodes very poorly for me, but I don't have the time to deal with it right now.

On my shoulders, Hank settles down, curling his warm

scales against my neck and purr-buzzing into my skin. I reach up to run my fingers over the spiky top of his head.

"All right, that's the last of it," Briareus says, clapping his hands together and coming round from the back of the RV. Rune hastens after him. Clover slumps, arms crossed, against the metal siding. "We're ready to go whenever you are, Your Holiness."

I look at Enzo, stoic and silent and refusing to meet my eye.

Rory and I exchange a weighty glance. I watch her try to tuck away the tremors in her hands before I notice them.

We are not ready. And still, I turn to my parishioners and say, "Let's get this over with."

In hindsight, I really should have pushed harder for teleporting.

The Ether is a wasteland.

No, that isn't quite right. The Ether is *thriving*, as far as I can tell. It does look eerily like the world we just came back from. In fact, when we leave the palace grounds, the keepers drive us through a stretch of jam-packed highway that reminds me of Spaghetti Junction back in Atlanta. There are billboards and businesses and people going about their lives. We could still be on Earth, except for the few differences here and there. The animals aren't quite the same. The fashion is different. The products advertised on the billboards are for things like TRUTH TONIC: YOU NEVER HAVE TO GUESS WHAT THEY'RE THINKING EVER AGAIN!

The *land*, though . . . the foundation of this world, the dirt and hills and life that should make it what it is . . .

It's bad. Everything is flattened. I don't see a single tree. I tell myself it's because we're in a city, but even when we drive farther out, onto a long rural road, there's just nothing. It isn't even like seeing the desert, where there's sand and cacti and some kind of life slithering between the dunes. What used to be forest and mountain and fields of wildflowers have been razed to the ground. And instead of the earth returning, rising up from the ash and becoming something new, it just . . . stayed dead.

And the people of the Ether have built right over it. So many generations have passed now that no one still breathing would have any memory of what this world was like when the land was alive.

Sometimes, Gem Echols thought the land in Gracie was trying to talk to them. That the earth there, where Mvskoke was spoken by its ancestral caretakers, was trying to send a message in a language we just couldn't quite make out. Now it seems a childish thought, conjured by a childish mind. But it felt important then. I can still feel the resonance of its importance, even if the weight of it is now beyond my grasp.

But the land in the Ether *did* have a voice once. It sang for its people with the Mountain's mouth, and it hasn't just gone silent while its god has been away. The Shade cut its tongue out.

The Ether is a crime scene.

The Librarian's eyes watch through every window, taking in more detail than anyone else can see. The Shade does not look at anyone or anything. The Evergod whispers to Hank from his bottom bunk.

And the Mountain locks themself away, dead bolt snapping on the bedroom door.

We're supposed to reach their kingdom by nightfall. Our first stop.

I sit next to the Shade. Careful with my words, knowing

we're in earshot of the Amarith family, I ask him, "What will we find tonight?"

"How would I know? This world isn't mine anymore." And still, he does not look at me.

The zombies are a good distraction from the decimated environment. When the keepers warned of the Shade's soldiers crawling across the Ether, hunting anyone who was disloyal to their god, I hadn't been entirely sure what that meant.

Apparently, it meant the walking dead.

Well, not *literally* dead. Not actual zombies, I guess. More like . . . robots? Like Roombas whose owners walked away and left them running into the wall over and over again for the last few years. Except the Roombas used to be people.

What do you call it when someone loses their entire personality and freedom of thought and everything that makes them who they are, and they become a hollowed-out ghoul no one seems to know what to do with?

The answer is Gem Echols's sophomore year of high school, but the answer is also the Shade's army.

And I don't know if it's something he's doing, and he's just not telling me—entirely possible, given his attitude today—or if the brainwashed horde just senses, somehow, that he's in the RV. But as we drive, we start collecting an entourage. They don't move quite as fast as a car, but they move faster than *people*. And they follow behind us, catching up whenever we stop at a light or get gas.

Clover sits at the tiny kitchen table, leaning against the window so she can watch the trail of them on the highway behind us. When she catches me staring, she scowls.

"Is that judgment I see on your face, *Chosen One*?" I ask.

"Looking down on those who would follow their god any-where . . . Do you think you're any better than they are?"

Her answer isn't what I'd expected.

"No." Her jaw tightens. "And that's the problem."

While the sun sets, Rune parks the RV in a pulloff so thoroughly abandoned it could be mistaken for an archaeological dig. The city is long behind us now. We haven't seen another car, or busi-ness, or living thing for miles and miles.

"This is as far as we can go," he tells me, standing up from the driver's seat.

I raise an eyebrow, frowning. "Are we out of gas?"

"Oh. No, Your Holiness, we have plenty of fuel. It's just—" he stammers, looking to his husband for relief once more.

Briareus explains, "You wanted to spend your night in the ruins of the Mountain. But we should not get any closer than this. For safety's sake."

The ruins of the Mountain.

I don't know if they can hear the words from where they've locked themself in the bedroom. Maybe they just sense how close we are, or they know we must be done driving when the engine rolls off. Either way, Rory comes storming down the center of the RV seconds later. They don't stop to address anyone, don't spare me a glance, before slamming the door behind themself and marching into the distance. In the direction of their palace.

No. Their ruins.

"What are they going to find?" I demand of Enzo again. I watch the way his throat bobs, the way his ashen cheeks seem to sink in, instantly becoming even more gaunt on his beautiful face. And still, no answer comes. With a growl, I follow the Mountain.

"Rory!" I call at her back, but she doesn't turn to me.

Smoke.

The closer we get to our destination, the thicker with smoke the air becomes, until its black plumes are the only thing I can see or breathe.

"RORY!" I call again, but I can barely hear myself over the roaring of embers—how close is this fire? I can't see it through the black smoke, but I know it must be right in front of me. I can feel it on my face.

The Cyclone's power blows like a gale in my chest. I set it free, letting the rush of wind explode from within me. Violent and eager, it pushes the smoke away, clearing my line of vision.

Rory stands directly in front of me, no more than two feet between our bodies.

Directly in front of her is a moat. Someone, at some point in time, dug this border. It's too wide and too deep for us to cross without having to swim.

And we shouldn't cross it, anyway. The moat is there not to protect what's inside the circle but to protect the rest of us. For inside is the once-kingdom of the god of land.

The ruins of the Mountain. Burning.

Everything is tar. This kingdom burned a long time ago, and the ash it left behind continued to burn in its wake. And now there is nothing but blackness and decay and rock formed of fire, one thousand years of it. The immortal, godly fire of the Inferno. Stolen from the Siren's husband. And used to torture her sister's kingdom, for the last thousand years.

I don't know *how* I know, but I suspect, if this moat hadn't been dug, the fire would have continued to spread until it had eaten this world alive.

"Rory . . ." I touch the crease over her elbow, tear my eyes from the flame to look into her face.

She turns around, but her eyes skirt right over my head. She looks beyond me when she says, "You ruin everything you touch."

Enzo has followed us. He stops at her accusation, a few yards away, tilting his chin up. His body tenses. Finally, for the first time in hours, he speaks, saying, "You were not here to feel it. Forgive me if I don't pity you, Mountain."

"You think I don't feel this?" Their growl sounds like that of a bear, the warning that their territory has been breached, that an attack is next to come. Beneath our feet, the ground begins to rumble and shake. "YOU HAVE TAKEN EVERYTHING FROM ME!"

The impossible black eyes of the Shade widen. He opens his mouth, baring those hideous teeth. "I've taken from you? I've ... taken ... from *YOU*?"

Behind him, the mindless army begins to fold in, shuffling into order, perfectly still as they await their leader's command. Farther still on the horizon, the sun is setting, casting the world in the most beautiful colors.

"YOU STOLE *EVERYTHING* FROM *ME*!" he screams, words punctuated by that forked tongue flicking against a dozen fangs. "I WAS LEFT WITH NOTHING! And now you know how that feels—almost. You still have *them*."

My eyes dart between Enzo's face and Rory's, watching these ancient gods in their new-old bodies unravel a high school grudge that's been brewing for a millennium. When the ground begins to crack and split, my attention is drawn away.

I want to warn the Mountain that her quake could hurt more than the Shade—but this is not an earthquake at all. Something buried deep beneath us is beginning to *move*.

When caverns fall open in the crust of the earth, and *screams* rise from the abyss of their pits, my stomach drops.

"Rory, what is—"

"Maybe not for long," they whisper to him. "They won't forgive me for what I'm going to do to you now."

"Rory—"

From the Ether's core, trees erupt. Not fresh saplings but fully formed, ancient trees, with roots tied to the very center of this world. They spring free, towering hundreds of feet in the air over the Mountain's head.

But that is not the part making me dizzy.

The bark of these trees is not made from wood but from *flesh*. They are covered in muscle and ligament, oozing blood like sap, their limbs twisted bones stretched over with skin, and the screams are coming *from them*. From these abominable things that should not exist, but do, somehow.

This is the Ether out of balance. This is the Mountain's pain gone unchecked.

"Rory," I urge, over the sound of the trees' awful wailing. "You cannot do this! He's practically human, this isn't a fair fight!"

"Do not pretend you've started to care about fairness again, Magician," they snarl. Their black pupils slit into thin lines as sharp as razors. "Besides, *look* at him. There is nothing human about him."

My head snaps toward Enzo. At least two dozen unmoving soldiers flank him, but I know that isn't what Rory's talking about.

The Shade hasn't been able to use his power since the scales were tipped out of existence. The Reaper in Poppy's body called him *neutered*. Naïvely, I feared he was too vulnerable to survive in the Ether.

He smiles, and I know. There is nothing vulnerable about my demon.

He is not *without* his power at all—it has only been lying in wait.

I watch, the trees still screaming, as the sunset begins to grow nearer . . . and nearer. And in a rush that feels like gravity has dropped, the sunlight itself, in a collage of orange and pink, is *sucked* to the ground, leaving nothing but an endless stretch of blackness overhead. It would mirror the endless night of the Shade's eyes, if not for the stars still overhead.

The brilliant colors of the setting sun flood the space between us, a sentient flame that moves like water, beautiful and seductive. It could almost be tempting to reach out and touch it. But something as old as the world tells me that one brush of my skin against its surface would change me forever.

"You're both right," the god of things forbidden, of life, of night and day, of fire, of strength, the conquering king and most wanted fugitive of this world, whispers. "I am not human. And this is not a fair fight."

The Mountain roars and charges forward.

The Shade beckons them as they do.

And I know there is nothing I can do to stop this clash. It has already waited long enough.

20

STUPID, ROMANTIC HUMAN

YOUR GREED DESTROYED OUR WORLD!"

I don't know if the howl comes from Rory's mouth or from the trees. It erupts like a thousand wailing voices all at once, as a massive limb of bone shard and fat comes swinging at the Shade's head.

The demon turns to shadow in the same second it should have hit him, body nothing but black mist. Half of his mindless army is swept off their feet, though. The tree screams, but the soldiers are silent as they're thrown directly into the Inferno's fire.

He rematerializes, lips pulling back over those grotesque teeth. "My greed is child's play compared to yours, Mountain. Be honest—if not with Gem, at least with yourself. You aren't angry with me for what I did. You're angry because I wouldn't let you be part of it."

From over his shoulder, Enzo plucks a star directly from the night sky. He balls it into his fist and throws it at Rory's face, the impossible, lethal white light of it spinning and spinning as it nears them and—

And Rory catches it with their *teeth*. The god of land gnashes the star to dust between their incisors, with the agonizing, screaming grind of rock against bone. They spit the sludge left behind at the Shade's feet, as one of their screaming trees wheels down toward them. A dozen different hands, all sprouting from the same limb, like mushroom spores growing along bark, grab for the Mountain's massive frame. They lift her up, up, into the air, until she stands atop the highest branch, staring down at us.

No, not us. In this moment, I know, they only have eyes for Enzo.

"I came to you begging for an alliance to *save our world*," they snarl, those slit pupils flaring. "Because I knew you would be its ruin—and I was *right*! You call that greed?"

For a brief moment, I'm confused. The Mountain, begging the Shade for an alliance?

The memory clicks into place before I can question it, though. Not that I think either of them would hear me if I did.

"I wanted to know if he could be convinced to let me live."

"I could not. Though the offer was . . . enticing."

Right. Before the Mountain came to me, helping me scheme to escape my own alliance with the Shade, they'd gone to our demon himself. They'd offered themself up to the monster who'd killed their sister's husband. And he'd rejected them.

I still don't know the whole story. I don't know why the idea of hearing it makes me nervous.

From the corner of my eye, something moves in the surface of the water. My head snaps to the side, gaze narrowing in on the moat surrounding the eternally burning kingdom.

Cautious but curious, I take a step forward.

Watching the show, Siren? Which one of them do you want to see buried by the other? Or are you hoping they'll take each other out so you'll never have to worry about either again?

Whatever it was I saw, it doesn't move again. The only thing in the water is ash floating on the surface and strings of gooey blood fallen from the Mountain's awful trees.

I look back to the others—and bile slicks along the roof of my mouth.

The Shade's mindless battalion has charged forward and is tearing at the trunks of the Mountain's trees. The soldiers use their bare hands and teeth to rip strips of skin away, revealing the sinew beneath, more blood pouring when they do. The trees scream louder and louder. One soldier tears away a hunk of flesh and reveals a bloated face beneath, mottled black and blue with bruises, and I realize it's *screaming*. It's screaming, and even when the soldier begins to rip it apart and toss pieces of it away, the rest of the screaming doesn't stop. Because it's coming from other faces, other heads buried in the bark of the trees, or scattered along its clobbered-together limbs.

I don't want to know what I know but I do. These trees are made from the bodies of *people*. They were human once. Where did they come from? How did they become this?

My eyes move back to the forever-burning kingdom. I wonder what happened to the people who lived there, to the Mountain's most loyal subjects ...

Behind me, Enzo sounds almost bored when he speaks. "You came to me begging for an alliance to save *your life*. You would have done anything for me, given me anything I asked of you, if it meant keeping yourself in power. You only went crawling to the Magician when you realized that, without that power, you had nothing of interest to me."

When I look to him, I find my demon king forging a staircase from the light he snuffed from the sky. He glides more than he walks, floating one step at a time, and the sunset dapples a path beneath his feet as he does. He makes the world by stepping into it. And I realize, as he ascends until he's level with Rory again, standing on a pillar carved of sunlight, if I am Icarus, Enzo is Apollo.

What a stupidly romantic musing. What a humiliatingly human thing to think in earnest.

The Mountain tilts their head back, narrowing their eyes and huffing around a mouthful of tusks.

The Shade continues, "And I knew a thousand years ago it would be easier to kill you and claim the land for myself than it would be to bond your fate to mine. Because you have no allegiance greater than the one to yourself. Not to any people or any other god—not even the ones you claim to love so fervently. Unlike you, I have always been perfectly honest, even when my words weren't welcome. And I've told you the truth already, Mountain, I just don't know if you were listening."

"What truth?" she demands like a whispered warning. And though it is Enzo whose tongue is forked, it's Rory who sounds like the serpent.

As soon as the thought occurs to me, black *scales* begin to appear on the flesh covering the trees. They glitter in the dim glow of the Shade's impossible sunset, spreading until they cover every inch of what was once skin. Their limbs twist and shift together, their screaming growing louder and louder until it ceases all at once, until the branches of these holy trees morph into heads. Three giant snake heads rise over Rory's body, hissing, staring down at the god of things forbidden.

A hydra.

"Land is neither good nor evil, it just *is*," Enzo snarls. As I watch, fire begins to eat its way across his back, erupting from nothing and flowing out in a jagged pattern from his spine. *Wings*. With wings of flame, the Shade begins to rise from his

podium until he hovers over the Mountain's head, over her serpentine protectors, until he is nothing but darkness shrouded
in darkness and illuminated in the dark sky by his own blasphe-
mous inferno. "The land is loyal to no one!"

The Mountain's hydra rears its heads to strike. An arrow
of fire blooms in the Shade's hand. I raise my own hands, not
knowing *what* I intend to do but certain I will not let them
destroy each other.

Before I have the option of doing anything, though, Rory
says, nearly so quiet it can't be heard, "That isn't true."

The snakes still.

Enzo hesitates to loose his arrow, lifting his brows.

I wait, watching.

Rory looks down at the serpent whose back she stands upon.
A frown tugs at the corner of her mouth, worsened when she
looks back to the raging fire that was once their kingdom. After
touching their fingers to the snake's scales, silently communi-
cating to her monster, she is lowered to the ground. She tilts
her head up, looking at the god framed by the endless black of
the sky above us, and says, "Get down here, you clown."

It takes me so off guard, I think I must have misheard her.
Enzo, too, just hovers in the sky.

But after a moment, his body lowers in front of theirs. The
wings of flame are extinguished, and the fading sunset is shaken
free, its dim twilight scattering back to the horizon.

"The land is not good or evil. It just is." She sounds tired. "But
that doesn't mean it isn't *loyal*. The land protects its protectors
and starves its thieves. It speaks to those who learn to listen and
asks for *exactly* what it needs."

Something buried in me threatens to climb from the grave.
I push it down.

"An alliance with the land is so much bigger than just striking a bargain or making some crossroads deal. I was offering you the chance to become the rightful steward of this land. You make it sound like some cheap, desperate ploy, but it was . . . it was something . . ."

"Sacred," Enzo answers. He's staring beyond them, at the fire. It dances in his bottomless eyes. "You offered me something sacred and I laughed in your face."

"Yes." She sniffs. "That was the moment I knew you were going to lay waste to this world, and I had to find a way out. But a thousand years later, and I still don't really understand why. Why didn't you take me up on my offer?"

"Is my hesitance really so confusing? You explained it clearly, just moments ago." Enzo raises his hand, and the Mountain flinches with the expectation of a blow, even as the fire behind her dissipates to smoke. He is not fast enough to hide his pained expression over her fear. "I ruin everything I touch."

Rory turns around, facing the memory of her kingdom; the black tar and ash and molten rock that was once her home. Her serpents fall to the ground, burrowing beneath the earth the same way the trees appeared. Without them or the screams or the crackling of an ageless fire, it seems too quiet.

They turn back to Enzo. "Even if I wanted to mean that, I didn't. We both know it isn't true."

"Do we?"

I don't understand a lot of what just happened here, the unspoken part of this fight that means they're no longer trying to kill each other. But what does it mean if Enzo looks at *me* when he asks *that*?

The thing in the moat catches my attention again, darting in the corner of my eye. But it's just my reflection staring at me in the water now. High cheekbones and a perfectly sloped nose and thick, immaculately groomed eyebrows and eyes the color of two shards of raw amethyst. In this world, I am *beautiful.*

My stomach churns.

When I look away, I realize we've gathered an audience. Hank makes a dramatic squeal of a noise and flaps his wings, jumping from Clover's shoulders and flying across the gap to land on mine. The Amarith family stands awkwardly a few yards away. With them, the Librarian's eyes take in everything there is to see here, while the Evergod hums a tune I almost recognize.

"We, um—" Rune coughs into his fist. "We thought we'd give you three a chance to work through that together."

I think about killing him, but it's such a boring idea that it doesn't stick. No one responds, though.

When the silence stretches too long and too loud, Briareus adds, "We'll be ready to set out at dawn, Your Holiness. Earlier, if you'd like."

Dawn. I think of the sunset pulled from the sky and still say nothing.

Clover rolls her eyes. "Well, are you *hungry?*"

My stomach gnaws itself. Hank squawks an affirmative. I reach up to stroke the pads of my fingers along his scaled belly. "Starving, actually."

"Great!" Rune says, before his face turns ghostly pale. "No—no, it isn't great that you're starving. I just meant—um—"

"Dad, stop." Clover turns toward the RV, shaking her head. "He just meant we have a shitload of instant ramen."

The keepers sleep in the RV, but the gods lounge by the still-cooling tar long after dinner has ended and the world's been put to bed. Hank breathes in deep, his eyes closed, spread out over my thighs. The Evergod dozes next to Enzo, his head on my demon's shoulder. Rory studies a rock she collected from the smolder. The Librarian studies everything everywhere all at once.

I don't exactly *know* it's coming, but I'm not at all surprised when Enzo says "Creature?" and I look to him and he asks, "Can you show me Earth again?"

Too many of the Librarian's eyes snap toward me. Rory pauses in her geological analysis, waiting for my answer. Neither Hank nor the Evergod stops snoring.

"Why?" I ask and wish I didn't.

Rory winces, curling her fist around the rock and tucking it into a fold of her tunic.

Enzo's black eyes flick with something darker than pitch. But as quickly as I think I've seen it, it's gone. He shakes his head. "Do I need to convince you?"

"I'm just . . . not sure it's good for you, is all." I wrap my fingers around Hank's throat, focusing on the soothing rise and fall of his chest, the warmth of his fire-bellied scales under my skin. "You shouldn't cling to something that's gone."

"Shouldn't I?" Sometimes, a question can be a threat. "That's how I got you back."

Knowing I'm going to regret this, I stand and stomp my way back to the moat.

The water is dirty and still and surprisingly cool for its proximity to fire for the last thousand years. I kneel at the edge, hesitant to dip my dinner bowl in to rinse it off. The Siren may not have reared her head during the battle of the millennium, but that doesn't mean she *isn't* watching. And I know exactly how keen she would be to hold my head under.

Feeling the eyes of the Librarian on my back, knowing any

weakness will be cataloged for later, I force myself to get over it. I make quick work of rinsing the bowl out and refilling it, bringing it back to the campsite where the others have gathered.

The Evergod is awake now, Enzo having abandoned his post, and the old man blinks up from his spot on the ground when I step over him. His giggle sets my teeth on edge.

Rory and Enzo have settled on either side of the space I vacated, and I slide perfectly in between them. My shoulders slot just beneath his, and well below hers. I'm used to feeling small next to Rory, but Enzo being taller than me is weird.

The anger hits even before the realization does—fury with myself for yet another ridiculous human thought. *Enzo* isn't taller than me, but the *Shade* is. And he *always* has been.

I use too much force when I set the bowl down on the ground in front of us, and too much water sloshes over the wooden edge. Fuck me. Whatever, it's fine, it'll be fine. I just need enough to dip my fingertips in.

Rory presses her palm to my thigh. She is so warm and so close and the softness and strength of her have never begged for my body to sink in so deep. And here I am, playing this game with the scrying bowl instead.

But on my other side, Enzo is tense and still and I know he needs this, even if I can't allow myself to understand why.

I lean forward and press my fingertips to the water's surface.

As last time, there's nothing at first. And when there *is* something, it appears slowly, pushing its way through the ash and muck from the dirty moat water. Finally, as the Librarian steps closer, hovering over me to look into the bowl for himself, the image comes clearly into view.

We're back in Gracie Hospital. Back in Enzo's room, with

the nurse. His father isn't there, but his mother is. She's reading from an old book of poetry propped up on her knees, and the curtains are thrown wide open to let in the sun.

"'Brighter shone the golden shadows; / On the cool wind softly came / The low, sweet tones of happy flowers, / Singing little Violet's name. / 'Mong the green trees was it whispered, / And the bright waves bore it on / To the lonely forest flowers, / Where the glad news had not gone.'"

She glances up from the page, studying Enzo's face where he lies unmoving in bed. As good as dead. Her breath struggling to fall back into place, she returns to her book.

"'Thus the Frost-King lost his kingdom . . .'"

The nurse slowly backs away, slipping from the door. The image in the pool begins to shift, following him into the hallway.

"No," the Enzo at my side whispers, leaning forward and gripping my arm with his hand, claws digging into my skin. "No, please, make it go back. I need to see her."

I tug out of his grip. But as I intend to swirl my own nails against the water's surface, the nurse steps into another room.

At my side, Rory gasps.

In the bowl, she sleeps in her hospital bed. I wondered if their body might be alone, with their grandparents gone. But there are two others in the room. A tall woman with long black hair pinned back with an alabaster clip carved into the shape of a whale, and a short man with no hair and a beaded sealskin vest over his T-shirt. They sit on either side of Rory's bed, hands gripping each other over her middle, both of them watching her face, as if they think she might open her eyes at any moment.

None of us here in the Ether say anything for a long moment. I'm the one to finally break the silence. "These are your parents."

I don't even know how I know, but I do.

Rory's voice is not that of a god, but that of a seventeen-year-old girl, when she answers, "Yeah."

The nurse checks her vitals before slipping out again, as quickly and quietly as he came.

"Wait," she whispers. "Please, I need to—"

He pushes open another door, and I catch sight of a flash of dark, braided hair in the bed, *too familiar,* and I shove the bowl away before I can stop myself. Emptied, the wooden bowl rolls on its side, while the water pools underneath it. Dead and dirty and becoming mud.

"I'm sorry. I didn't mean to—" My heart is doing a thousand things right now, and none of them make any sense. I want to cry, but I don't know why. I want to run away, but I don't know why. I want to be held, and that's just ridiculous, because *I am the god of gods.*

That can't actually have been me in that bed, can it? I'm dead.

No, I mean—*I'm* alive, but Gem Echols is dead. Right?

"It's okay." Rory sniffs. "It's okay, um. You're probably right. We shouldn't cling."

Enzo does the unthinkable when he says, "You look like your mother, kitten."

"Shut the fuck up, hellhound," Rory snaps from over my head.

"*Hellhound?*" Enzo and I ask with one voice.

She groans and drops her head into her hands.

A moment later, Enzo's knuckles brush against my jaw and I turn my head to look at him.

"*I'm* sorry." Somehow, those terrifying eyes are soft. It makes them frightening in a new way. "I . . . It's been difficult, coming back here. Everything is the way I left it, but it isn't. *I'm* not. But I know you're right. I know we need to let it go."

I press my hand against the back of his, taking a deep breath and relishing the cool touch of his skin on mine. I've missed him. I don't understand how that's possible when we've been together this whole time. Maybe because he's disappeared into himself. Maybe because I have. Maybe because every moment that I'm not buried in his skin feels like a crime. Maybe because I'm just pathetic. But it doesn't matter; I have, I've missed him so much.

"You have all the time in the world," I remind him. "We're gods."

His smile is sad and tender when he leans in to brush a kiss against my mouth. The hair on the nape of my neck rises when I make out the ghost of his teeth against my lips.

Any further excitement is derailed by the Librarian chiming in, "I wouldn't have believed this, if I weren't seeing it with my own eyes. The Shade has been cursed by a human life filled with *love.* And it has completely *nerfed* him."

The humanity of that phrase itself isn't lost on me. I scowl, leveling a glare on the god of knowledge. "I'm sure that goes right over your head, when there's nothing about your miserable mortal life to miss."

"Hm." The Librarian shrugs. His eyes move out of sync, flicking this way and that; he is always the scholar. "I only wish I'd had more time. I could've transformed that world—and that family."

Time. I glance to the Evergod, perturbed to find he's already staring back at me.

He smiles. "One hundred and twelve years and sixteen days from now, a little girl named Eliza Cotter will find Buck Wheeler's bones at the bottom of an empty well on what used to be farmland. Don't worry—I left her a note."

Everyone stares at him. His smile doesn't falter.

"Um." I sigh. "Okay."

My fingers tighten over Rory's arm, and she raises her head to look down at me. I don't say anything about the redness in her eyes. Instead, I bring her hand to my mouth and kiss her knuckles. She touches her tusks to the back of my skull.

I've missed *them*, too, and somehow in a completely different way. I've missed her the way a patient strapped to their sickbed begins to miss walking outside and drinking in the outside air, and the grass under their toes, and the sun on their neck. I've missed her like life.

From inside my cloak's inner pocket, the Ouroboros burns a flash, reminding me of its existence. The space in my ribs, the same space where Gem Echols stabbed themself to death, gives a painful throb. I know it's all in my head. It doesn't stop it from hurting.

"We should get some rest," I tell the others. "You all know what tomorrow's going to bring."

The gods groan their displeasure. Even Hank squeaks and shivers in his sleep, twitching in my lap. I don't blame them. Crossing through other territories to get to the Shade's might be inevitable, but tomorrow has the potential to be even worse than today.

Tomorrow, it'll be a Battle to the Death.

21

THEY'RE ALREADY DEAD

Well, no one would dare call the next day's ride *enjoyable*, but it isn't nearly as bad as the first—at least, not in the beginning. Enzo and Rory are talking again. Considering the way things have gone since I landed back in the Ether, I'll choose to be grateful for small favors.

The silent horde of the Shade's followers continues to grow, replenishing the number lost to the fire and then some. They follow the RV's tire tracks, *too* fast, always in the rearview.

Rune and Briareus keep trying to talk to me, but neither of them has anything to say. For most of the drive, we listen to Taylor Swift's latest pop-screamo album. At one point, Clover pulls out a tiny laptop and sets it up on the kitchenette table, and we all watch *Toy Story 4*—in the Ether, it's a true-crime documentary.

The Evergod sleeps and sleeps and one of the Librarian's eyes is always on me.

GEM!

I catch the word from the corner of my eye like a jump

scare, twisting in my seat to find the source. It's on a billboard looming high in the air, a hundred yards away.

RARE GEMS! HEALING GEMS! ROMANCE GEMS!
100% AUTHENTIC CRYSTAL MAGIC, NEXT EXIT!

Something the Reaper once said to me floats to the forefront of my mind, like a memory of a memory, like something from another lifetime altogether.

"How could a stupid rock be more powerful than me, *you know?"*

I tilt my head to look at Clover, curled up in the booth, staring out the opposite window. Still watching the army as it collects behind us. She looks dead behind her boring eyes.

"And on a keeper's seventeenth birthday," she'd told me, when I woke up in my new-old body, *"they come to the garden of the gods, and they ask you to bring magic back to the Ether."*

"What did you mean?" I ask her. Rune and Briareus look back at me from the front of the RV. Rory glances up from where she's petting Hank's spikes. Enzo raises an eyebrow. The Librarian is always watching and the sleeping Evergod knows this conversation already, has known it would play out since before humans existed in our world. Clover doesn't look at me until I continue, "When you said I was supposed to bring magic back—what does that mean?"

There is no spark in her expression when she stares at me. The fear and reverence she might've felt in the beginning has long since worn away. I know I've disappointed her. She can take a number and get in line.

"Humans have been trying to re-create your magic for a thousand years." She doesn't sound particularly interested in the conversation, either. "But it isn't the same. We use alchemy, divination, herbs and rocks and . . . But it isn't the same."

"Well, that's because what you're describing isn't magic at all. And of course it isn't. You're human." Puzzled, I raise a hand and wave at the space between us. "Magic belongs to the gods."

And only because I allow it. Magic comes from *me*. It's mine, my sandbox. I just deign to let the rest of the pantheon play here—with constraints.

I don't know where that thought comes from. I don't know how true it is, either.

Clover huffs. "Yeah, okay. But you used to give magical gifts to your followers, right? So, humans *used* to be able to do magic."

I blink.

She blinks.

"I never did that," I tell her. "And I never would."

I look away from her, glancing at Briareus, then Rune. On their faces, I watch a thousand years of mistranslation and warped idolatry as it begins to crumble.

The Magician these keepers have worshipped all their lives is a god who existed only in their heads. They wanted a being to love, so they made one, casting me in whatever image told the best story, able to rewrite my existence however suited them because I wasn't here. And oh, how the truth of me must pale compared to the god of their own invention.

Gem Echols spent their entire high school career being loved and wanted for the person their peers turned them into. The small town's queer awakening. Mysterious and laid-back and just rough enough around the edges. Always down for anything. Unafraid, and unbothered, and ready, and willing, and a *complete* fraud. They spent so much time worrying that no one would ever love them if they got close enough to see through the smoke screen.

And then they got really, really lucky with Rory and Enzo.

A spike of panic pitter-patters around in my mitral valve. *Gem* got really lucky with Rory and Enzo, but can the same be said about *me*? It would be a lie to pretend things haven't felt different since we got to the Ether, that there hasn't existed some tension, or distance, that the thread binding us to each other hasn't felt like it was fraying, and I don't know how to fix it.

Because I am not the god that exists in the minds of others. The reality of me is always disappointing.

Take a number, get in line, rinse, repeat. For an eternity.

"What the *fuck* is this?"

The *this* in question appears to be a giant wall.

We've been riding all day and have finally reached the outskirts of the kingdom of Battle. There's been nothing and nothing for miles, not since the last big city we left behind, and now there's a *wall*. Made of thick stone, it has to be at least fifty feet high, maybe a lot more. I can't quite make out the top when I tilt my head back and squint up, the glare of the setting sun's rays catching in my line of vision. It's the only thing anywhere around, the only thing interrupting the flat horizon in any direction we look.

Enzo slaps his palm against the stone, turning to look at Rune and Briareus, as if accusing them. Following up his first question, he asks, "Why is this here?"

Rune looks like he's going to shit himself because the Shade just addressed him directly, but Briareus manages to string together a whole thought. "It is the Wall."

Well, almost a whole thought.

Enzo blinks, then looks at me. I don't think I'm actually reading his mind, but I swear I hear his voice in my head. "*Can we kill them?*"

I sigh.

"Look, I don't— Hey, what are you doing? Hey! Hank!"

The wyvern launches himself from his post on my shoulder, leaping into the air and flapping his leathery wings. His scales glint different colors in the sun as he lifts himself higher into the air, belching a tiny ball of smoke as he does.

"HANK!"

When he disappears over the top of the wall, swallowed by the flare of sunlight when he does, I think, *Not again.* This dog is trying to get me killed.

Oh well. I press my palm against the warm stone, and magic floods to the surface of my skin, as ready as if it were waiting by the phone for a call.

Knock, knock, Lionheart. Ready or not, here we are.

The wall turns to dust beneath my touch.

Behind me, Clover screams before she and her fathers scramble back to the RV. Probably for the best. The humans should ride through the blood-torn streets of this city. But the gods can walk.

Inside the once-kingdom of Battle is a *legion* of the Shade's army. There must be thousands of them, too many for the city to hold. What were once houses, businesses, schools, and parks are now all overrun with the bodies of these brainwashed animals, just waiting for their master's orders. There are so many of them that they trample over each other in pockets, not seeming to notice or care when they walk across the fallen, bloated bodies of their comrades. Corpses litter every inch of these streets. Whether from being overcrowded or from starvation—can these things starve?—or from other injuries, their dead lie, rotting and forgotten, in the open air. Most of the horde, though, was pressed against the wall, wailing in desperation for escape. When it disappears, they're left standing with nothing in front of them. Their hands are still bloodied from trying to claw their way out.

Every pair of eyes in the city turns to face us, finally falling on Enzo. The army freezes, stoic and silent. There is no relief at having finally been reunited with their god. There is nothing but a dead-eyed pause, while they wait for their next command.

Just like the moat outside the Mountain's ruins, this stone wall was not built for the protection of those inside. It was built to protect the rest of the world from what it contained. The citizens of Battle, the last threads of warriors left, must have given *everything* they had to trap this much of the army here.

I glance at Enzo. His face is unreadable, and intentionally so, that perfectly impassive and unfeeling mask tightly secured to his sharp cheekbones. I find Rory's eyes when she looks away from him, both of us having studied his expression. She gives the smallest shake of her head. My chest hurts.

"We need to find Hank," I say, and I step past the line of dark ash where the wall once stood, making my way into the prison of the damned.

The soldiers step aside as we trudge through, gathering around the center road, hovering at the edges. We walk slowly, taking in the detail, no sound in the city but our breathing and the slow roll of tires over dirt and dead bodies as the RV creeps along behind us.

I'm not sure how I'm sure, but I know the Lionheart isn't here. Maybe she was. Maybe she came here as soon as she shrugged off the last of her porcelain shell back in the garden, and she found her kingdom—not burning, not like the Mountain's, but its own kind of ruin. This isn't her home anymore. Maybe she'll be back, eventually, but I'm certain she's not here now.

"Hank!" The sound of my shouting echoes off the walls of

the old buildings, untouched by life for at least a decade, maybe more. I don't know how long after the Shade's departure they created this place, but I have a feeling it wasn't long. This is a ghost town.

And speaking of ghosts:

"Is that—" Rory begins.

"Death?" I finish for her. "Looks like it."

On the road ahead of us, a barbed-wire fence erupts from the dirt, a massive metal gate at the center. There are two armed guards just past it, humans dressed in long white coats with assault rifles in their hands. Beyond them, there are medic tents that stretch on forever, a massive makeshift hospital with doctors and nurses scurrying back and forth.

Even this far away, it smells of formaldehyde and decay.

"I have a feeling I should not be seen here," Enzo mutters.

He doesn't give anyone a chance to disagree with him before he turns to shadow. It happens so quickly it makes me jump in surprise, my neck snapping to search the ground for him, even realizing I won't find him here. What remains of the Shade is little more than a suggestion of darkness that clings to the dirt under our feet. I can *feel* him, I *know* he's still here, in his own way, but not being able to see him makes my stomach churn.

Rory lifts her hood, bringing it low over her face to hide her unmistakable appearance.

I glance at the Librarian's too-many eyes. Some of them glance back at me. He doesn't bother trying to hide.

Whatever.

"Hey, what are you doing?" one of the armed guards demands, the closer we get to the fence. "You aren't supposed to be here!"

"Yes, I am," I counter without pause.

"Oh. Of course."

I'm close enough now to watch the way they blink into the realization, that unsettling acceptance of unreality beginning to fog their eyes. "My mistake. Let me help you."

Too easy. Something rattles around in my rib cage like a warning.

They slide the lock from the gate on their side, and their coworker helps them pull it open wide so we can step through, the RV following behind us. They are careful to make sure to lock out any of the Shade's soldiers, though. The army screeches from behind us, clawing at the sharp fence posts. I don't look back at them.

No one past the gate bothers to give us a second glance, maybe assuming we must belong here if we're here at all. Or maybe they're just too busy to care, bouncing between tents, buzzing conversations back and forth about IV drips and post-surgical care.

The kingdoms of Battle and Death have long stood like twin cities, their stories linked, their foundations interwoven. But it was never like this, not in eon after eon I spent watching over this world.

In the times before, Battle's city was a hall of kingmaking. It was a hub where the brightest minds, the fiercest competitors, the most brilliant leaders from across our world could come to hone their skills. They would learn the arts of violence and governance from the very god who conceived of both. It was a brutal place, but not an ugly one. Rather than a feral wasteland, it was a sharply sophisticated and thriving city where the best of the best knew their own worth—and so did anyone who dared show up and try to forge an alliance with them.

Meanwhile, its shadow city, the kingdom of the Reaper, was

sacrosanct. The denizens of Death took holy vows to honor the passage from one life to the next. They were watchers, guardians, guides. They helped to prepare those who stood at the looming mouth of the unknown to leap forward into their next chapter. Death, for those arcane teachers, was not a threat meant to be feared. It was an inevitable becoming, a passage from one shell to the next, a transformation that could not be avoided forever and therefore should be embraced.

If Battle's home was where kings were forged to conquer the game of life, Death's was where those kings were finally free to set down the heavy weight of their crown.

And now . . . this. This frantic, sterile hub of medicine and white coats and *stench*. There is nothing holy about this place. Instead, everything about it gives me the ick.

A feeling made infinitely worse when the Librarian says, too calmly, at my side, "Their patients are the Shade's soldiers."

I scowl at him. There is no way that could be true. It wouldn't make any sense. But when Rory gasps, so quiet I almost miss it, I lower myself to actually investigate the claim. As we pass, I peer fast tent flaps, eyes searching for faces in beds.

My heart crawls into my throat.

There's . . . No, that doesn't make any *sense*. They must just be people, just regular, *human* people, and they're just sick, and they're not right in the head, and that's why their eyes are glossy, and their skin is ashen, and they jerk forward as if to crawl toward the shadow at my feet whenever we pass. That's why they're all wearing chains, locking them in their hospital beds.

What is going on here?

"Whose goddamn pet is this?!" a familiar voice yells from a tent a few paces up the road. A moment later, a medic in a white coat emerges from inside, with Hank curled around her forearm.

My heart falls out of my throat and into my stomach. My blood turns cold. I think Rory might say something, but I can't hear anything over my own pulse.

"*In some ways, the Ether is like an alternate version of Earth,*" Rory once explained to me, on the floor of Gem's bedroom, when I was so lost and ancient truths were so new. "*I'm not sure when exactly it branched off. But some things are the same— languages, and food, even some people appear in both.*"

Evil Tom Hanks. Screamo Taylor Swift. And Catherine Echols. My mother.

No, Gem's mother. *Gem's* mother. Standing just a few feet away, with my wyvern dog curled around her arm, nuzzling her like he's missed her, like he knows her, because he *does,* even if he doesn't.

Her eyes catch mine. She must feel me staring. She frowns.

We don't look the same here, in this world. This body I'm walking around in, my *real* body, has no similarities to hers. But she looks almost exactly the same as she does on Earth.

She looks so much like Gem.

"Who are you?" she demands, those dark eyes narrowing with suspicion. She glances at the Librarian over my shoulder. I can see her counting the eyes in her head.

"No one important." I don't know how I manage to speak when my throat feels like someone's squeezing it. I don't know why it would be a problem, anyway. I don't care that she's here. It obviously doesn't matter that she's here. She is no one important. She is nothing to me. "The wyvern's mine."

She glances from him to me, skeptical. She brings her arm

in closer to her stomach, like she's worried I'm some kind of freak who's going to do something weird to him if I take him.

I sniff. "Hank."

The reptilian dog makes a grumbling kind of sound, blinking his eyes to glance over at me. He *sighs,* irritated in the way only a pet can be, and unravels himself from her, floating lazily toward me and landing on my shoulder again.

"See?"

"Fine." She rolls her eyes. "I don't recognize any of you. What are you doing here? Do you have clearance to be here?"

"We must, if we're here." I'm speaking, but I'm not. I recognize that my mouth is moving and words are coming out of it, but I cannot feel my body, and I don't think I'm in control of it. Someone else is driving the ship, someone else is talking, I am sitting in my mind's eye, watching my life and wondering why it doesn't feel like my life at all.

There is no reason to lie to her. What would she do, if she knew she was in the presence of long-dead gods? Would she laugh, a scientist's reaction? Would she kneel? And it wouldn't matter, either way, because she could do nothing to any of us. None of these people could do anything to any of us. We could level this city, and the city of Battle, and any of the cities that lie between us and the Shade's palace, and no one could do anything about it.

We are gods, and I am the god of gods, and no one can do anything to me. No one can touch me here, not even my mom.

And yet, what I find myself saying to her is "We're on our way out. We just came to observe. It's an interesting program you have here."

She frowns. She looks at me again, then Rory, the Evergod, the Librarian. At my feet, the shadow that is Enzo shifts, but doesn't call attention to itself.

"Yeah, well." Catherine clears her throat. "I'm really proud of it. I think we're on the brink of a real breakthrough. Come back in a few months, and you might be able to meet the very first patient finally cured of the Shade's influence."

Cured. They're trying to cure them. To undo the brainwashing that turned them into an army to begin with. They're trying to hand them back their humanity.

All around us, the mindless soldiers scream their protests, fighting to get to the shadow clinging to me. They are not being cured.

"I'd be surprised if that were true," I tell her honestly. "Most of them look half dead already. Isn't the curse the only thing that's keeping them alive?"

She shrugs. "They're still human. They eat, and sleep, and die just like the rest of us. Honestly? The Shade's curse works more like a drug than any magic. They're addicted to him, and now they can't get their fix. You're right that adrenaline is keeping some of them going—and they won't make it through the treatment. But others will. They can have full lives when we're done with them."

And because I can't seem to help myself, I ask, "Why bother doing any of this? They don't have anything to offer you. Why not just let them die?"

Across lifetimes and worlds and realities, the Reaper's voice mocks me in a whisper, but I pretend I cannot hear her.

Catherine scowls. "They don't need to offer me anything—they're *people.* They're people, and they're sick, and they can get better. They can go back to who they used to be. That's reason enough in itself, isn't it?"

I turn my head over my shoulder, looking to the barbed-wire fence we came through. Looking to the ravaged city of

Battle, where the sick have turned their fingers to stumps as they tried to claw their way outside, where they've spent years trailing over the bodies of other humans, where they now are shredding the skin of their arms and faces as they try to break through the barrier.

Swallowing, I look back to Catherine. "No. Even if they can get better, they will never go back to being who they were before."

My mother watches us as we walk away, and Rory's knuckles brush my own, and Enzo's weight presses into the air around me. And although it does not entirely feel like it, I leave the kingdom of Death alive.

22

NEVER SHOULD HAVE COME HERE TO BEGIN WITH

That night, we get lost wandering the desert.

It would be comical if it were any less true. We're headed in one direction, bound for the Heartkeeper's kingdom, hours of silence on the road—and then suddenly we're turned around, right back where we started, Death's grim city hovering behind us.

When it happens a second time, we abandon the RV and travel on foot. I study the map. Something isn't adding up.

"This doesn't make any sense."

"What?" Rory asks, narrowed eyes searching the distant horizon. Sand whips in her hair, kicked up by the wind.

Am I doing that? I don't mean to be. I tell it to still, and the earth goes quiet.

The Librarian's eyes all blink rapidly and out of sync. "Thank you. That was beginning to sting."

"This map doesn't make any sense," I continue, shoving it at Rory's chest. "It can't be right, can it?"

She looks at the paper, eyebrows tight, then back at me. "I don't get it. This looks right to me. What are you confused about?"

"Has the Ether always been so . . . small?"

The Evergod laughs. "Always! Always! Always!"

Enzo scowls at him before taking the map from Rory's hand. He studies it for a moment before looking up at me and shrugging. "It's the world we created."

"It used to feel . . . bigger." Something tugs at the edge of my thoughts, but I swat it away. "And anyway, that's not the only problem."

I point to Death's kingdom on the map's surface, trailing my claw across the page to touch the asylum of Love. "There is no desert between these cities. Not on *this* map and not on any map from a thousand years ago."

The others frown, one after the other. All of them except the Evergod. He smiles at me, bigger and bigger. Tick, tick, tick.

"So, where the hell are we?"

When we find ourselves having accidentally circled back to Death's border for the third time, we give up. The RV is waiting, with the Amarith family inside. We rejoin them, ignoring their curious stares.

This will be a problem we solve tomorrow.

Unfortunately, tomorrow comes with problems of its own.

I wake alone in the bed at the back of the RV, sunlight speckling the backs of my eyelids until it draws me into the world of the waking. My fingers twist in the sheets, searching for lovers who aren't there. I listen for their voices, wondering where they've slunk away to.

But it is the Reaper's voice I hear. The whimsical music of a graveyard xylophone jingles just outside my window.

There is no getting out of bed. I don't rise, don't dress, don't hurry through the RV to get outside. I hear the sound of her laughter and all at once my body is there before hers.

The empty sockets of her eyes gaze up at me from beneath her veil. The harsh ivory of her almost-mouth twists as if attempting a smile.

"You've no business here, Reaper," I warn her.

"Me?" She tilts her head—the skull swings in a full three-sixty, lurching across her chest before righting itself over her neck again. "You broke into my house."

That . . . isn't entirely unfair.

"We haven't come to see you dethroned *today*, Magician."

The Lionheart's voice rumbles from her lover's side, and only then do I become aware that Death and I are not alone. I find Battle's eyes watching me closely. "*Some people just have to die.*"

The memory of stardust, as thick and charred as ash, coats my tongue. I'm still unclear on whether or not our cosmic duel happened entirely in my head. Maybe it doesn't matter.

Behind me, Rory's voice chimes in. "We have apparently already crossed over into the Heartkeeper's kingdom. These two were explaining that there's a cease-fire on her land. Any issues between us get left at the border."

"How convenient for her." I wonder if that's why we could not seem to move beyond the first stretch of this place, forever winding back, over and over—like the Ouroboros eating its own tail. There are too many issues in our caravan. "How does the god of Love think to enforce such a truce?"

Reaper laughs. Her finger bones twinkle as she taps at the armor sutured into the Lionheart's chest.

I see. So, that's why these two are here.

"We never should have come here to begin with," Enzo growls. "And still, we can leave. We are only at the edge of her realm for now—the closer to her city's heart we get, the stronger her pull becomes, and the deeper we may fall under her sway. We should leave now, while we still can."

"You speak like someone with firsthand experience." The Librarian's voice is sharp. I imagine a dozen of his eyes on Enzo, though I don't dare look away from our guests to see for myself. "What did the Heartkeeper do to you, Shade?"

Enzo doesn't answer.

"Directly through her city center is the fastest route to your palace," Rory counters. "You said that was where we needed to be. You said we would be safe there."

"There is another way. We can take a boat, cross the sea—"

"And send ourselves directly to a watery grave, thanks to the Siren."

"Perhaps if you would simply reconcile with your sister—"

"I would think very carefully about the next words to leave your mouth, *hound*."

The Reaper giggles. I glare at her, but she seems as unbothered as she ever does.

At length, Enzo continues, "Gem could teleport us. That was always an option, wasn't it? Our magic is working just fine. There's nothing to be afraid of. We could be there in minutes."

"There is *everything* to be afraid of," Rory snaps. "Gem is not Gem and their magic is not their magic, and do you really want to ask a single thing of them right now?"

"Hey." Finally, I turn to face them. "That was unkind."

Rory's expression falls, as if they hadn't considered the weight of their words until they'd left their mouth. "I'm sorry."

"Thank—"

"But I'm not wrong, either."

Silence hangs until it stretches into discomfort. The Reaper whistles and brushes past me to join the others, where they're stretched out on folding chairs or beach towels in the sand. She sweeps onto the floor in a pool of swathing blackness, cradled in her own chasm of nothing.

"*Anyway*," Death rattles, "it doesn't matter. She knows you're here now. The city's as safe as anywhere else."

Enzo looks on the verge of a breakdown. I sigh, moving over to his chair and sliding between his legs. I lean back, tilting my head into his chest. He finds my shoulders with his claws, steadying himself on me. Good.

In the uneasy quiet that settles over the group, my eyes find Clover Amarith's face and I nearly choke on a laugh. Her eyes are bugging out of her boring face, her cheeks white, her mouth open. She's staring at the Reaper like she's seeing . . .

Well, a corpse, I suppose.

"What?" I demand of the Chosen One, as the Lionheart joins her lover on the sandy desert floor. "Afraid of death, Lucky Clover?"

Very slowly, her eyes drag from the Reaper to me. "I . . ."

I've not actually seen this girl speechless. I do think I like her this way. Perhaps we should've invited Death along sooner.

"If it makes you feel any better, she wasn't much easier on the eyes as a human." I glance in the Reaper's direction. "Worse, actually. So much neon."

"For the entire catalog of your sins, Magician, do you know the worst of them all?" She sighs, a breeze blowing through her open sternum. "You were a boring human, and you are a boring god."

"We can't all be Poppy White," Rory offers up. She scoots, hesitantly, a little closer to Enzo and me. There's a question in her eyes, watching us.

I take her hand, the only answer I can offer.

"Oh, no one could be Poppy White." The Reaper laughs. "Oh. I'm going to miss her."

"Me too," the Lionheart agrees. She balances her shield in front of her lover's not-body, using it to tighten their bones to one another. "But I would trade this for nothing."

"Ew," I inform them.

"What was your favorite memory from being human?"

The question startles me—not its content so much as its asker. Enzo leans forward, claws digging into my shoulders as he watches the couple across from us.

Why is he asking this question?

The Reaper hums. "*Oh.* In 2019, I used my Make-A-Wish wish to go to the Met Gala."

"Of course you did." Enzo sounds like he's smiling. "That's perfect."

"March twenty-first, 1413," the Librarian says, "I had the best sandwich ever made."

"Sandwiches did not exist in the 1400s." The Lionheart rolls her eyes. "And that was the day Henry the Fifth became king of England."

"Sandwiches didn't exist for *you* in the 1400s," the Librarian counters. "You were too busy caring about kings."

She scoffs. Then adds, "I did really love the politics. Humans are . . . clever little strategists, in their own way."

"I really loved cows." That is the single most coherent thought I've ever heard the Evergod utter.

"When I woke up from top surgery." Enzo swallows. "My parents were there, and I—I just started . . ."

He can't finish the thought. I wonder if it's because it's too difficult for him, or because he doesn't want the others to see how deep that weakness runs.

Rory comes to his rescue. "The day I got those tattoos."

I don't have to look at her to know she's touching her chin, fingertips ghosting against the skin where her human body was decorated.

She clears her throat, tone shifting as if to brush off the seriousness of what she just said. "I miss dogs, though."

Hank squawks.

"And what about you, Mage?" The Librarian's voice taunts me, sounding too close to my ear. "What was your favorite moment from being human?"

I don't like this game.

I *hate* this game, actually, and I don't want to play.

"Being human feels more like a dream than a memory," I retort. "I can hardly recall any details. None worth dwelling on, anyway."

Enzo's hands tighten even more on my shoulders. Beside me, Rory tenses.

The Reaper shakes her skull in disapproval. "Bad at being a human, and bad at being a god."

You have always been dead.

23

LIKE A GIFT HE'S NERVOUS TO GIVE

At noon, we enter the city center of the Heart.

It wasn't a choice, really, when it came down to it. Especially not after spending our morning with the Reaper and the Lionheart and all their cryptic messages.

I am the god of gods, but I am not *omniscient*. And the god who is keeps dozing off in the middle of his sentences. Ultimately, it seems too much of a risk to appear in the Shade's palace, abandoned for almost two decades, with no idea what we might be arriving in the middle of. On foot, we can at least assess as we go, and bail if it starts to look like something unsavory is waiting for us there. Or prepare to slaughter whatever it is.

Going over the ocean is a ridiculous idea. I still have no clue where exactly I *banished* the Siren to, but I have a feeling I'm the last person she'd like to grant safe passage. If not me, the Shade. If not him, the Mountain. And we'd all be crammed in a boat together, like sacrificial lambs. No thank you.

All morning, the closer we get to the city of Love, the more the mood changes—in the RV and outside of it.

Now that we've been instructed to leave our baggage at the door, so to speak, the road stops sending us in circles. Finally, the scenery begins to change. Unlike our first couple of days of driving, the billboards on the side of the highway start advertising fewer and fewer *things* for people to spend all their money on, and more and more *experiences* for people to spend all their money on. Meditation retreats and family vacations and professional romantic encounters. And there are more people. Within a couple hours of the Heartkeeper's actual home *city*, the population begins to boom, rapidly growing the closer we get, apartment buildings and suburban neighborhoods replacing the long stretches of barren nothing that I've become used to.

While the rest of the Ether seems to be hanging in something like limbo, no longer pressed beneath the Shade's thumb but not ready or able to leap forward into whatever comes next, this part of the world has moved on. At least on the surface. There are communities here. There's life here, in a way there doesn't seem to be anywhere else.

I don't understand why Enzo was so adamant about not coming anywhere near this place.

And he's being weird, too. He's twitchy and on edge, constantly darting around the RV and looking out the windows, like he's waiting for someone to attack, despite the fact that nothing bad is actually happening. After long enough watching this, Rory begins to make fun of him.

"Sit, puppy." She chuckles. "You'll get your walkies later."

"I cannot stand you."

"Then it seems like it would be a great idea for you to *sit*."

I laugh, because it's funny, and Enzo shoots me a wounded look.

"Aw, come on." I touch my fingertips under his chin, and smile. When he relaxes a hair, I say, "Not the *puppy-dog* eyes."

He groans and shoves my hand away while Rory howls with laughter. Across the RV, even Clover manages a quiet chuckle. I wasn't aware she had a sense of humor at all.

But really, she's been in a better mood all day than I've seen her since my arrival. She keeps letting her guard slip, though I don't think she intends to. I've seen her sitting with her dads and smiling, chatting animatedly about whatever it is terribly boring people care a lot about. And her dads seem happier, too. Or at least, way less on edge. They've been holding hands over the center of the RV since we got back on the road. Briareus keeps bursting into song at random.

It's kind of cute.

The Librarian seems to suffer from the same shot of anxiety that's got Enzo worked up, though. Maybe because there's suddenly a lot more to see outside of the RV, and his eyes are going rapid-fire in every direction. But he's pacing, too, eyes on the world outside our windows.

I feel totally unaffected by whatever's got everyone's feelings in a tailspin. I suspect the Evergod does as well, but only because he's been sleeping all day.

At noon, though, almost as soon as the tires pass over into the city itself, our surroundings quickly shift from thriving neighborhoods to thick throngs of people gathered in the streets, too many of them for us to keep driving. There are booths set up along either side of the road, selling food and crafts and ten-minute sessions with fortune tellers. There's art displayed, and loud music, and people dancing and laughing. Someone in an orange vest waves us down and directs us to park the RV on the shoulder.

"There's some kind of festival happening," Rune explains.

"I'm so sorry I didn't know anything about this sooner, I would have chosen a different route."

"It's all right. You didn't choose this route, I did," I remind him. "We can take the rest of the way by foot. We're almost there, anyway."

Even if we have to walk through the crowds, we'll get to the edge of the Shade's kingdom by nightfall. We'll be through the gates of his demented palace by midmorning tomorrow.

Because, apparently, the Ether is tiny. And apparently, I'm the only one who still thinks that's weird.

Rune gives me an odd look, though I don't know what the meaning of it is supposed to be. After a moment of silence, *I'm* the one who looks away.

"Well, come on." I clap my hands together. "Let's get going, then. Who knows, there's a lot going on out there—maybe we'll even enjoy ourselves."

"I am not having a good time," Enzo lies, while Rory paints his face in a dark alleyway of the festival, tucked out of sight of any onlookers.

And I know he's lying, because he can't stop smiling, as much as he's trying. It pulls at the corner of his mouth like a secret, like a gift he's nervous to give, and his black eyes keep dancing between Rory's face and mine.

"Oh, hush," they chuckle, the face-painting kit they stole from a children's booth balanced in the palm of one hand while they use the also-stolen brush to swirl a red circle over his nose. Actual clown makeup, for our own personal clown. "You're the one who said you were worried about being recognized."

"Not *worried*," he flounders. "Just *aware* it was a possibility."

"Mm-hmm." They smirk, casting me a look through their

eyelashes. "Gem, honey, is that the impression you got? That he was just being *aware*?"

I chuckle, taking a sip of the ginger and cardamom soda from the brown bottle in my hand. "Be nice to him, babe. He's got *so* many issues."

"Yeah, yeah, I know," they muse, wiping the red off on their sleeve to go in for an eggplant purple to color in his eyelids.

"You are both terribly mean to me," Enzo complains, without a drop of anger behind the words.

"*Mean?* And here I am, giving you a makeover for free," Rory drawls, clicking their tongue in a *tsk tsk tsk* against the roof of their mouth. "You wound my heart, you really do."

"Well, we can't have that." Enzo tilts his head back against the brick wall of the building behind him. "And you really shouldn't give away your services for free. Tell me, kitten, how can I repay you?"

The soft bristles of their stolen brush pause over the corner of Enzo's eye, the dip where eyebrow meets temple, where the journey to his cheekbone begins. I watch him as he watches them as Rory's mouth parts. The air is so warm and thick, and it smells of the best foods, and past the sound barrier of the brick walls closing in on the alleyway, I can still make out the sounds of music and laughter and celebration.

And I realize I want to see them kiss. And as soon as I realize it, I feel like a terrible pervert, like some kind of awful voyeur, but I've already thought it and there's no unthinking it.

"Enzo," Rory says like a warning.

"Aurora," he replies like a dare.

The moment stretches on and on and when Rory looks at me instead of leaning in, I find myself biting back a sound of disappointment.

"Well, what do you think? How's he look?" They step back, too quick to put distance between their body and Enzo's.

I need to know what they're thinking. But I don't know if it's my place to ask. And even if it is, I don't know if this is the right moment.

So, I don't. Instead, I finish my drink with one long sip, and step forward to consider their work. The white face paint with the red nose and the purple eye shadow and a thin stripe of green over his upper lip, like the worst, most ironic mustache ever.

"I think . . . I always did say you were going to clown college," I remind him. But I still raise my hand to touch his throat, feeling the way his pulse jumps beneath my fingers, as if his heart wants to meet my palm.

He reaches up and touches my wrist, eyes holding mine. "I was the top of my class at clown college."

"And I was proud of you." I grin. "My boyfriend, the *actor*."

"God, you say it like a slur." He's grinning.

"Well." I offer him my most condoling face. "I wouldn't say that. I mean, it wouldn't be less true just because I didn't say it, but I wouldn't have said it."

"I've missed you."

He's still smiling, but there's something tucked underneath the expression that I can't quite read, and I don't think it has anything to do with the makeup.

And even though it feels like a lie, even though I know it's the truth, I tell him, "I haven't gone anywhere. I've been right here the whole time."

"No." He squeezes my wrist. "Not the whole time."

I think, maybe, I know what he means, but I'm too chicken-shit to ask, so I don't. Instead, I do what Rory wouldn't, and lean forward to press my mouth to his. And there is a very stupid, very human part of me that wants to cry at the feeling of his mouth on mine. It feels like lifetimes have passed since we've kissed, and I don't understand how it's only been a couple of days.

His ridiculous green mustache is smeared when I pull back.

"Oops," I mutter, pressing my thumb to the corner of his mouth.

He chuckles, unbothered.

I tilt my head to look at Rory. They're watching us, making no attempt to hide the eager interest in their stare. Without thinking, I lean in to kiss them too. They groan into it, grabbing my waist and dragging me closer. A small sound of surprise bubbles out of my throat, and my hands find their shoulders, fingers curling into their shirt while they press our bodies together in the most impossibly tight line. I can feel every bit of them against me, every hard muscle and soft curve that turns me to liquid. When their tongue touches mine, I wonder if they can taste Enzo's mouth. The thought sends fireworks through the very center of me.

When we finally pull apart, their own lips are stained green.

"Oops," I say again, unapologetic.

They struggle to catch their breath, pupils huge and perfectly round.

Enzo audibly swallows.

I'm not sure what might've happened next, if we'd been left to our own devices, but we aren't given the opportunity to find out. From the opening of the alleyway, someone clears their throat. I wheel around, furious at being interrupted, to find Clover watching us. Hank is curled around the back of her neck, sleeping on her shoulder.

"Sorry." She doesn't sound particularly sorry, either. "But we can't find the Librarian or the Evergod anywhere. And you three . . . well, we were worried when we couldn't find you either, but apparently you just had *something to do*."

There are a million vile things I would like to say to this rotten child, and all of them jump to the tip of my tongue at once, fighting it out for who gets to be spoken. No one wins, though.

Enzo pushes himself off the wall, straightening his posture and moving toward Clover. "We should find them. The Evergod's probably passed out in a booth somewhere, but I don't trust the god of knowledge. Especially not when he's still got all my thoughts in his head."

And to that point, fair enough. Still, I point out, "I thought you two became friends or something. During those two weeks when I was . . . away."

He frowns. "Yeah, we did. But we're back now. Everyone's different here. Aren't we?"

"Right." Yeah, of course. They were Enzo and Rhett when they became friends. They aren't . . . they aren't those people anymore.

Obviously.

Out in the street, the music seems louder than it was before, the crowds thicker and more cramped. I end up squished between Clover and Rory as we try to force our way through the throng, following Enzo.

There is a group of dancers, gathered on a stage at the center of the street, and he pauses in front of them. Clearly part of some kind of troupe, dressed in the same baggy but colorful clothing, they're in the middle of performing a choreographed number. They sway in perfect sync with the music, as it it's coming from *them* and not the speakers. It's hypnotic. We can't help watching.

"Hey," someone whispers at my back.

It takes everything in me to pull my eyes away from the dancers, to turn around and face the voice.

The Muse stands on the street in front of me, a curled fist in front of his mouth. He unfurls his hand to reveal a pile of brightly colored powder in his palm. "Boo."

Color explodes in my face and the world goes black.

I don't wake up, but I do come to.

There is no festival. I'm standing in the center of the same street, but it's empty except for me and Rory and Enzo and Clover. There is no music, no food, no dancers. The air is cold and still. Down the street, Rune and Briareus turn toward us, confusion all over their faces—clearly, the same celebration just disappeared from right in front of them.

"Sorry to cut the party short." I wheel around, and find the Muse walking up the steps of that center stage. "But I thought it was time we all reconnected."

On his way up the stairs, he passes the Evergod, the old man whistling the same tune that was just playing on the speakers. He moves past the Reaper and the Lionheart, standing shoulder to shoulder at the edge of the stage, to join the Librarian at the back.

And at the heart of it all is a breathtaking being. Sitting on a giant, cloudlike pillow of bright red and gold, she's draped in sheer, multicolored fabrics and adorned with more jewelry than I've ever seen one person wear. Her black hair is long enough to curl down to the bottoms of her bare feet, and every visible inch of her dark brown skin is decorated with intricate white-ink tattoos—*moving* tattoos, each one a portrait telling a living story. Her brown eyes are too big for her face, taking up twice the space they should, and they're locked directly on me.

"Hello, love." The Heartkeeper smiles. "It really has been too long."

And then everything, *everything*, comes back to me at once.

24

THE WORST THING THAT COULD HAVE HAPPENED TO GEM

I open my eyes for the first time, and it is her face staring down at me.

"Where am I?" I ask, in a voice I don't recognize, in a language I've never spoken.

"You're home." She smiles when she reaches for my hand, helping me stagger to my feet.

We are nowhere and everywhere all at once; floating in space, surrounded by nothing but the light and dust of distant galaxies as they flow past.

I run my fingertips through a belt of stars. "What's home?"

"Whatever you want it to be."

I stare into the vast everything of the universe and breathe out and the Ether begins to unfold around us.

The Heartkeeper squeezes my hand. "We're safe now."

"Who is he?" I ask her on a laugh, lounging on the bank of a still-forming river, when our world is so new.

She runs her fingers through my hair and chuckles. Across

the way, on the docks, a beautiful boy with a brilliant smile invents music, to the delight of his crowd of onlookers. "The Muse. The god of art."

"Where did he come from?" I lean against her shoulder, wrapping an arm around hers.

"I loved him into existence." Her smile is as dazzling as his when she grins down at me. "Just like you."

We are not lovers, though the whispers of insinuation follow us wherever we go. I know the other gods suspect. I don't care.

I know it is because they don't understand us. Friendship, for a god, is as intangible as grasping at smoke. They cannot fathom the trust she and I have in each other.

But magic is love and love is magic. We are one in the same. I could never be without her.

And if I were to think about it, I have no reason *not* to take the Heartkeeper as a lover. She is as close to me as the blood in my own veins, her voice as familiar as the sound of my own heart's beat. She is beautiful beyond any compare. She is safety, and comfort, and exhilaration, and joy.

She is as soft as cloud and stronger than any stone. She is the heart of this world, and she is *my* heart beyond my body's cage.

"You will come to regret this," she tells me, standing in the garden at the center of my palace.

I've just told her my plan—to create a weapon capable of killing a god.

"I don't intend to use it," I press, desperate for her to understand. "It's only meant to be a safeguard. There are those among us who cannot be trusted with their own power, and it is my role to keep the balance. If I am pushed into a corner, I have to have a way to do that."

Tears well in her eyes. I want to shred my immortal body out of existence.

"How do you not see you are building your own corner?"

"I didn't think you would come."

Tonight is the night I execute my plan. I will bring the Ouroboros into the world, the most powerful piece of magic ever to exist. I am alone in my chamber, the blade I've forged laid on my altar table, when the Heartkeeper joins me.

She says nothing for a long moment. She moves closer, examining the knife. One hand reaches forward, and she touches the tips of her fingers to the snake's silver scales.

"Forever consuming itself," she finally whispers. "The cycle never ends."

My shoulders stiffen. "*Why* did you come?"

"I know what your sacrifice will be, if you go through with this, Magician." She tilts her chin toward me. "I wanted to give you one last chance to stop."

My pulse thunders. For so long, as I've nurtured this secret scheme, I've wondered what the balance would demand of me in return. I've feared it, but pushed forward, regardless. And now she claims to know? "How?"

"Because it is your heart." She pulls her hand away from the knife, straightening to her full height and staring down at me. "Should you go through with this, you will never know a moment of peace. You will spend an eternity at war with yourself, halved in two—the part of you who hates that you could have given life to this weapon, and the part who descends *because* of it. Every step you take, you will feel as though you are divided between two worlds, because you *will be.*"

The Heartkeeper touches my shoulder, and I flinch. "We are tied together, you and I. We have been tethered as one since the dawn of this world. If you go through with this, you sever that tie. And you will never know your own heart again."

I stare into her eyes. My beloved friend. The other half of me. Somehow, I know what she's saying is true.

And slowly, my eyes move back to the Ouroboros on the altar.

> The pain of my loss is so heavy that I cannot carry it.
>> And so, to protect myself, I forget it exists.
>> I forget her entirely.

. . . .

> *The pain of my loss is so heavy that I cannot carry it.*
>> *And so, to protect myself, I forget it exists.*
>> *I forget him entirely.*

I cannot breathe.

An ancient wound reopens, something coming undone at the very core of me, and there's nothing I can do to stop it. *This is how I'm going to die,* I realize. *This is how I should have died a long time ago.*

It's clear now that forgetting held me aloft, just out of reach of the hand of death, but it didn't allow me to keep living. Not really. All this time, ages upon ages, I've wondered at the truth of who I am. Of why my heart is never still, why it is never satisfied, why I am always hungry and tired and alone and afraid of the whole world, even when I was the one who shaped it.

God or human, it didn't matter. I have always known only one thing to be a certain truth—

I don't know my own heart. And no one else does, either. And if anyone ever did, they would surely leave me.

Because *she* did.

Who is the Magician when no one is watching?

Empty. I am not the god of gods—I am nothing more than the shell of one.

The whole of me unhooks from the ropes I've long used to bind myself to my own existence, and I cannot breathe. I've always known my bonds were fragile but I was never sure when they would snap. And because I cannot breathe, and because I am unbound from my own self, and because there is a gaping hole at the center of me, Enzo is able to reach into the folds of my cloak and pull out the Ouroboros.

"Bitch," he snarls, and then disappears into shadow.

"Well," the Reaper breathes in a voice like a spider's legs skittering over a tombstone. "That was impolite."

She moves with such vicious and precise speed that it would be impossible to understand her movements—or maybe it's only impossible in this moment for *me*, the long-dying god, the overdue ghost. Whatever the case, I can't wrap my head around what I'm seeing as she flies from the stage and shoots one skeletal hand into the empty air above her.

Not until Enzo reappears, a shadow blooming to light in that space, and the Reaper's got her bony hand buried in his chest cavity.

"*NO!*" Rory howls. They don't need magic or godhood to bring back one oversized fist and send it flying toward the back of the Reaper's skull.

I didn't even notice the Lionheart's approach, but her shield slams against their knuckles, blocking the blow before it can land. Battle shakes her head like a scolding parent. I can almost hear the *Now, you know better than that.*

Enzo hits his knees at the Reaper's feet, blood spilling from one corner of his mouth as the god of death sinks her fingers into the meat of his heart. And still, he has eyes only for the Heartkeeper—and she has eyes only for me.

I can't look away from those big eyes. I know I have to, I know I'm supposed to. I'm supposed to save them, I'm supposed to win this fight, I'm supposed to be the god of gods. What am I doing? This isn't even a *fight.* They are nothing compared to me, no one is anything compared to me, and

And

And yet.

I don't feel like the god of gods. And I can't seem to make myself move. I still haven't taken a breath.

"You ally with her and you court your own damnation," the Shade warns, spitting a glob of his own blood onto the stage floor. "Do you have any idea what she has done?"

"Do you mean the millennium she spent keeping this world from collapsing despite your best efforts to drag it to the brink?" the Muse demands. "Or all she has done in the years since, trying to rebuild the Ether from the waste you left behind?"

"Cherub," the Heartkeeper warns. "Remember what we spoke about."

The Muse growls, turning and stalking away, jumping from the stage at the back. He storms to the edge of the street, near the bay where boats are docked by the shore, and raises his hands to the setting sun.

I watch, enchanted and frozen in equal measure, as the god of art makes shadows dance in the dipping light. The wind blows at his back, making windowpanes creak and tree limbs shake, sending littered glass bottles and forgotten coins stumbling down the street. All of it joins together in one song, growing louder and louder beneath the eye of their immortal conductor. At his feet, the whole world is a stage, and everything in it a performer.

Like a child sent to calm themself down by banging on pots and pans on the kitchen floor. All the more accurate because he *is* her child, or the closest thing to one any god has ever had.

And Indy tried to tell me himself, once, I realize.

"*Art is an act of* love," he'd told me in that attic, while time stood in surrender, while I still had the choice to let Zephyr Beauregard live. "*And I have known and loved all of you for a very long time—even when I hated you.*"

Indy tried to save Gem Echols because he loved them. Because the worst thing that could have happened to Gem was for them to become . . . me.

"No," Enzo answers the Muse, showing off row after row of those horrible, bloodstained teeth. "I'm talking about when she came to me, all those years ago, and told me about the knife herself."

Well, that simply can't be right.

And I don't think I'm the only one who thinks that. The Reaper and the Lionheart exchange a weighty look. The Librarian's eyes bounce all over the place. Rory turns their head to look at me, but I have no answer. The only ones who seem unsurprised are the Evergod, the Muse, and the Heartkeeper herself.

In the silence that follows, Enzo asks, "What? She didn't tell her new friends about that? About how I would never even have known the knife existed if she hadn't brought it to my attention?"

"Is this true?" the Lionheart demands, tilting back her head to stare down her chin at the god of love.

"Yes." She doesn't even hesitate, makes no attempt at all to deny it. Those too-big brown eyes are still on my face. I can feel them burning holes in my cheeks. "The Ouroboros was the Magician's most ugly secret, born of their most private pain. I'd naïvely hoped that the god of things forbidden would force their secret into the light. That they would be called to face themself and reckon with what they'd done—and how they'd gotten where they did. Unfortunately . . . I never could have foreseen the way things truly unfolded."

"I did!" the Evergod pipes up, suddenly sitting ramrod straight, as if he'd fallen asleep and been jolted back into consciousness. "Does anyone want to know what happens next?"

Everyone looks to him. Even the Muse stops sculpting the skyline and turns to raise his eyebrows in the god of time's direction.

"The gods will fall, felled by their own kind, blood staining the hands of those who loved them. And the Ether as we know it will forever be destroyed." He smiles.

After a long moment, the Lionheart looks back to Enzo. "She did what she believed was right. She was trying to save us."

"*I DID WHAT* I *THOUGHT WAS RIGHT!*" The Shade wails his agony, and his blood pulses, brighter and thicker, over his lower lip. "All this time, you have chosen not to understand. But you brought this on yourselves. You locked me away, forced me into the shadows of this world, because you didn't want to look at me. But I was a *part* of you. I was one of your fold, and you had every intention to *extinguish* me. Why? Because of your shame? Because it was easier to starve me out than face where I was bred?"

Slowly, the Reaper's bloody finger bones tug free of his ribs. She steps back into her lover's side.

Enzo, his chest an open gash of scarlet, pushes himself unsteadily to his feet. He stands over the Heartkeeper with the Ouroboros still tight in his fist.

Behind her, the Muse turns back toward the stage. The Librarian crouches at her back, as if poised to whisper a lethal secret in her ear.

She seems unmoved. To the Reaper, she says, "Do not allow him to manipulate you. Remember, that's what he does."

"Me?" Enzo demands, voice thready and faltering. "You have a lot of nerve to call *me* the manipulator. You, who can puppet the very hearts of those around you. I've felt the weight of your vile power since before we even arrived in this city."

The shift in mood in the RV.

I catch Rory glancing at the ground, masking a wince. Thinking of their almost-something moment in the alleyway? A work of the Heartkeeper's manipulation?

"It is true, I can influence those around me to act on their feelings in ways they never would have otherwise. But I cannot *invent* feelings. There has to be a seed before something can bloom." She sighs and tilts her head to finally meet his eyes. "For example, there was already a *minuscule* part of you that loved the Magician. And because there was, *I* was able to grow it into something powerful enough that you were finally compelled to leave our world and find them."

I cannot breathe.

25

SALT AND GRIEF

Water sloshes over the side of the boat, a wave as tall and angry as I am, soaking us like drowned rats. Rune and Briareus desperately scoop it back into the sea, desperately use their hands and clothes to try to keep us from being sent under. Clover kneels in front of me. She's screaming. I can't hear her over the sound of the storm raging on the ocean's surface. I think she might be begging for our lives.

I can do nothing for her.

Shouldn't they all know that by now?

Enzo smiles at me through the laptop screen, lying on his stomach in his bed in Brooklyn while I lean against my pillows in my bed in Gracie. It's late, too late, and we should both be asleep. We have class in the morning. I can't make myself log off.

"Ivy just got their own apartment," he tells me. "I'm gonna help them get things set up this weekend, but they sent me some pictures from the listing. It's so cute. I mean, it's tiny and dirty and someone definitely died there, but it's *so* cute. And all

I could think about was how I can't wait for you to be here. I can't wait for us to have our own place."

My heart threatens to give out. I've never wanted anything more than the life he keeps promising me. I will claw my way out of Gracie with air in my lungs, no matter what it takes, just so I can get to what comes next. To my real life. With Enzo.

Sometimes, I still don't understand how it's possible. How it feels like we've known each other forever, how it feels like he can see me more clearly than anyone else ever has and he's never even seen me without a screen between us. It's like I've been waiting for him and I didn't even know it until I'd found him.

He knows this, of course. He doesn't know how sometimes I worry that while I was waiting for him, *he* wasn't waiting for *me*. He doesn't know how sometimes I lie awake and panic that he doesn't see me, not really, and that when he finally does—when he's finally close enough to look through all the smoke and mirrors—he'll realize he's made a huge mistake.

The Shade whispers, "You torment me, creature. Even when I hate you, I want you."

And I don't mind that he hates me. His hatred makes our game more fun. If he didn't hate me a little, I don't know that the whisper of his teeth on my throat would be nearly so exciting.

This is what I tell myself, at least.

The sea screams, or maybe that's Clover still. I blink. All I see is gray and blue and wet. Lightning erupts across the sky overhead and I taste the memory of it in my mouth.

What is happening to my magic? What is happening to

the balance? What can I do and what can I not and how is the answer to both of those questions *nothing at all*?

Our boat is thrown back and forth between the waves, tossed like a toy between the Siren's palms.

Briareus roars something and drags his daughter and husband to his chest.

We go under.

I don't think the Shade hates me anymore, and there is a part of me that is terrified to acknowledge that belief, even in the back of my own mind. What if I'm wrong? I desperately do not want to be wrong.

But things are different now. We sneak soft touches and lingering kisses in between macabre torture scenes, in between the assassinations of our own kind. We fall into his bed, into the tender liquid of his sheets, and I don't worry if he really loves me, because I pretend he does, anyway.

"We've lived such long lives. There is little I thought could surprise me anymore." The Shade runs his claws down my side, and I arch my back like an offering. "But you . . . you took me by surprise."

I want him to be finished talking. I want his hands and mouth on every part of me. I want to know what he feels like when he abandons this half-human facade and truly becomes one with shadow.

Still, I tease, "And how did I surprise you, demon?"

His eyes glitter silver and gold when he looks down at me. "You have seen what my hands are capable of. Yet you do not flinch when they reach for you."

My lips part. My heart thunders, a brewing storm in my chest.

I want to ask him if this means he's come to *care* for me. I want to beg him to tell me where his own secrets are hidden, and if I am one of them. I want to know if he is trying to be soft for me, when we're alone together, like this, and tell him he doesn't have to.

And I want to tell him the sentiment is just as true from the other side. We are two monsters who were lucky to find each other—after all, who else would have us?

Instead of admitting my own weak depravity aloud, I pull his lips to mine.

....

"Do you ever worry they're going to figure it out?"

Enzo asks the question, seemingly unprompted, on FaceTime. It's the night before his junior play, the biggest performance of his high school career. He's anxious, pacing back and forth in his bedroom, and we're up too late again.

"I have no idea what you're talking about," I tell him, watching as he fiddles with his costume hanging on a mannequin bust in the middle of the room.

"You know, people. People at your school. Do you ever worry they're gonna realize that you're just, like . . . bullshitting your way through everything?" It's an awfully rude thing to say to someone, but it doesn't sound like an insult when it comes from Enzo. Maybe because his hands are shaking and his eyes are wet, and he wheels toward the camera to look at me, big-eyed, in the screen. He's too upset to remember to be pretentious right now, so I know it's really bad. "Like . . . like I worry all the time that everyone can see through me. That they're gonna figure out this

whole thing is an act. That they won't . . . won't want any-
thing to do with me once they clock it."

I sniff, sitting up straighter. I worry about this con-
stantly; every minute of every miserable day. And of course
he knows that.

Instead of saying it out loud, I tell him, "I think they
probably already clocked it. You're not that good of an
actor."

He's so taken aback that he laughs, cracking a sur-
prised smile. "Well, fuck you, darling."

"I love you, too," I reply, because I do, and because I
know he does. I know he does.

We are both awful, scared, pathetic little liars. But we
love each other. I know that much is true.

The current pulls me deeper and deeper, dragging me toward
the ocean floor.

I hear the Siren's rage in my head and open my mouth to
scream my own agony, salt water flooding my lungs when I do.

*YOU'RE A FOOL, SIREN! DON'T YOU KNOW I'M
DEAD ALREADY?*

And the whole world is made of salt and grief.

I lie awake all night, pressed between Rory's and Enzo's bodies, listening to the sounds of the swamp outside the window.
Even though my *mind* doesn't feel like I've been gone for two
weeks, trapped in whatever unconscious state the Evergod suspended me in, my *body* has missed these two. I can't make myself fall asleep, can't bring myself to miss a single second of their
breathing, and their warmth, and the solid *realness* of them.

They're alive and they're here and we're together and it's okay, we're going to be okay, things will work out just fine, because they're here, and I have them, and they have me.

They have me. They *want* me. They looked for me every moment I was gone. I don't know how I got so lucky. I don't understand how I deserve this, and I'm pretty sure I don't.

I am not a good person. I think I can admit that now, in the quiet, in the alone, at least inside my own head. I'm not a good person, even though I never wanted to be a *bad* person, even though I always thought I was *trying* to be a good person. Good people don't make the kinds of choices I do. They don't let the world bleed the way I do. And, honestly, if being a good person means letting bad things happen to me and the people I love, maybe I don't actually want to be a good person anyway.

And maybe I *can't* be a good person anyway. There is something broken in me, something deeply, grotesquely fucked up. It's been there since I was a kid, a monster always under the bed, a secret I couldn't name because I was too ashamed even to look at it.

A good person should be able to say *no* to people. I've always wondered why I can't say no to people. Why my body felt more like a way station covered in strangers' graffiti than it did a home for me to live in. And I realize now, they could *smell it on me*— somehow, the kinds of people who would use my body, the kinds of people who would *hurt* my body, they could always tell *I* was the kind of person who would *let them*. I've always wondered why I was like this, but somehow, even when I didn't know, *they* did. Therapists with wedding bands and older boys with cameras on their phones and strangers who looked at me and saw my shame, saw the shadow of it on my face, even when I couldn't. They knew I was already broken. They knew I was already dirty beyond repair, so it wouldn't matter how many stains they left behind.

But I can see it now. I can see all of it, all of their handprints and all of the shadows, and the monster under my bed finally has a face. And I don't think there's any coming back from this. I don't think I can ever get clean, not really.

And Rory and Enzo are here, anyway.

They know. Maybe not everything, maybe not every awful detail I'm only just starting to piece together myself, but they know. They've always been able to see the shadow under my bed, even if they didn't know its name. They know I'm dirty. They know they cannot wipe me clean. And they don't want to try. They just want to love me anyway.

They just love me anyway. I am deeply, grotesquely fucked up, and I am *so* loved. I am *seen,* and I am so loved, and it is terrifying, and perfect, and I don't know how I'll ever sleep again.

Salt water burns my lungs and eyes, and I think of Icarus.

Was it really hubris that allowed him to be seduced by Apollo's beckoning hand?

Or was that just the story Daedalus told himself as he lost his child to the sea?

Maybe it was easier to think his son impulsive and naïve than wonder why he might have chosen to fall. Because maybe Icarus knew, even if they escaped, there was a part of him that would be imprisoned in the Labyrinth forever.

Maybe it was Poseidon's kingdom, and the promise of rest at the bottom of the ocean, that he was after all along.

. . .

I am neither dead nor drowning. I'm freezing, though, and my clothes are soaked through. The fire doesn't help much. And I don't know who built the fire, the one I'm sitting in front of, the one that's keeping me from *actually* freezing or dying but can't get me warm.

I blink. Clover is wedged between her dads, the three of them huddled together on the other side of the flame.

We're on the shore. We're on an island.

Okay. So, we stole a boat. I remember that, now. We ran from the Heartkeeper's kingdom, ignoring the Shade's screams and the Mountain's roars. We ran, and we stole, and we fled into the open ocean, because I needed to get away from him. In that moment, the Siren's sea was far less frightening than the Heartkeeper's truth.

My own keepers are watching me.

"We shouldn't have pulled you back," Clover says between chattering teeth.

I say nothing. We both know she's right.

Maybe I wanted to drown.

26

A WELCOME GRAVE

The island in question is the long-abandoned kingdom of the Sun. I realize this the next morning, watching the way light filters in through the trees, listening to the sounds of birdcalls and vicious waves clawing at the sand.

Rune and Briareus discover a cluster of tiny houses on the other side of the key. No one can speak to who the inhabitants might have been, but whoever they were, they're not here anymore. The Amarith family disappears into one home without extending an invitation for me to join them.

I know the keepers have lost their faith. They don't want to be trapped on this island with a useless god any more than I want to *be* a useless god. But we all have our roles to play. I disappear into my own stolen home, disappear from the glare of the high-hung sun, from the sound of the ocean's screaming as it assaults the shore.

The little house is cold and empty, cobwebs in every corner and filling every inch of the fireplace. There are dirty dishes still in the sink, and a nest of blankets on the floor. As if the owner thought they would be right back. As if they were just running out to work, or to see a friend, or let the dog out. And then they never returned.

The blankets smell of mold and sharp sickness. I sit with my back to the wall on the other side of the room, still shivering. I pretend I cannot see the shadows moving all around me, brought to life by the outstretched hand of sunlight through the window.

"Gem?"

I blink. I don't know when I fell asleep or how, but I must have. My eyes struggle to adjust to the half-light, making out shapes and suggestions before I realize there's a face directly in front of my own. I blink again.

"Rory?"

She sighs, touching her palm to my cheek. The warmth of her is so unexpected, so starkly different from the cold I've been living in, that I *moan*, my face sinking into her hand. She brushes her thumb under my eye, easing my chill, bringing me back into my body. I close my eyes again and let myself be held in this simple touch, her skin on mine.

When I open my eyes again, she's still watching me. There are dark circles beneath hers, like she hasn't slept in a while. And she's soaked, her own clothes dripping water onto the floor beneath us.

"How did you find me?"

Her fingertips stroke the place behind my ear. "I took my own boat."

The Mountain sailed, alone, across the ocean, with no idea where she was going. She faced the Siren's wrath for me, on nothing but *hope* that she might actually be able to find me.

And she paid the price for it. Her wet hair clings to her skin, hiding her face behind its strands, but I can make out enough to recognize the hollowed-out expression in her eyes. Rory is haunted by whatever she saw on her sister's sea.

"How did you *find* me?" I ask again, touching my own hand to the underside of her jaw, brushing the pad of my thumb over her chin. A memory of tattooed lines floats across the surface of my thoughts, but I don't scoop it up. I let it continue to drift, carried downstream on the wind.

Her eyes, heavy and hurt, flare with some unspeakable emotion. "How many times do I have to explain this? I will always find you. I will *always* bring you back."

A voice from another world whispers, "*Let your people help you come back to yourself.*"

My chest aches so sharply I want to cry.

"I can't come back," I tell her, but I don't know which one of them I'm actually talking to. "I don't know how. I'm not . . . I don't belong anymore."

Rory shifts her weight to settle next to me against the wall. She curls an arm around my back, dragging me into her side. I let myself fall into the soft escape of her body, let myself be comforted and held by its warmth.

"That's just not true," she disagrees. "Of course you belong. After all we've been through, do you really still have no idea how wanted you are?"

"Not *me*." I sniff. "A lie—a person who doesn't even exist."

"Just because there's *more* to the story doesn't mean the rest isn't still true." Rory sighs. She squeezes me, kisses the top of my head. "You can't hide forever."

Maybe not. Probably not. But I can hide for a while longer.

I tuck into her side even tighter, burying myself in the Land like a welcome grave.

When I wake again, there's a fire in the fireplace, and Rory's clothes are dry. I don't move at first. I watch her from where I'm lying on the cool ground, as she crouches in front of the flame, poking at it with a stick. The embers dance in her dark eyes and cast shadows on the lines of her face.

I wonder what she sees when she looks into the fire. I wonder if she sees her kingdom burning.

Finally, I push myself up, scrubbing sleep from my eyes with a curled fist. Rory glances over at me, but her eyes don't linger, and she goes back to tending her fire.

"Morning, honey."

"Mornin'." I don't know that it is, actually. The sun is still out, or out again, maybe a little lower in the sky than it was before. But this island gets only a couple of hours of dark each day. The sun being up doesn't mean much.

"Are you hungry?"

I think I should be. I'm not sure how much time has passed. At least a day. Maybe two. Maybe more. But my stomach is a maze of knots and pits of acid and I don't think I could eat if I tried.

"I'm okay."

Not the same thing, and not the truth. But it's what I say, anyway.

Rory nods, though I suspect she knows I'm lying. A moment later, she finally stands, discarding her poking stick. She picks up a bowl from the kitchen counter and brings it over to me, setting it down on the floor in front of us when she slides back into her spot at my side.

I open my mouth to protest, thinking it's food. But the words splinter and fall apart when I realize it's just water. Just a bowl of water.

I look at Rory. She looks at me. I know what she's saying without saying it, but I can't do this. How does she not realize I can't do this?

"No," I tell her.

"Yes," she argues.

"I'm not ready."

"You're never going to be ready." She touches her palm to my knee. "If you wait until you're ready, you'll die like this. Is that what you want?"

I don't know. I don't know. *I don't know.*

I look back to the bowl. And even knowing this is a terrible idea, I reach out and press my fingertips to the surface of the water.

My mother sits with Rory's and Enzo's in the yellowing-white hospital cafeteria. She has a paper cup of coffee between her hands, her head bowed, her face a lithograph of worry lines and long-flaked makeup. The three women are silent, Rory's mother staring at the clock over their heads, Enzo's pushing cold meat loaf around her tray with a plastic spork.

It seems odd to see them like this, sitting together in an almost companionable quiet, when they're strangers. But they aren't strangers, I guess. How long have they been together in this hospital? How long did it take for them to find each other in the halls, mourners walking the same funeral procession with different ghosts?

Three Native women from three different Nations, and each of them waiting for a child to come home. It isn't *lost* on me, how this scene is not actually a new one at all, how this moment has played out over and over again for mothers like these and children like us, for the last five hundred years.

No, they aren't strangers. They never could have been.

A fourth joins their table, my grandmother pulling out a chair and sitting down at my mother's side. Back straight, dark eyes sharp, she considers the women in front of her.

"You are losing hope?"

Rory's mother whimpers. My own presses her hands to her face. Enzo's meets my grandmother's eyes. "You aren't? There's been no change. The doctors have given up, even if they won't say it—they already let Poppy and Marian go home to die."

"You trust what these doctors have to say?" she asks. The question, which, from someone else, might have dripped with condescension, is instead genuinely puzzled from her. "You put your faith in their ability to fix what they've admitted they do not understand?"

"Ecke," my mother breathes, shaking her head. "*We* don't understand it, either."

"I just wanted them to know we never stopped looking." Rory's mother groans, tilting her head back and biting her lip to fight away tears. She stares at the fluorescent-lit ceiling above, shoulders shaking. "They can't leave this world without knowing that—that we missed them *every day* they were gone. That we never gave up. That we never would have."

Enzo's mother presses her hand to the top of the other woman's. It's enough to finally send Rory's mom over the edge, and she lets loose a jagged sob, sinking forward to put her own head in her hands. Mrs. Truly rubs her back.

My mom sits up straighter, dropping her hands to her knees, looking at the two women in front of her before looking at her own mother. "Whatever you think this is, it isn't. Something's been going on for a long time, and I think . . . maybe this is how it ends. Maybe—"

Her voice catches in her throat. She has to take a breath, and swallow it back, before she can continue.

"Maybe we were always going to lose Gem, no matter how hard we fought."

My grandmother's eyes narrow, a dangerous set to her spine as she stares down at the withering, grief-stricken shell of her daughter. She snaps something I don't understand, something brutal and beautiful in the language that was almost stolen from her. To the end, she adds, "This world is cruel to our children, but it is *their* world. No matter how deep in the shadows they are forced to walk, they will always find their way back. *They are coming home.*"

She turns her face away from my mother's, staring out into nothing. If I let myself, I could almost pretend she was looking through worlds to find me.

My whole body winces, and the image ripples and fades from the water bowl. Rory sniffs, wiping her knuckles under her eyes.

"I don't understand how I'm still alive," I tell her.

"Your attempt wasn't as successful as you thought. It wasn't your *death* that brought us back here."

"Then what was it?"

She hesitates, lips trembling. "I don't know."

Everything feels like it's happening too far away. Or maybe too close. Fuzzy and distorted, and I can't make out the whole picture, no matter how hard I try. And haven't I been trying? Haven't I tried so hard?

I don't know how to keep doing this.

"But I know this. Gem—you are so wanted."

I want to cry. Instead, my fingertips graze the water again.

I would recognize the Shade's palace anywhere, even after a thousand years. Darkness hollows in every pocket of air, secrets and sacrilege twined in matrimony along every stretch of black stone.

Enzo stands at the center of his throne room. He looks awful, like he hasn't slept since the last time he lay next to me. The Shade's curls are a nest of frizz, shooting up at all sides of his skull. His black eyes are massive, his cheeks are gaunt, his expression is harried, and he's beside himself as he screams.

"TELL ME WHERE THEY ARE!"

It is the Evergod he's railing against. The old man stands in front of him, a detached smile on his ancient face. Staring at his expression, I can't help wondering if the other angels smirked when they witnessed Lucifer's descent to hell.

Enzo grabs for his shoulders, shaking his frail body. The Evergod's neck whips back and forth, his head threatening to give way and go rolling—and still he laughs. He giggles that awful, sadistic giggle, and reaches up to take the god-king's hands beneath his own.

"I tried to warn you this would hurt." His voice is not that of an old man, nor that of Buck Wheeler. It is the deep, impossible timbre of time itself, opening up like a black hole. Even through the scrying bowl, it makes my stomach drop. "The Shade was never meant to be happy."

Enzo howls and howls and drops his hands from the Evergod's body and wheels away, his nails dragging bloodied rivets into the sides of his face, his fingers twisting in his hair and tugging until it threatens to come out by the handful. And still, the god of time dares to laugh.

Not for long, though.

The Shade turns back to him, body shaking, voice quavering when he whispers, "If you won't tell me, I'll get the answers myself."

The Ouroboros sits in his palm.

"NO!" I scream, careful not to knock over the scrying bowl when I shoot to my feet.

Every instinct in me screeches at once, warning that *this* is the worst thing that could ever happen, *this* is the thing we cannot come back from, *this* is how my worlds end. I reach for my magic, my broken, confusing, unbalanced magic, and demand that it bring the Ouroboros to me.

And it does. Silver forges itself into life in my palm, a perfectly lethal dagger with a serpent wrapped around it, forever eating its own tail.

But there is no relief. Because this is not the blade, but instead a perfect replica. Just like the one I gave to Rory before prom.

In the scrying bowl, Enzo is still holding the god-killing knife.

The Evergod does not attempt to move away, though I know he could. I know he has seen this coming, know he has known since the dawn of his own creation that this was how it would end, know he could simply step aside and change his fate. But he doesn't. Instead, he laughs, and laughs, and laughs, even as the blade sinks into his chest. He laughs until his laughter is nothing but a blood-soaked gurgle.

The knife slides free. The Evergod hits his knees and whispers, in a voice that carries throughout all of the Ether, "*Finally.*"

Our eyes meet through the scrying bowl.

Looking right at me, the god of time winks before he crumples.

And all of his power, the knowledge of everything that has ever been and everything that will come to pass, crawls its way into the Shade's body, instead. And Enzo screams, and screams, and screams, until his screams become silence. Until he, too, sinks to the floor, wide eyes unfocused on the shadows above him.

"He's breaking," my voice says, though I don't know if I'm the one speaking. "His mind is going to collapse."

Rory is already standing. "I'll get the boat. We can be there in hours. We can save him."

I don't know what she sees when she looks at me, but she grips my arms and says, "Gem, listen to me. We can save him, and we're going to."

She leaves.

I know I'm supposed to follow her. We're going to save him. *We're going to save him.* It's going to be okay.

But I can't seem to make myself move. Frozen. Useless.

"Magician?"

I blink. Clover stands in the doorway.

She waits for me to say something, and, when I don't, huffs and steps inside. "We need to talk. Look, I get it. You're going through it, or whatever."

No, I don't think she does get it. I don't think she has any idea. I blink again, watching her, still unable to make myself move.

"But we're stranded here because of you. Okay? And—and frankly, we didn't do anything except help you, so . . . So, you need to get your shit together and help us get home." She crosses her arms and juts out her chin, staring me down.

I blink. The ice in my veins thaws when it touches the fire of rage.

"You would speak to me like this?" My voice doesn't shake. I still don't know if I'm the one speaking. "Do you not realize the sacrilege in that? Do you not know that I am the god of gods? And you think I would concern myself with helping *you*?"

My magic is not useless. It is not broken. It is whatever the fuck I want it to be, just like the rest of this world.

"Gem?" Rory asks, back at the door. "Gem, come on, we have to go *now*."

But I am not Gem. I am the Magician. I've lowered myself to Gem Echols for too long.

I stalk closer to Clover.

"Do you not see that you elevate yourself, and your pointless human life, to godhood?"

Her eyes grow bigger and bigger the closer I move. A single thread of shivering rage holds every atom of me together. She shivers for entirely different reasons.

When she backs into the wall, I press my hand to the brick behind her head, caging her.

I am not a good person. *I am the Magician.* And the whole world can bleed for me, as long as the ones I love are safe.

"If you wish to rise as a false god, Clover Amarith . . ." The replicated Ouroboros glints in the dying light from the fire. She does not scream when it plunges through the protective bramble of her ribs. Blood begins to gurgle over her teeth. ". . . then you can fall like one."

In a wave of dark fabric, I spin away from her, grabbing Rory's hand and teleporting us away. Without a second thought, I leave the Chosen One to die.

27

I DON'T WANT TO DO THIS

We do not die, which is convenient.

As soon as I've done it, the stupidity of teleporting away hits me like another of the Siren's waves. All this time, I avoided flexing that power, unsure of what we might walk into, or how my magic might *hurt* more than it helped. In my rash need to get to Enzo, in my off-the-handle rage at Clover for speaking the truth out loud, I allowed my impulsivity to win *again*. Just like it did in that church attic, and just like it did in the Gracie High School parking lot during prom. And I could've lost Rory for it.

But she's fine. At least, she seems fine. We reappear in the courtyard, in the Garden of Death that has haunted my dreams ever since I fled the Ether all those lifetimes ago. We stand at the center of brown, wilted grass, and blackened, twisted trees, with an inky, still pond at the center. Rory's reflection shimmers on the black water. I catch it staring at me before I raise my eyes to her face, confused by the hurt looking back at me.

"Are you okay?" I ask, trying to assess for signs of a wound.

She takes a step back. "We don't have time for this."

Without looking at me again, she turns and flees in the direction of the cave mouth, the jagged rock face that guards the Shade's palace, the cryptic kingdom hidden within the crag's shell.

From the corner of my eye, I watch the black pond water ripple, though there is no breeze. *You again, Siren? Come to finish the job? You'll have to wait.*

I race to follow the Mountain into the belly of the mountain, refusing to allow myself to get sentimental or creeped out. I refuse to think about carving open the Sun's body as I dash down the rocky hallway, that same path I walked more than a thousand years ago, the night I stepped into the dark with the god of things forbidden. I refuse to think of all the nights I spent retracing my steps, coming back here to this same empire, never certain if I would be met with bloodshed or devotion or, as was more often the case, both.

Near the end of the tunnel, it gets too dark for me to see until I drag my claws against the stalactite, and it sparks to life, five miniature bolts of lightning dancing at the tips of my fingers and illuminating our way. Rory barrels forward, not stopping even as we approach the massive black door made of stone and ancient magic. They don't hesitate, slamming their shoulder right into it, and it gives way beneath them, bursting apart in a spray of shrapnel that slices their skin and mine.

And still, neither of us hesitates. The Shade's cold and cavernous bedchamber sits empty on the other side of the door. Rory races straight through, to the other side of the room and into the heart of the palace. I wonder, briefly, how they know where they're going—but remember just as quickly that they've been here before. If not more often, I know with certainty that they were here at least once. The night they tried to make a deal with the devil.

"*Fuck*," they bite out on a half whisper, finally coming to a halt in front of me.

I put my hand over their arm, moving around them.

It's exactly what it was in the scrying bowl. The Evergod is dead. The Shade is breaking. And the real Ouroboros lies on the floor between them.

Hitting my knees next to Enzo's body, I press my hand to the side of his face. He doesn't know I'm here, eyes glazed over, taking in the entire history and future of our worlds. He's still in there, but he's buried underneath his own mind, and now we have to dig him out.

We have to. But how? How?

"What do we do?" Rory asks, sinking to their knees on his other side, their hand reaching down to touch one of his.

What do we do?

What do we . . .

My eyes drift to the knife on the floor. My stomach lurches at the very beginnings of the thought threatening to push its way to the forefront. I can't do that. I can't.

But it might be the only way to bring him back.

"We have to get rid of Time's magic . . ." I swallow. "We have to . . . take it away from him. He wasn't supposed to—it's too much for anyone."

"Take it away?" Rory frowns. "How do we . . ."

My hand curls around the Ouroboros's handle. Their eyes widen. I can see it on the tip of their tongue, the protest, the demand that I not do this, that I *can't* do this. And there is a part of me that wants them to say it. I want them to tell me to stop, I want them to force me to put the knife down, because I don't want to do this. I don't know if I *can* do this.

But they don't. They say nothing, and I bring the god-killing blade to Enzo's sternum, resting the tip in the center of his chest. He doesn't seem to register that it's happening, doesn't react at all to the cold steel on his body.

No one says anything. Rory and I stare into one another's eyes, and I silently plead with them to stay my hand.

Finally, they look away. They turn to watch Enzo's face, squeezing his hand tighter in their own. And they say, "Do it. Now."

When I press the blade into the Shade's body, I have the most ridiculous of human thoughts. This is the exact spot where Enzo's top-surgery scars don't quite meet in the middle.

"If she were to survive, and even a *fraction* of her power were to remain within her, it could be catastrophic."

The Shade tells me this when we stand together in the underbelly of the Caretaker's kingdom. The god of life is strapped to the table in front of me, and I've carved into every inch of her body, turning her from a god into a broken-open piñata, organs spilling like candy all over the place.

"All of this, all that she has already suffered, would be for naught. We cannot risk that, can we?"

The same is true now, only in reverse. I have to use the Ouroboros like a scalpel, to find every mutated cell of the Evergod's power, and cut it out.

But I *cannot* take anything else. If my knife stays too long or cuts too deep, I could do the very thing Enzo feared I'd done already, ripping his power out of him.

Or I could do so much worse than that. I could kill him. *Really* kill him, forever.

Leave any shred of the Evergod, and his mind may never

recover. Cut away too much and remove a vital piece of the Shade himself, and he may cease to exist at all.

Everything else falls away because it has to, because I can focus on nothing but the knife in my hand and the skin beneath the knife, and the muscle beneath the skin. When his blood blooms into my touch, someone *whines* like a kicked animal. I don't know which of the three of us it is. The blade tip slides between his ribs, curls lower, into his gut, splitting him open underneath me. Like using a letter opener to unwrap a gift.

I press my fingertips to his navel, then slide my hand past the unnatural slit of his flesh, dipping into the sloppy heat inside of him. My claws take care to trace, gently, at the swell of his iliac crest. There. Right there. The knife follows my hand, pressing down, carving into him like a poacher carving porcelain from their trophy kill.

Time stands still. Or maybe it only seems to because I'm holding it at knifepoint. I don't know how long we spend like this, my hand searching him for cancerous magic, my dagger carving away stolen pieces like tumors. I know Rory never leaves us, not even when the cloudy expression in Enzo's eyes begins to fade, and he begins to *feel* what's happening to him, and in his pain and his confusion, he starts to fight back.

The knife slips inside his body as he struggles, slicing open an artery that wasn't meant to be cut. Blood flows and flows and—and bodies shouldn't bleed this much, I think.

"I'm sorry, I'm sorry, I'm sorry," Rory whispers, and they hold their other hand over his mouth, suffocating him until his eyes roll back in his head and he loses consciousness.

There's more, I know there's more. I haven't saved him, not yet. If I leave any piece of the Evergod behind, I don't know what might happen. I have to find it, have to find this last shred of time trapped inside him, and have to do it before he wakes up and forces me to kill him instead.

His blood coats my arm up to the shoulder, my hand wrapping around his clavicle, fingertips stroking the length of his thoracic outlet, then deeper to his aorta and—

There. Right there.

The Ouroboros follows, both of my arms now wedged inside the Shade's body. I press the tip into his muscle, his pulse in my hand as I do.

Ba-bum, ba-bum, ba-bum.

And I slice away a piece of my boyfriend's heart.

Ba-bum . . . ba-bum . . . ba . . .

28

THE MAGICIAN IS JUST GOING TO KEEP MAKING EVERYTHING WORSE

By the time Enzo wakes up, I've loosed the Evergod's power into the world like a helium balloon without a weight, and used my own to heal his body. He blinks himself back to us, slowly at first, his pitch-black eyes squinting from even the low light in his bedroom. He shifts in bed, wincing when he does.

"Are you still in pain?" I demand, my grip on his hand tightening.

"G-Gem . . . ?" He frowns, tilting his head toward me. "You're here?"

I only squeeze his hand tighter in response.

"Hey, they asked you a question," Rory pipes up from where she's sitting on his other side. We've both taken up our posts, sitting at the edge of his bed, watching over him, one of his hands in each of ours. "Are you in pain?"

"I'm . . . a little . . ." He frowns. "Mostly just sore. What happ—"

Rory leans forward and presses their mouth to his. Enzo makes a quiet sound of surprise, tensing up for only half a second before groaning into it, slanting his head and opening his mouth for them. Their hands twist together, white-knuckled and desperate, in Rory's lap.

Something in me gives a sigh of relief.

When Rory finally pulls away, her eyes are wet. "You are a fucking clown, Enzo Truly. And you will never do anything like this to me again. Do you understand?"

He blinks. "Yes, Aurora."

"*Good.* Because if you do, I will kill you myself."

A beat passes. I run my fingers along his knuckles, staring down at his hand in my lap. My chest hurts, and I'm not even the one who was carved open.

"Gem?" he says again, even quieter this time.

I sniff, and tilt my head up to find his eyes. "Yeah, hey."

"I . . . What you heard . . . What that *bitch* said—"

"We don't have to talk about it." I shrug. I don't want to keep looking at his face. It hurts, and I hate that it hurts, and I hate that I can't even tell myself why. "She was lying, right? I mean . . . of course she was lying."

He stares at me.

The moment drags on for too long.

"Oh." My hands fall away from his. I stand, leaving his bed. "So, she . . . wasn't, actually. I see."

"Gem, please, I need you to listen to me. You have to understand—she was telling the truth, but that doesn't change how I feel about you." He raises his now-abandoned hand, pressing his palm to his chest. His own dark eyes shine. "I am so in love with you. I would follow you to the end of *any* world and back again. *You* are the future I have been fighting for."

"Minuscule," I remind him, throat like a rope bridge shaking under the weight of my words. "That's what she called it. That's how much you loved me."

"No!" Enzo sits up straighter, holding out that hand to me, desperation clawing at his face. "That is how much the *Shade* loved the *Magician*."

My head feels like it's full of sand. I wonder if it got trapped in there when the Siren was trying to drown me.

"I don't understand. You *are* the Shade. I *am* the Magician."

"Yeah." He sucks in a breath, running the back of his hand under his nose. "Yeah, okay. That's true. But it isn't the whole story. 'Cause I'm not *just* the Shade anymore."

My eyes flick to Rory. Their smile is as sad as it's ever been. Their words play back in my head. "*Just because there's* more *to the story doesn't mean the rest isn't still true.*"

Enzo keeps going. "I don't know if I *could* have loved you before I was Enzo. Definitely not like this. I needed to be him—to be *me*, before I could have anything that felt this good. Back then, that thing I was, it was just . . . just a black hole of pain. A black hole can't love *anyone*, not really. Even when I got close. Even when I wanted it, *so* bad. The pain was always going to come first."

I shake my head, looking back to him. "I still don't get it. I mean—okay, fine. You didn't really love me, and it was a you problem, sure. But how is any of that different now?"

"Because Enzo got to have what the Shade didn't. A family that wanted him. Friends who loved him. A place where he belonged. And when he met you, he was ready." Enzo swallows. "And I fell so fucking in love with you. Over wake-up texts and FaceTime calls and care packages and inside jokes—I fell *so* in love with you. That doesn't . . . that doesn't stop mattering now. That doesn't become less real just because we're here."

It feels wrong, and I can't explain why. It makes me want to cry, and I don't know how to make him understand. Finally, I say, "That's so . . . human."

Enzo tilts his head at me. "You want an epic love. A lifetime-after-lifetime, withstanding-epochs, godly love. Is that what you mean?"

"You make that sound dirty," I snap. "Like I should be embarrassed for wanting to be loved the same way *I* have loved *you* for a thousand years."

"No, darling, I don't think it's dirty. And I don't think you should be embarrassed. I just think you're not hearing me." Enzo takes a deep breath, letting it out slow and shaky through his sharp teeth. "My *human* love for you has changed the very fabric of who I am. By loving me, you have undone a grief so big it consumed a world. When they granted me the gift of their heart, *Gem Echols* felled the most lethal monster to ever live."

I do cry then. Tears slip from the corners of my eyes without my consent, and I push them away, face heating. I take a deep breath, trying to steady the shaking of my bones.

Finally, I say, "The *second*-most-lethal monster."

A beat passes. Rory chuckles. Enzo barks out a laugh. I smile, despite myself.

Enzo breathes heavily and looks to Rory. They meet his gaze and nod, something silent passing between the two of them.

When she looks back to me, she says, "We have all been changed by humanity. We are not the gods we were when we last lived in the Ether, and we will never be those gods again. And that's why . . . I think . . ."

She hesitates. Enzo squeezes her hand.

"What?" I frown.

"That's why," she repeats, "I think we need to go home."

I blink. She can't possibly mean what it sounds like she means. That wouldn't make any sense.

But they're both staring at me, expectantly. And I realize she can, because she does.

Whatever Enzo sees on my face, he's quick to say, "I know we left things in an upheaval. There's a lot we'll have to fix. But rebuilding our human lives will be nothing compared to trying to rebuild the Ether. Anything we did here, I think—I think we might just break it more."

"But I don't . . . That doesn't . . . This *is* our home."

"This *was* our home," Rory agrees. "When we were these people. But look what we did to it. You've seen what it's become, and we all had a role to play in this. I don't know that we *deserve* to call this place home, Gem."

If I only ever got exactly what I deserved, what would I be left with?

"But it's *ours*." I feel like my chest is wrapped with a zip tie, and it's yanking tighter and tighter. "I am the god of gods. I am the Magician. This is *my* world. Why—why would you want me to go back? I was nothing. Gem Echols was nothing, they were barely even a *person*. They were just—they were ten diagnoses in a trench coat, and they were afraid all the time, and—and now I never have to be afraid again, because I am the most powerful thing that exists. Nothing can hurt me here."

Rory and Enzo exchange another look.

"But that's . . . that's just not true." Rory looks back at me and gives a sad shake of their head. "*You* can hurt you here. And you are."

"I'm fine," I argue, the weight of the lie almost too much to swallow. "I don't know what you're talking about."

"You've been walking through a fog since you got here." Rory sighs. "I know you may not see how bad it's gotten, but . . . but that's part of the problem. I don't think you're seeing anything clearly right now."

"You are the most powerful thing that exists." Enzo nods. "But I don't know that you *should* be. Because Gem can get better. They can figure their shit out and fight for the future we've been planning. They can live. But the Magician . . . Darling, I'm scared the Magician is just going to keep making everything worse."

"And the whole of the Ether might pay the price." Rory winces.

I step away from them. I back toward the door. I can't be here right now. I need—

Well, I don't know. I don't have any idea what I need.

"Give me . . . give me a minute." Rory rises to her feet, as if thinking to follow me, and I shake my head. "Please, just . . . I'll be back, I'm not gonna do anything stupid, I just . . . Give me a minute, okay?"

Slowly, she lowers herself back to Enzo's side.

And I turn and leave, the whole world trapped like a ball in my throat.

They don't trust me with my power. They want to force me to go back to Earth, to become human, because they think I'm going to destroy the Ether. Because I've already destroyed the Ether.

How can they love me if they don't trust me? They must not love me. It hasn't ever made sense, how I got so lucky, how I ended up with two people I don't deserve, and this explains it.

But—no. No, it doesn't. Because they do love me. They do, I know they do.

Rory is my home. They are the roots I grew from, and the seed of new life left at the center of me when the rest is whittled away. They are the steady ground beneath my feet, and the warmth of things meant to be. When we kiss, I taste the language of the land on their tongue.

And I am their adventure. Their god of bedlam, their Viking raider, their saint of blood and new beginnings. I am the spark in their eye and the crack of a whip in their hand. I am a cool, deep breath after running for our lives. When they look at me, I think they see an eternity of forevers.

Enzo is my reverie. He is the dream I've been chasing since before I knew his face. He is fantasy made real, power and sex and magic, an impossibility in the body of a boy. He is every falling star I've ever wished on, and when he touches me, I burn.

And I am his truth. I am a mirror held up to the heart of him. I am the one waiting backstage when the makeup is smeared away and the lights are turned off. My name is the gospel he cannot avoid, and when he hears it, he remembers he's still human.

I don't know yet what they are to each other. I don't know if they've had time to figure it out, either. But I know we fit. I know they love me. Even when it hurts, they love me.

So, why? Why demand we go back? Why can we not just love each other here—here, where we will never grow old, and never die, and where no one can ever hurt us again, because we are too powerful to touch? Why is that so bad?

"Hello, Gem."

I jump, spinning around. The Siren stands at the edge of the water, watching me.

29

HAPPY, PATHETIC, BORING HUMAN

How long have I been walking? I must've wandered right out of the palace doors, my head somewhere else, my body called away. I'm outside again. I'm on the shore.

A moment stretches on. I swallow.

"Are you going to try and kill me again?"

The Siren tilts her head. Water slicks off the thin layer of fur covering her skull. She doesn't answer my question. Instead, she says, "I saw what you did to the Shade."

I frown, narrowing my eyes. "How?"

"Human bodies are eighty percent water." She shrugs one shoulder. "It's a little different, for gods. But only a little."

The implication of her words is horrifying. To avoid throwing up, I ask, "What do you want?"

"I want exactly what I've always wanted. To be human."

"Listen, I don't have time for—"

"I want you to cut my magic out of me, the way you did for

the Shade." She stands up taller, squaring her shoulders. "And then I want you to send me home."

In my waistband, the Ouroboros begins to thrum, heating against my skin, knowing it's been summoned. I press my hand against it through the fabric of my pants.

"You don't know what you're asking for," I warn.

"Yes, I do." Her fists curl. A tremor flutters over her strange, silken body. "You can take it. All of it. My magic, my immortality, my godhood. You can carve it all out of me and do whatever you want with it. All I want in return is to live a human life, on Earth, with the people I love."

I can't do this. Why is my hand curling around the dagger's handle? "It'll hurt."

She shows me her teeth. "Don't worry. I'm used to pain by now."

I don't even know I'm going to say yes, not consciously, not really. I don't know it, but I'm stepping forward, and the knife is at her belly, and then all I can think about is a terrible joke that ends with the punch line *gut you like a fish.*

There's salt water tucked in the notches of her lymph nodes, and the tip of my blade looses a flood to rival the sobs of any Earthly god.

Fresh water coats the walls of her lungs. It drips down the gem-encrusted handle until it spills over my hand. I press my mouth to my wrist and lap at the wellspring of the Siren's life.

The tides move back and forth through her veins, pushed and pulled by the full moon of her heart. Flecks of crimson decorate my fingertips like grisly constellations.

Her immortality stretches and curls along the grooves of

her spine. I pry forever from her bones, a pseudo-archaeologist without concern for the sanctity of the buried.

Her godhood hides, quivering under her tongue.

I take it all, slicing and carving and taking everything this once-god offered me. To her credit, she only screams a lot.

In the end, she lies at my feet, desecrated and powerless, the white sand of the beach stained a shocking red. She lost consciousness some time ago.

The knife tip trails from the mutilated corner of her mouth, over her throat, toward the wide-open cavity of her chest. She has nothing left to give.

But she has *nothing left to give.* Why would I send her back to Earth?

What reason would I have to grant her what she'd asked for, to send her home and let her live her happy, pathetic, boring human life? Why does she think she has earned the right to be boring and pathetic and happy, while the rest of us have to deal with what our world has become?

I am never going to be happy. Why does she deserve what I can never have?

Selfish Siren. The blunt edge of the Ouroboros presses against her heart, and blood spurts, almost cartoonish, from the vena cava. *Maybe I'll do you one better. How would you like to be reunited with your beloved husband?*

I am the Magician. I am the god of gods, and I am not a good person. She should have known better than to willingly crawl under my hands.

The sharpened edge twists, turning toward her pulmonary artery. I press the razor-sharp blade to her beating muscle—

My hand stills.

I stare at it. The dagger in my palm. The Siren's blood soaking my fingers, my sleeve.

Murphy's blood all over my hands.

The blood of *Rory's sister* all over my hands.

Hey. Hey, self?

What the fuck are you doing?

Slowly, I pull the knife away from her unconscious body and shove it back into the folds of my clothes.

The trembling sets in as I realize why the others want to leave.

I am the Magician. I am the god of gods, and I am not a good person.

But I am also Gem Echols. I *am* Gem Echols. And I do not have to spend another eternity being defined by the worst things I've ever done. I do not have to live the rest of my forevers carrying the weight of every awful thing that's ever happened to me, or haunted by the ghosts of things I had to do to survive.

I may not be a good person, not yet, but I don't have to resign myself to being a villain, either. Just because there's already blood on my hands. Just because that's all some people will see when they look at me.

I can still fight like hell to get clean.

From the serpent on the knife's face, I give the ocean back its own magic. Once I've scrubbed my hands off on my shirt, I reach forward and press my fingertips to the Siren's forehead. Under my touch, her wounds stitch themselves together. In moments, she sucks in a deep breath and shoots up, eyes popping open. Her hands fly to her chest, feeling her own scales, stroking up to her neck and down to her belly, her thighs.

"It's done," I promise. "You aren't the Siren anymore. You're just Murphy."

And Murphy deserves to be happy. To cheer at the championship football game. To graduate valedictorian of her class. To marry her high school boyfriend, or go on to an Ivy League before becoming president someday, or both. To call out sick on the days when her pain flares and spend hours in her pool. To hug her parents. To laugh at viral videos and walk dogs and stay up too late and wake up earlier than I ever would.

Murphy deserves purple-pink sunsets and summer drives with the windows down and her favorite playlist coming through the speakers. She deserves to love, and to live.

She deserves to live.

So did Clover Amarith.

So did Zeke King. And maybe so did Zephyr Beauregard and everyone else whose life ended under this damn knife.

Keeper of the scales my ass—who the hell am *I* to decide who deserves to live or die? I stand on shaking knees, and Murphy slowly rises, confusion on her face.

"But—my body?"

It takes me a moment to realize what she's asking. "Oh. Um, you'll wake up in your other body, when I send you back."

"What do you mean, *when you send her back*?"

Murphy's eyes flick behind me, over my shoulder.

Guilt, as heavy as an anvil, makes a cradle of my chest. I turn, slowly, to find Rory standing in the spot where forest meets beach. The rocky exterior of the Shade's palace looms over her head.

"I . . . I thought you weren't going to follow me."

"Yeah, that was before I heard the *screaming*." She narrows her eyes, gaze darting between Murphy and me. "What did you do? Gem, what did you fucking do?"

"Don't be angry with them." Murphy sighs. "Gem has done exactly what I asked them to. It was an act of kindness."

The guilt becomes twin anvils.

Rory stares at her sister, open-mouthed. I can see the pieces shoving together in her mind, see as she starts to realize what's happening. "No. No."

"Rory—"

"She can't leave!" Rory interrupts me, her face an open wound. "We—we're all tethered together. We're bound to each other. You can't send one of us back without—"

"We aren't." I answer, my tongue the unwilling weapon. "The spell that took us all to Earth the first time has come full circle. That tether was broken when we came back to the Ether. And—and even if it wasn't . . ."

"I'm not a god anymore." Murphy shakes her head. "I can finally have exactly what I've always wanted—to be human. To have my wonderfully imperfect human life, with people who love me."

"*I* love you," Rory whispers. "I have always loved you."

"I know." Murphy sniffs and looks down at her webbed hands, the scales on her arms, the waves licking the bloody sand beneath her feet. When she raises her head to meet Rory's eyes again, she continues, "But it hurts me to be loved by you."

The animal whine that breaks from Rory's chest is so pathetic that I have to look away. My teeth clench until I taste my own blood.

"Our lives have been so long, and so ugly, and full of so much pain. I don't want this." Murphy waves a hand over her monstrous body. "I haven't wanted this for a long time. I don't want to fight for every moment of peace and tenderness. If you loved me—if you truly loved me—you would see I've earned my rest. I deserve *softness*. Let me have that now, in the last chapter of a life that's been too long. *Please*."

It is not fair that sometimes the most loving thing we can do for someone is to let them leave.

Rory has blood on her hands. Just like Enzo. Just like me. It doesn't mean any of us are undeserving of another chance. But maybe it means we don't get to demand that chance from the same people whose blood it is.

No, it's not fair, but it is *just*. The Lionheart would be proud. I think I'm finally beginning to understand the difference.

I don't know what I would do, if Rory turned to me and told me not to send her sister away. If she begged me to keep her here, bound to us for the rest of her human life, forcing her to die alone in the Ether instead of in the home she's made on Earth. I want to believe I would love her enough to give her what she *needed*, even when it was the very opposite of what she was demanding. I know the Mountain has loved the Siren since they were formed together in the womb of this world, and I know Rory wants Murphy to be happy more than anything else, even if it means losing her.

But I don't exactly have the best track record of helping the people I love make healthy choices. And it was only about ten minutes ago that I was thinking of cutting the Siren's head off just for the hell of it.

Luckily, for everyone's sake, I don't have to find out. Because Rory, after a long and painful moment of silence, steps onto the shore and says, "Okay."

"Okay?" I repeat, watching the way the ocean waves kiss the sand, watching salt water bathe my lover's bare feet.

"I hope it is everything you deserve," the Mountain whispers, with eyes only for her sister.

Murphy's smile is neither kind nor cruel when she answers, "I hope the same for you."

I raise my hands, palms facing the no-longer-god of water, Gracie High School's head cheerleader, and once more utter, "Go home."

And the Siren is no more.

The only evidence she was ever here is the footprints left at the mouth of the ocean. And seconds later, those, too, are swallowed by the deep, disappearing beneath a wash of foam.

Rory sinks to the ground, her claws digging into the sand. I take one step toward her, but think better of it as seaweed, carried by the tide, begins to curl itself like a bandage over her body.

I leave again, unsure where I'm going now. And behind me, the Mountain feeds her grief to the sea.

30

WHAT ARE YOU DOING HERE?

The Heartkeeper's kingdom is quiet. At least it is by the boardwalk where I find myself. There are a few people out, food vendors at the ends of their shifts, couples holding hands, but not the same crowds we saw the day of the festival. Did that festival even happen? Was it an illusion by the Muse? I don't know. Maybe I'll never know. Maybe it doesn't matter.

It should be impossible, how quickly I got back here. But the idea that anything might be impossible seems naïve lately.

"Hank?"

The familiar wyvern is bounding through the air toward me, bouncing up and down and shaking the entire lower half of his scaly body. He slams right into my chest, so hard I lose my breath, and my arms curl around him.

"Holy shit, hey." In all the chaos of the last couple of days, I hadn't even stopped to wonder what happened to him. "I'm so sorry, buddy. Did you get left here?"

"It was an unusual day," a beautiful voice says from the direction he came. "There was a lot going on."

Hank squeaks a happy little sound and presses his face into my throat. I stare out over him. The Heartkeeper stands a few feet away, silhouetted by the sun over the water. Once again, the Librarian and the Muse are together at her back.

"What, no lesbians today?" I swallow, brushing my fingertips down Hank's long neck.

"Death and Battle, too, have a lot going on." The Heartkeeper inclines her head, slim shoulders rising and falling. "You've seen what's become of their lands."

More guilt. Every time I think it's maxed out, there's always more at the bottom of the barrel.

"They've gone home to try and resolve things with the locals." She takes a deep breath, turning away from me. Slowly, she begins to make her way toward the dock. Indy and Rhett join her. Over her shoulder, she says, "Come. I'd like to meet this Gem Echols I've heard so much about."

And because I don't have any reason not to, and because maybe it's the whole reason I came back here at all, I follow her.

She sits at the pier's ledge, overlooking the ocean. Rhett and Indy hang back, sitting on opposite sides of the walkway, so I have to pass through the hallway of their bodies to get to her.

"Dude, stop looking at me," I tell Rhett.

He rolls a dozen of his eyes.

I sit next to my oldest friend, the complete stranger who's trying to rebuild this world. Our shoulders touch, and I don't move away.

"I've missed you," I tell her, because I think it's true. Even though this whole thing is fucking weird.

She touches my knee. "I've missed you, too."

"Your kid tried to sleep with me, you know." I jerk my thumb over my shoulder at Indy. "Like, that's disgusting, right?"

The Heartkeeper's perfect little button nose scrunches up. She shoots her son a disparaging look.

In the Ether, Indy's body is ever-changing. It's impossible to know what he looks like, exactly, because his features are in a continual shift. It's like watching a TV when someone's just holding the channel button down, all the images fading into each other as they swirl past.

The indescribable god holds up the palms of his hands and shrugs. "It was a different time."

Which I suppose is true. But *still.*

Rhett makes a sound of pure disgust and tilts his head back. If he's trying for nonchalance, it would probably be more convincing if several of his eyes weren't still glaring at me. I flip them off.

"Yes, well." The Heartkeeper finally sighs, looking back to me. "I did know that, actually. The Muse and I had some time to reconnect before you found your way here. He told me about you, Gem."

"Probably nothing good. Unfortunately, it's all true." I rub my hands on my thighs, fingers brushing hers when I do. Wait a second. Something finally occurs to me. "You had his statue. It was here—so he would be here when he woke up."

She nods. "I visited the garden several times after your disappearances. I checked on you. There was a part of me who hoped, someday, you would return. I wanted to make sure nothing happened to him, so he could always come back."

I think I feel jealous about that. About the way she protected him, and not me.

I also know it's ridiculous, so I don't say anything out loud.

"Gotta be honest, it's very weird that you told your mom about your almost-sex life." I make a face at Indy. "Like . . . boundaries, you know? Consider some healthy boundaries."

He rolls his eyes and looks at Rhett. "We never actually—"

"*Boundaries,*" Rhett snaps.

Hank snores where he's curled around my neck. The Heart-keeper runs her knuckle down his back before she clarifies, "He wasn't trying to tell me about any almost-sex life. He was just telling me about you. And you're wrong. There was a lot of good. A surprising amount."

I think that's an insult, but it's worded like a compliment, so I'm not entirely sure.

"You've changed," she continues. "He told me he could see it, but I wasn't sure. Not until I'd seen you myself. You are not who you were when you left the Ether."

I look out across the ocean. I wonder if Murphy made it back okay.

Too late, I realize I should've told her to give a message to my mom.

"No, I'm not." Something almost forgotten tugs at the back of my mind. "My heart is human now."

"I can see that." She touches that knuckle to the corner of my jaw. Her white-ink tattoos perform their own choreographed motions along her skin. "And I am so proud of you. I know how hard it was to get here."

Why does that make me want to cry again? Why does everything make me want to cry lately? It's pitiful. I brush a stupid tear away when it escapes. "Yeah, well. It wasn't exactly a quick process. I had a lot of lifetimes of being a huge dick before I thought about trying something else."

Thought about. Not always successfully, though. Gem Echols is far from perfect.

"It doesn't surprise me, you know," Indy pipes up. "That this is the first life where I haven't wanted to strangle you at every opportunity. I mean, it's also the first time you haven't just been sitting pretty. You're not just some spoiled brat with a silver spoon in their mouth. You've been through shit this time, and it's obvious."

I blink over at him, raising one eyebrow.

He seems unfazed. "What?"

"You really don't hear how messed up that is?"

"*What?*" He presses again. "Suffering builds character. It makes for good art."

"Dude." I shake my head. "Fuck that. What are you even talking about? You sound like a wall plaque from Hobby Lobby—*God gives his toughest battles to his strongest soldiers,* or some bullshit."

Rhett says, "They have a point," though I think he might just be agreeing with me because he and Indy are in a fight right now.

Hank nuzzles the underside of my chin.

I sniff and don't look at anything but the ocean. "I didn't get molested and have my whole life turned upside down just so I could be a better person. And honestly, if I did, it wasn't worth it. So, I'm glad you found me less annoying in this lifetime, or whatever. But I would've preferred being a bitchy, spoiled brat who still managed to learn the power of friendship some other way."

Indy doesn't respond. I imagine a dozen different expressions on his ever-changing face, but I can't bring myself to actually investigate.

At length, Rhett has something to say. "Have you ever considered that you weren't less annoying in this lifetime—because this is actually the only life you've ever lived?"

"Um." I can't help it, I laugh. "No. Huh?"

"You've never wondered if maybe Gem Echols is all you really are, and all you've ever been?"

"You know, for the god of knowledge, you're asking some really stupid questions." I raise my eyebrows. "I mean—yeah. I thought I was one-and-done Gem Echols, before I *remembered everything*."

"Right, but . . . well, that just proves my point, doesn't it?" Rhett lifts an eyebrow. "You already know your memories can't be trusted. What if *this* is what you're wrong about?"

"That doesn't . . . make any sense." And, frankly, it makes my stomach hurt. "Look around. We're literally *here*. Of course this is real."

The Heartkeeper brushes her palm down my back. "I think I understand what he's saying. It's an interesting thought."

"Maybe someone could unpack it for me," Indy mumbles.

She nods, eyes far away, like she's mulling over the Librarian's suggestion. Finally, slowly, she explains, "All magic comes through you. The rest of us don't exist without it. And I was there, at the birth of this world, and I remember nothing from before I found you. Maybe we are all *your* creation. Have you never considered that? After all, you speak of this pain from Gem's past . . . Is it so impossible that our existence was born from that pain? That the Ether itself was invented in the mind of a scared child who needed a place to escape? It would make sense, wouldn't it? That you might create a world where you were not only a god, but the most powerful of all gods—because you felt powerless in your real life."

How much bigger this world used to feel, the last time I was here.

"Maybe we're all just figments of Gem Echols's imagination," Rhett adds.

"Fuck you," Indy answers.

But I watch the horizon, and let myself consider it.

"It is *you* who has abandoned *me*," the Heartkeeper cries, just before a stray bolt of the Cyclone's lightning barrels into my chest.

I scream—not in pain or fear, but in frustration. I wrench the lightning from my body and smash it between my hands until it forms a blade. With a roar, I send it spinning through the air, spinning back toward the Cyclone.

He laughs, disappearing behind a gray storm cloud.

I whirl on the Heartkeeper, throwing out my arm toward the raging storm behind us. "You know my heart as no one else ever has, so how is it that you cannot understand why I need this? How do you not see that I am only barely holding this world together? I alone have been given the impossible responsibility of keeping the balance, and I am going to *break.* Is my destruction so much easier for you to swallow than my corruption?"

The Heartkeeper winces and looks away, the truth of my accusation in her pained face. All around us, the wind howls its own empathetic rage.

. . . .

I threaten to tell my parents only one time.

"You would do that to your dad?" Paul asks me. He levels me with a look burdened with so much disappointment that it makes me nauseous. "It would destroy him. He would never be able to look at either of us again. I can't believe you would take away the only family he has left."

Arguments form and knot and die in the back of my mouth. I dig my nails into my own hands. I want to scream. Nothing comes out.

The cross necklace around Paul's neck dangles in my

face when he hovers over me. "You're so special. You're the strongest person I know. And this family needs you to keep holding it together. To be strong like only you can. For your mom, and your dad, and for me. We're all counting on you. And if you start freaking out like that? I mean . . . the whole family just falls out of balance. You don't wanna be responsible for that, do you?"

Outside of the bedroom, locked in the hallway, Hank whines and scratches at the door. I wish I could tell him I'm okay. I wish saying it could make it true.

I'm standing at the foot of Paul's bed, watching him sleep. In one fist, I clutch the stolen kitchen knife I've kept under my pillow across the hall for weeks.

"What are you doing here?" I ask the Evergod, who's sitting in my windowsill. "You're dead."

"Not yet." He smiles.

I guess that's true. "What am I doing here? I already lived through this part."

"Did you?" He frowns, looking down at his hands. He starts counting on his fingers. "I thought you were still sleeping."

The room flickers and fades, and now we're in the Wheeler barn, and I'm standing over my own unconscious body.

My head hurts. "Why did you keep me hidden for two weeks?"

"Maybe I forgot that you existed." Buck sighs. "*Oh, oh, oh, wait*—maybe we're building the world."

I blink. The others are watching me, as if waiting for some revelation.

But I don't have one for them.

Maybe I was a god who breathed a new world into existence and crumbled under the weight of its gravity and destroyed everything I'd built. Maybe Gem Echols was a whisper of that god, an echo of their former life, forced to hold ancient sins that were too heavy for human hands.

Or maybe I was just a kid with a knife I couldn't use, desperate to be loved in a way that didn't feel like a sacrifice. Maybe I built a world for myself where the land spoke in a language I *could* understand, and I was protected by every living thing that walked its surface. A world where I could face my demons, the shadows I was forbidden to talk about, and could hand *them* the knife—so they might finally be set loose in the light.

Or maybe time has never been linear. Maybe all of this happened at once. Maybe it's happening even now. Maybe all of my past lives feel like they're pressing in on me because they're still unfolding, all together, growing more tangled the longer they spin.

Maybe Icarus was arrogant, and maybe he was just tired.

And maybe it doesn't matter. Maybe there are things I can't understand and will never know and maybe how I got here isn't as important as how I get out.

And to that end, at least, I think I finally have my answer.

31

BEFORE TURNING BACK AND DESCENDING INTO THE DARK

Hank and I are alone when we reappear in the bedroom where I last saw Enzo. The wyvern coos, sliding down my shoulder and drifting toward the bed, rolling around in the sheets to make a nest around his scaled body.

I leave him to his comfort, stepping into the hallway and calling out, "Rory? Enzo?"

Nothing. Have they gone to look for me? Did Rory tell Enzo what I'd done—are they angry with me, both of them? I *know* it was the right thing, but the right thing isn't always the *right* thing. Is that what's happening now?

The Shade's palace is cold and quiet and dark. When I slip into the throne room, I note that the Evergod's body is gone. Perhaps one of the others disposed of it, getting rid of the corpse before it started to stink. Or maybe he just stood up and let himself out. At this point, neither would surprise me.

The god of time is not here, but neither are my boyfriend and girlfriend. Again, I call out, "Enzo? Rory?" And again, no one answers.

Branching off from the throne room is a thick, winding staircase that leads through the chest of the mountain. I let my hand brush the stony black railing, claws scraping rock, as I make my way up. I've never actually been up this way before. I'm not sure where I'm taking myself.

At the very crest of the stairs is a single, simple door, cut into the mountainside. I push it open and light spills in, illuminating the flecks of dust in the air and glinting off the fragments of gemstone in the rock walls inside. Beyond the threshold is the very top of the mountain, the high tower of the Shade's palace, a flattened balcony overlooking his kingdom and those that border it.

Here, Rory and Enzo are standing at the edge of the balcony, staring down at the mountainside. They both turn when I join them, and relief shudders through me that neither looks angry to see me here.

"You're back," Enzo whispers, and a frightened kind of hope lingers in his stare.

"Yeah." I let the door to the palace close behind me. "I am."

"Are you okay?" Rory asks.

"I think so." And if I'm not, I will be. I'm really starting to believe that. "Are *you*?"

They sigh, and nod, and hold out a hand for me. "I think so. But we do have a situation."

I slip my fingers into theirs and step forward, joining the both of them at the balcony's edge. Looking down, I grimace at the sight. "Oh. That's not ideal."

You know, it hadn't occurred to me to wonder where the Shade's soldiers had disappeared to, while I was taking my depression vacation to the island, or playing the world's worst game of Operation with my boyfriend's body. But here they are. They're covering every square inch of the mountainside, as far as I can tell, completely silent and uncomfortably still, staring down at the ground under them.

And on the ground, there is a cluster of—humans? Looks like humans. And they're—

"Wait." I shake my head. "What am I looking at?"

"They arrived a couple of hours ago," Enzo explains poorly. "They seem to be some kind of . . . rebellion? They're wanting to lead a coup, maybe? I'm pretty sure they're here to kill me."

"Clover appears to be leading them," Rory tells me, slanting their eyes in my direction.

"Clover is alive?!" I lean forward until I almost stumble and lose my footing, Enzo's hand shooting out to grab my waist to keep me from tumbling down the mountain like an idiot. When I spot the most unremarkable face in the world, staring up at us with a vicious glare, I loose a sigh. "Oh, thank fuck."

One less drop of blood I'll have to scrub off my hands.

"The soldiers are keeping them out?"

"Mm." Enzo nods. "They won't fight them. The keepers must have gone back to Death, and told the medics there what was happening. There are some in the crowd. I think they're afraid to attack and hurt anyone."

"Because they believe they can cure them."

"Right." He sighs. "But I don't know how much longer they'll be held off. And if there really is a chance the doctors are right, and the army can be cured . . . I won't order them to stay and die for me."

I reach for the hand on my waist, squeezing his fingers in mine. "You won't need to. We're not going to be here for much longer."

"What?" Rory turns away from the ledge, facing me. "What do you mean?"

Breathing deep, I let go of them both and take a step back, holding out my palms as if in surrender. "You're right. We have to go back. Our human lives weren't perfect, and I have no idea how we're going to solve the problems we just got away from, but . . . I think there's only one way to save the Ether. And it's the same way we save Gem."

Rory and Enzo exchange a look before they both turn back to me.

"Thank you," Enzo offers.

"You don't need to thank me. I don't know what I would've become, if it weren't for you."

"Yeah, well." He swallows. "Same, though."

I study the sharp planes of his face before looking to Rory, finding those wild, expressive eyes. She offers me a subdued smile.

"Either of you," I remind her.

We have always been like this, and we always will be. Each of us holding out a hand to the others, across lifetimes and realities, each of us always pulling the others forward, even if it took a millennium to see the ripple effect play out.

I used to hate this idea of inevitability, desperate to believe I was the only one in charge of my own future. It was furiously unfair to think anything might have been predetermined, to think I might have to relinquish autonomy, or control, to the invisible hand of fate. After feeling so powerless for so long, all I wanted was a life of my own choosing.

But I think I just didn't understand it then. The truth is, the three of us have always been inevitable—*because* we were always going to choose each other.

"I have a plan," I tell them. "I've already spoken to the Heart-keeper. She's going to gather the others, and they'll be here by morning. We just have to make it one more night."

"One more night," Rory agrees. "We can do that."

Enzo nods. "Yeah. What's the worst that could happen in one night?"

"Dude," I groan. "Please don't say shit like that."

He grins and Rory chuckles and we offer one last look toward the stoic soldiers and the growing rebellion before turning back and descending into the dark palace.

Despite Enzo's best attempts to jinx us, we're still alive by midnight. I shuffle Hank out into the hallway and ignore his wounded expression, while Rory turns out the lights in favor of the candles Enzo's lit.

There is a strange sort of heaviness to the air, a recognition that none of us has spoken aloud but I know we're all trying to parse through. This is our last night in the Ether. I am certain of this. We will not return here. We will never know this home, this world we created together, formed by our own joy and pain and magic in equal measure, again. What does one do, on their last night in the first home that ever held them? When they know they can't ever go back again?

Maybe I'd like to see the kingdom of magic one last time, to walk through the halls of that palace, to smell the flowers in the garden at its center. Maybe Rory would like to walk the cooled embers of their empire's wasteland, to feel the rock beneath their feet, to grieve and say goodbye.

But it feels fitting that our story should come to a close here, in the most shadowy corner of this world. Of course we would spend our last night in the same brutal darkness where our end began.

The Shade's realm has festered like a wound in the Ether for so long now. There were those who thought to amputate it, to cauterize the infected limb so the rest might be saved. There were others who thought ignoring it might make the pain lessen, that it might heal on its own. And still, that infection continued to spread, ravaging the healthy tissue all around it, destroying the same way it had been destroyed.

After tonight, I think this place will finally start to heal. I wish I could see it for myself—but I guess that's kind of the point. This kind of magic, the kind that *doesn't* hurt everything it touches, really does always require a sacrifice.

"Gem?"

Pulled from my thoughts, I look up to realize Rory and Enzo are both watching me. My cheeks flush and I rub a hand over the back of my neck. "Sorry. Just . . . you know."

"I do." Rory inclines her head. "I was asking if you were ready for bed."

"Right. Yeah, I guess we should sleep."

None of us move, each of us watching the others, balanced on the edge of a moment, waiting to see who blinks first. Enzo swallows. Rory's fingers twitch at her side. My stomach pitches with anticipation.

It's Enzo who finally breaks the spell. He takes a step toward the bed, placing his palm against the headboard, eyes dancing between her and me.

"This is the last night we'll ever spend in the bodies of gods . . ." His forked tongue flicks across his mouth. "Are we really intending to get a full night's sleep?"

Rory's eyes meet mine again, something searching in her gaze. I'm not sure what she finds there. But her voice is as soft and unflinching as the rest of her when she answers, "I'm not."

"No," I agree, moving forward before I've told my feet to go, my hands already outstretched. "No, I'm wide awake."

Enzo's teeth sinking into my throat. Rory's deft fingers twisted possessively in his hair. The spark of magic in my claws marking a trail lower and lower down the crests of her body.

He kisses her like salvation, like he might find something holy beneath her tongue, like he's tucking penance in her mouth. She kisses me like reclamation, as if one kiss might burn hot enough to brand the thousands that came before it. I kiss him like desperation, a starving creature who might swallow him whole.

There is no configuration in which we do not fit, no single way our bodies cannot hold each other. When shadows feast on my flesh, the room comes alight in bolts of lightning and the starry glow of Enzo's eyes, my magic glimmering in a sheen on his lips. When Rory plants herself like a seed in my belly, my hands tend the land, slow and steady, until she blooms. And when the Mountain quakes, so does the mountain itself, threatening to bring the seat of the Shade's empire to ruin inside.

For one last night, I am the god of gods. I spun this world like cotton candy from the sugary beginnings of a fledgling galaxy, breathed it into existence from the wombs of stars long since dead, and built a sanctum from the very bones of infinity. And here, on the eve of my long-overdue crucifixion, one thing is clear.

There is nothing, in this world or any other, as powerful as the human heart.

32

WE CAN NEVER COME BACK FROM THIS

On the morning of the Magician's death, the last remnants of a once-great pantheon stand in front of me in the throne room of the Shade's palace.

"Thank you for coming," I offer, though it sounds awkward and incorrect from my mouth. I *want* to mean it.

"An invitation into the belly of the beast?" The Reaper's voice clinks like coins dancing between bony fingers, the lilt of it its own kind of unnatural magic. "Who could resist?"

She leans against a far pillar in the throne room, as much distance between herself and me as she can manage. I might mistake this stance for an act of fear, if I weren't certain she was only barely keeping herself from flying across the room and peeling my skin away.

Unbeknownst to her, there will be plenty of time for that later.

"The Siren has returned to Earth," I tell them, shoulders back, watching the ripple of curiosity flick across the others as the news hits their ears.

Battle and Death exchange a long glance, the Lionheart's hungry eyes holding the empty sockets of her lover's eternal corpse. Indy raises his eyebrows, the color of them shifting wildly over his own ever-changing eyes. Both the Librarian and the Heartkeeper seem unsurprised to learn this information, though she does exchange a look with the eye on his shoulder—I wonder if she meant to incline her head in a silent nod, or if I'm imagining things.

"And the Evergod is no more." I try not to think of Buck Wheeler, as I face my own ancient enemies in the same spot where he died.

"What do you mean by that, Magician?" the Lionheart drawls, turning away from the Reaper to glower in my direction. She stands empty-handed in the birthplace of demons, nothing but her shield strapped across her muscular back. If I were infinitely more foolish, I might believe this actually put her at a disadvantage.

Enzo, from just behind me, clears his throat. "I killed him."

At my side, Rory tenses, shoulder stiffening, arms tightening—consciously or not, she prepares to throw herself between him and whoever might think to avenge the god of time.

None of the others move, though.

Rhett does ask, "How are you at all coherent?"

Clever Knowledge. When Enzo does not answer, I glance to him and find him staring at me. Though his lips are parted as if to speak, the words cannot seem to form on his tongue.

I look back to the others. This is, after all, my own ill-advised plan. I suppose I should be the one to explain it.

"He wasn't; not at first. The Evergod was *born* to sit at the watchtower of eternity, and even his mind could not hold everything he saw there—not without fraying at its edges.

No one else could have taken the power of Time." I swallow. I imagine the pool of blood in the very center of this room. I swear I can still smell copper. "So, I cut it out of him. I used the Ouroboros to remove that magic, and set it free. Time now belongs only to itself."

The Librarian tilts his head with interest. The Lionheart raises a hand to her jaw, stroking her thumb against the underside of her chin, a Battle as inquisitive as any god of knowledge.

I take a deep breath. "And I did the same to the magic of the ocean, when I cut it free from Murphy's body."

The Reaper moves like a flickering light, a sharp whirl of darkness, at once leaning against the pillar and then, as suddenly as blinking, standing only feet away from me. "You did what?"

"They did only what she asked them to do," Rory answers, and their hand lands heavy and warm and solid against the back of my neck. "Believe any other vile truth you will about me, Reaper, but you *know* there is no world where I would allow them to hurt her."

Not unless she'd begged me for it, the way she ultimately had.

"Hm." The bones in Death's mouth click and pop together with consideration.

I explain, "The Siren did not want this. She has made it clear for a long time now that we are not the family she's chosen. She chose Earth. And so, Earth is what I gave her. She allowed me to carve away her place in this pantheon, and her connection to our seas, and I sent her home."

"*Family,*" Indy repeats, his faces scrunching up with disgust— or maybe contrition. "Are we a family, Magician? Is that what you'd call us?"

"Yeah, a family from an episode of *Jerry Springer,* maybe." When the Reaper mumbles, it sounds like a shovel scooping dirt from a newly growing grave.

"Or *Dateline,*" Rhett adds.

"We *are* a family." The Heartkeeper's eyes hook into mine. She smiles. There is joy there, somehow, even if it's quiet. "And that can mean or not mean something different to each of us. But it doesn't stop being true."

The others glance to and away from her, but no one argues. I get the impression there is respect there, even if begrudging. Of course, there must be—she's the only reason any of them would have walked into this palace, trusting it wasn't a trap.

"Clearly." The Lionheart tilts her head at me, waiting for the other shoe to drop. "You did not summon us here to say Hail Marys at the confessional, Magician. Why are you telling us any of this?"

"Because . . ." My mouth falters. I *know* this is the right thing, I *know* this is a decision I am supposed to make, I *know* there is no other option that leads to anything but damnation. It's just— there's a chance this option leads to damnation anyway, and my tongue hesitates to cast the spell for my own downfall. I curl my fists, pressing the tips of my claws into my palms. The pain is grounding. I force myself to continue. "We are waving the white flag, Battle. We are laying down our arms. And we're here with the terms of surrender."

"What," the Reaper clanks, "the fuck does that mean?"

I suck in a deep breath. Rory's hand tightens on my neck, and I can feel when Enzo steps in closer to my back. The two of them manage to keep me upright, and remind me why I'm doing this at all.

"For so long, we've been caught in this bloody cycle, each

of us believing we were doing the right thing at every turn. But sometimes, the right thing is not actually the right thing." I glance to the Lionheart. "Sometimes, fairness is not justice."

She narrows her eyes at me.

I continue, "We've gone round and round for lifetimes, always trying to fix things, and all we've done is make everything worse. More pain, more devastation—and now *this*. The world we built together has become a relic of what it once was, a mockery of what it could have been. The only option is for this cycle to finally end. And the only way that's going to happen is if we cannot hurt each other anymore. And the only way *that's* going to happen . . ."

"Is if we're worlds apart," Rhett finishes, all of his eyes watching me.

I nod. "We all had our roles to play, but it was my knife that carved this world open. I do not belong here anymore."

"It was their knife, but it was my hand." Enzo shakes his head. "Every mile marker of this world is a reminder of the worst things I've ever done. I don't want to be the Shade anymore—but I'll never be able to be anything else, not as long as I'm here."

Rory sniffs. "Their knife; his hand. But I was the coward who forced us to abandon the only home we'd ever known, instead of fighting to put out the fire."

"So, you just get to leave?" Indy asks, voice whipping against his teeth. "You just waltz back to Earth, gods among humans, and leave us to clean up your mess? How the fuck is that fair? How is that atoning for anything?"

"Cherub." The Heartkeeper reaches for his hand, squeezing gently. "I know how hard you fought to save Gem, and I know how heavy the hurt of that failure is. But you have to put it down. It's blocking your vision. You aren't seeing them clearly."

I stare at her for a long moment, stomach twisting back and forth, trying to eat itself. Finally, I nod a silent thank-you, and continue. "We won't be gods among humans, because we won't be gods at all. And *that's* why you're here."

When I tug the Ouroboros from the inner lapel of my cloak, the air in the room tenses and spits with anxious, violent energy. I can feel their stares, each of them watching the god killer with unease and awe.

"Here, in front of you, we will carve ourselves open and cut out the very thing that *makes us* gods. When we return to Earth, we will be *humans* among humans." My breath shakes. "We will surrender every drop of our magic—and because of that very sacrifice, you will witness the Ether's healing."

The Reaper and the Lionheart exchange another look. Battle reaches up to touch the back of her hand against her lover's cheek, such tenderness from a god whose severity is without match. After a moment, she looks back to me, and asks, "What happens when you make this sacrifice? You say you intend to surrender. What does that actually look like?"

"The Land will lay claim to itself," Rory tells them, voice firm. "It will fight to heal. And if you choose to make yourselves its ally, it will remember that."

"Day and night, fire and air, strength and peace," I list off. "Each of these will be returned to a world in desperate need of them all."

Enzo takes a step forward, steeling himself and raising his chin. "So, too, will that which is forbidden. Without a vessel to face subjugation, the secrets of this world will never again be forced to decay in shadow. You will all have to learn to face your demons in the light."

"And what of life?" Death's whisper echoes from the walls

of the chamber, coming from everywhere and nowhere at once. And though I am looking right at her as she stands across from me, I swear I feel her breath on the back of my neck.

"Life will return to Death." I do not deserve to cry, and I will not let myself indulge in the selfish cruelty of my own tears, not in front of the mourning Reaper. I do say, "And I am so sorry I made you wait as long as I did."

Her bones shake and shake and sing like wind chimes and I don't know if she's laughing or crying or both. But she does not accept my apology, and she does not say anything else.

"And magic?" the Librarian demands. "You are the keeper of the scales. You were meant to mind the balance. What will happen to *your* power when you leave this world?"

"Magic will fall to you. You five, the last remaining gods of this world, will have to keep each other in check. The job of balancing the scales should not fall to any one being, no more than any one of you could have held the endlessness of Time. There will be no *god of gods*. And when someone inevitably fucks up, the other four can hold them accountable." I frown. "Well, the other four, and one more person. I will leave behind *six* shards of my power. Humanity will have magic of its own—with Clover Amarith as its keeper."

"Who the fuck is Clover Amarith?" Indy asks.

"She's . . ." I can only laugh at the ridiculousness of my own words, half unbelieving that I'm saying them out loud. "She's the Chosen One."

"With this shard," Indy wonders aloud, "would we be able to move between *both* worlds? Earth is not without its problems, but I have a soft spot for that doomed little planet."

Rhett nods. "You may not want to be a god among humans, Mage, but I'm not nearly so humble. I'm not interested in pulling a Murphy—but I *do* have some unfinished business back in Gracie."

I shrug. "I can do anything I want. I suppose the same would be true for you—as long as you didn't get too cocky about it. That never ends well."

"In exchange for all we are giving up," Rory presses, drawing the attention back to our proposition, "we ask only for two things. The first: that you use your new magic to send *us* back to Earth."

"Only after you've gone under the knife," the Lionheart clarifies. She raises one eyebrow. "Does it not strike you as dangerous, to make yourselves that vulnerable? You will be powerless—butchered and left with no magic. What would stop us from letting you die? What reason would we possibly have for making good on a promise to send you back to your comfortable human lives?"

It tastes vile in my mouth, but I have to tell her the truth.

"You will send us back, because *you* are a good person." I sigh. "You have never once chosen cruelty for the sake of cruelty. You are the only truly righteous god I have ever known. And it is only in hindsight that I am beginning to unravel how many opportunities you tried to give me to stop my undoing before it was too late."

Genuine surprise makes the Lionheart balk.

"*And . . .*" I admit, "you will send us back because you are the most clever strategist in any world—and you know *I* am *not* a good person. You know I would not make myself as vulnerable as this plan appears to. You know there is always something tucked up my sleeve. And you know that giving me the human life I want is *infinitely* less annoying than dealing with whatever bullshit I might pull if you turned on me."

Silence stretches out in the throne room. I can sense the others shifting uncomfortably, but I do not look away from the Lionheart.

Finally, she scrubs a hand down her face and groans. "Fuck me. And what's the second ask?"

"When we have carved out our power and handed it away, you will use my magic to finally destroy the Ouroboros." When it hears its name, the blade burns like coiled lightning in my palm. "Because we are not gonna do this shit ever again."

Though I imagine there is a perverse curiosity about what is going to happen next, the other gods disperse, leaving us to our gruesome ritual. Only the Heartkeeper stays behind, hovering at the edge of the throne room, the white-ink tattoos swaying back and forth across her skin. She smiles at me when I approach her.

"You don't have to watch this." If I had the choice, *I* would leave. "It isn't going to be pretty."

"Love is not always pretty," she says with a shrug. The bright cloth draping her body drags on the ground alongside the ends of her hair as she moves in to press a kiss to my cheek. "To truly love someone is to be unencumbered by witnessing the ugliness of them. You are not a burden to behold, Gem. And I am not leaving you—not again."

"I wish we'd had more time." I'm crying again, stupid and pathetic, my throat threatening to close as tears slip over my cheeks. "I just got you back. And now I'll never see you again."

I know we can never come back from this, and I know it is the right thing. Knowing that doesn't make it hurt any less.

"Oh, my love." She touches her hand to my face, brushing one tear away with the pad of her thumb. "We both know that isn't true. You are leaving me with a piece of you, yes, but *you* will also carry *me* wherever you go. As long as you keep listening, you will hear me in every beat."

I reach up to the hand on my jaw, magic pulsing between us, our eyes locked to one another.

After too long, Enzo asks, "Gem?"

Despite how badly I don't want to, I turn to face him and Rory. They're both watching me, different shades of concern flickering on their faces. I drop the Heartkeeper's hand and move to join them at the center of the room. The Ouroboros pulses with anticipation.

"Okay." I suck in a deep breath. "So, uh. Who's going first?"

"I'll do it," Enzo answers, immediately. "I've done it once already. And—and there's a lot to get through in here, huh?"

My god of stolen empires. Yeah, we might be here awhile.

I clear my throat, fist tightening around the knife, and take a step forward. But Rory halts me, her hand on my elbow.

"I can do it," she offers. Her fingertips slide down the slope of my arm until they reach the dagger. I don't protest, letting her slip it from my hand and into hers. "He's right, he's done this already. And I've already watched *you* suffer through it. I don't know if I could do that again."

"Are you sure?"

"Yeah." She sniffs, glancing down at me. "Besides . . . someone's going to have to do me next."

I let her take the blade and step away, joining Enzo at the baptism of this heretical altar. And I know it is not just the loss of her at my side that makes my whole body go cold.

At a certain point, when it has witnessed enough pain and trauma, when it has surpassed the threshold of its own survival, the human mind ceases to comprehend what's going on around it. It compartmentalizes, shuffling boxes of the unnecessary and upsetting into the cobwebbed corners of itself, protecting its host from its own lived experiences. With enough digging, purposeful or by accident, these boxes can be uncovered. But, left alone, and they will disappear beneath layers of dust, piles of unmarked junk that a person may glance at and wonder at its contents, but never feel the need to touch.

For the most part, the minds of gods are not so benevolent. And because of that, I am perfectly and completely aware of every moment spent in that throne room. Enzo, and Rory, and me, and the Ouroboros between and against and inside us, and each of us using our already bloodied hands to turn each other into shreds of confetti. Top three worst birthday parties ever.

She scoops smoke and brimstone from his bone marrow. He might plead with her that he's given all he has, but it's hard to tell when his body is nothing but pulp.

I claw the howling tongues of beasts from her womb, and marvel at the grotesque and clumsy irony of the butterflies in her stomach.

Neither of them can hold a knife, and so my last act of magic in this world is to heal their no-longer-godly bodies, bringing them back from the edge of death so that they might deliver me to my own. I can think of no better use of my power than this.

He holds the blade, sculpting me like stone, and every searing bite of pain makes me wonder if he's yet revealed something new and beautiful. When he stares into my face and cannot bring himself to do what he knows must be done, she takes the knife from his hand. And once she has dug my eyes from my head, I scream into the empty nothing that it's over, it's done, they have finally taken the last of the Magician from me.

Rory presses the Ouroboros back into my palm and I clutch it against my mutilated, shaking body. They circle on either side of me, lifting me up between them.

"It's almost over," Enzo whispers into the side of my face.

The gods have rejoined us. I can feel them, even if I can't see them. I think I hear the rattle of Death's gasp when she accepts the gift of Life. Serpentine threads of magic slither away from me, finding their new masters, and I feel the loss of each one as clearly as the blade itself.

The blade.

Silver clatters to the ground of the throne room, tumbling from my hand to the feet of these gods.

"Now," I whisper through what's left of my bloodstained teeth, unsure if they can understand me. "Do it now."

Nothing. There is no sound, no light, no tremble beneath my feet to indicate that the act is done. Maybe they didn't hear me. I open my chapped lips wider, thinking perhaps I can scream—

Beside me, Rory nearly collapses when she sighs with relief. I believe only the task of keeping me upright actually keeps her on her feet. At my other side, Enzo releases a shaky breath, his grip on me tightening.

"It's done," the Lionheart tells me.

It's done.

"You have everything you've ever wanted," Rory says.

Enzo finishes, "Now send us back."

Something slips against what's left of my face. I think it must be blood, more blood, dripping from the holes that were once my eyes. I think this until I hear a familiar, pitiful whine. Scales brush my ruined skin.

"Hank," I whisper.

The wyvern whimpers, trying to curl himself around my broken arm. My hand twitches, fingers straining to comfort him.

He can't go with me this time.

Warm hands slide against his flank, pulling him free of me. He gives one last kiss to my knuckles as he's taken away.

"There's—" I almost choke on my tongue, and have to start again. "There's a woman named Catherine. A medic in the city of Death. He might—they might want to be together."

It feels impossible that anyone could understand the ghost of a whisper that actually manages to come out of me. And maybe they can't. But still, the Heartkeeper promises, "He will be loved, no matter what. He's a good boy."

Yeah, he is.

"Okay." The voice of the Librarian. "Let's get this over with."

"Let's," the Muse agrees.

"Gem, dear," the Reaper pipes up. "Do make sure they have the gaudiest memorial *ever* put up for me at the high school, won't you?"

I think maybe I try to laugh, and almost die instead.

"Okay." The Lionheart twists the word like a command. "It's time."

Rory and Enzo press even more fiercely against my sides. If I still had eyes, I might close them. And all together, the three of us hold our breath, praying to wake up again.

EPILOGUE

Eighteen Months Later

H ey!" I grin when the FaceTime call blinks to life, the screen of my phone split to show Rory on top and Enzo on the bottom. "Sorry I missed your call earlier. Mom and I were just leaving Dad's place."

"It's okay." Rory smiles, bringing a mug of tea to her mouth as she asks, "How's he doing?"

"Good. Like, really good, actually. I think the new meds are helping a lot."

Dad's been out of the hospital for about a year now, and living on his own for the last few months. Mom's been going over once a week or so to check on him, but tonight was the first time I got to see the place for myself. And I know he's never gonna be the dad I remember from before, but there were moments, tonight, over dinner, when I swear I saw that guy in flashes.

"That's great, babe." Enzo beams up at me, holding his phone over his head.

"Hellhound," Rory chuckles. "Are you in a *hammock*?"

He swishes back and forth, angling his phone to show off

the view of the palm trees and the sunset over the beach behind him. "It's *summer* here, kitten. Sorry we can't all be staying in an igloo for the holidays."

I roll my eyes at them, but smile, hooking my phone up to the car mount and turning the key in the ignition. I've got a long drive ahead of me.

"How's that going, by the way?" I ask Rory, keeping my eyes on the highway. "Being home again."

"It's . . . good? It's weird. There's just *so* many cousins and not a single person hears me when I say I don't wanna talk about being kidnapped and brainwashed. So." She laughs. "But, uh. It's good, too. I mean, I knew I missed my parents, but I kind of forgot how much I missed this *place*. It feels nice, just to be back in the snow."

"Can't relate," Enzo chimes in. "Well—about the snow, anyway. You wanna talk about cousins? I'm pretty sure I have not met like, a hundred of these people, but they've all seen my naked baby pictures."

Rory chuckles. "And how is Georgia?"

"Oh, you know. It's Georgia." I snicker. "Mom's heading down to Tampa tonight. I'm gonna fly out tomorrow and meet her there."

Just as soon as I'm done doing what I've gotta do.

"Did you see Murphy?"

I glance from the road to the phone, quickly scan the look on Rory's face before looking back. "Yeah. I mean, we didn't talk or anything, but I did see her at Piggly Wiggly. I guess she's back from school for break. She looks good."

"Good," Rory answers, and I know she means it.

"Oh, shit, you know who else I ran into?" I smirk. "Our friend, Officer Allen."

Enzo makes a pig noise.

When we got back from the Ether, there were a lot of *issues* we had to work through. The Gracie PD should've been the biggest one. But, taking everyone by surprise, Mrs. White came through in the end. She cleared up any confusion with the department about what happened in her daughter's attack, shifting the blame back to Zephyr—repayment, she told me, for slaughtering the little creep who'd killed her husband.

The family left Gracie not long after that. I have no idea where they went or what they're doing with the still-sleeping bodies of Poppy and Marian they took with them, but I sincerely hope we never cross paths again.

"Have either of you heard from Rhett or Indy?"

"I talked to Rhett a few days ago," Enzo answers. "As of our conversation, they were both Earthside. Apparently, the Clancy family came into some big money. Totally a stroke of luck and not at *all* the god of knowledge rigging the stock market or anything. But, uh, he was helping them put together some kind of trust or investments or—I don't know, I wasn't listening that closely. I *do* know he and Indigo are fighting."

"Again?" Rory groans.

"*Again.* So, I think the Muse is on a breakup tour—somewhere in Europe, maybe."

"Hm." I shake my head. That couple makes no sense to me, but to each their own. I would ask about the others, but the Reaper, and the Lionheart, and the Heartkeeper have all stayed in the Ether since we left. At least as far as any of us know.

For a moment, things get quiet. Rory drinks their tea and the waves wash against the shore on Enzo's beach and the highway zooms past my car window, and we sit in companionable, easy silence.

Finally, Rory says, "I miss you two. It's like, I'm not ready to leave *here*, but I also can't wait to be *back* for New Year's. You know?"

"We are going to have so much fun." I can hear the grin in Enzo's voice, even without looking at the screen. "Your first New York New Year's."

"Are we gonna watch the ball drop in Times Square?" I don't actually have any idea what Enzo has planned.

"Ew—god, no. What are we, tourists? That sounds miserable." He scoffs. "Don't worry. We're going to have fun."

"Oh, I'm worried," I tell him, and Rory laughs. "But I guess I trust you."

"Thanks, babe." He scoffs. "All right, I should probably head in, before some great-great-aunt comes out here and tries to feed me again or something."

"*Poor baby*," Rory mocks. "But actually, I should go, too. We're going sledding soon."

"Okay." I smile, tilting my eyes back to the screen for a millisecond. "I love you."

"I love you," they both parrot back at me.

Rory adds, "And have fun tonight, honey."

"Yeah." I can feel Enzo's smile, even with my eyes on the road. "Wish I was there. Let us know how it goes, won't you?"

"Sure." As much as I know they both want to be with me for this, it's something I have to do without them. I reach for the end button on the screen, finger hovering over it. "We'll talk soon."

Click.

The sun is setting here, too, the clock on the dash reading half past six. I've still got another three hours before my drive's over. I sync the phone up to the car's Bluetooth, and pull up the latest recording my grandmother sent me.

Through the speaker, she talks to me in Mvskoke, and I talk back to her, even if she can't hear me. Or maybe she can. She weirds me out sometimes with how much she seems to know.

Ever since I came back here, the land's been trying to speak to me again. I used to wish I could understand it, always mourning a connection I was so desperate to actually feel, but I never *did* anything about it. Not until last year, anyway. Now I'm done feeling sorry for myself. Instead, I'm taking back what was stolen from me.

I guess that's kind of the whole point of this drive.

It's almost ten when I pull into the adorable, cookie-cutter suburban neighborhood in Atlanta. I triple-check the address on my phone, car tires crawling down the residential street, until I stop in front of the one I'm looking for. It's cute. Red brick and a white porch. There's a big Christmas tree lit up in the front window. Even though it's getting late, there's a light on upstairs.

I park on the curb and walk up the driveway, between the red commuter car and white minivan. The healed scar across my rib cage throbs, angry at being cramped in the driver's seat for so long. I rub it absentmindedly through my shirt while checking the numbers over the front door one last time before I knock.

A minute later, it opens. A little girl, barely eight years old, with blond hair and big brown eyes and a smudge of candy cane remnant on her chin, frowns at me through the screen door.

"Um. Hi."

"Hi." I smile. She has nothing to fear from me. In fact, just the opposite. "Are you Hannah?"

"Uh . . . yeah." Her brow furrows. "Who are you?"

"I'm a friend." True, for her. "Could you go get your stepdad for me?"

A bleak look wisps across her face. Something so much older than her body claws to be set free behind those sad brown eyes. She doesn't say anything, though. She steps back, disappearing into the house.

I wait. The seconds tick into each other. I play back my grandmother's recordings, practicing in my head. I whistle when I reach into my pocket and pull out the knife.

Oh, the knife. The Ouroboros and its false twin, the mundane replica I'd used to stab Clover—one of them *was* destroyed in the Ether. The other came home with me. And it burns now, in the palm of my hand, my grip tightening around the gemstone-encrusted handle.

A stranger with my father's eyes comes to the door. When he sees me, he frowns. He is not afraid yet. "Can I help you?"

"I'm not sure. But I think so." I step forward, pressing my fingers into the tightly woven mesh of the screen door to pull it out of my way. "Tell me . . . what do you see when you look at me?"

"Hey, listen—" Whatever Paul meant to say dies at the back of his tongue. He tilts his head, confusion bleeding into fear as recognition dawns. And as he gasps my deadname like a desperate prayer to a vengeful god, I step over the threshold.

Clandestine magic, the seventh shard of the Magician, the secret tucked up my sleeve, flutters to the surface of my skin.

And I am not afraid anymore.

LIST OF CHARACTERS

LIVING GODS OF THE ETHER

The Heartkeeper, god of love

The Reaper, god of life and death, previously known as
Poppy White

The Lionheart, god of battle, previously known as Marian
Colquitt

The Muse, god of art, also known as Indigo Ramirez

The Librarian, god of knowledge, also known as Rhett
Clancy

DEAD GODS OF THE ETHER

The Sun, god of day

The Moon, god of night

The Inferno, god of fire

The Caretaker, god of life

The Stillness, god of peace

The Hammer, god of strength

The Cyclone, god of weather
The Evergod, god of time

NO LONGER GODS OF THE ETHER

Murphy Foster, not the god of the sea
Enzo Truly, not the god of things forbidden
Aurora Cook, not the god of land
Gem Echols, not the god of magic[1]

---

1 Well . . . about that . . .

ACKNOWLEDGMENTS

This book was an act of catharsis. For all the healing I hope my words might provide, they were still written in blood. And I know I wasn't the only one to bleed. On that note, every page of this story is dedicated to survivors of childhood sexual trauma.

Once again, I owe so much to the incredible team at Wednesday, for the unshakable support and enthusiasm they've shown this duology every step of the way. Special thanks to my phenomenal editor, Tiffany, for being sharp when the story needed it and gentle when I did.

Without my agents, Lee and Victoria, I never could've shared this story. Thank you, again and again and again.

Of course, I wouldn't be here at all if it weren't for the love of my chosen family, my own pantheon of wild queers both in the Pacific Northwest and around the world. Being seen is terrifying, but thank you for seeing me anyway, and for letting me see you in return.

For my cowboy. My coyote, my wishing star, my court jester. My leap of faith and my steady ground. Only you know how much I had to unearth to write this book. Only I know how you sat with me through it all and never once flinched. You are the sort of love I didn't actually think existed until I'd found it. And I will love you on purpose, forever and ever and every forever.

For Fin. I might've brought you into this world, but loving you brought me back to life. In one way or another, all of this is yours.

And for me. For every version of me who thought we wouldn't live to see our thirties and held on anyway. Thank you. I love you.

We're safe now.